P

PRODIGAL

John,

I have a weakness for this one ~

Love Irshad

Irshad AbdulKadir Oct 2, 2022

PICADOR INDIA

First published 2019 by Macmillan India
an imprint of Pan Macmillan Publishing India Private Limited,
707, Kailash Building
26 K. G. Marg, New Delhi – 110 001
www.panmacmillan.co.in

Pan Macmillan, 20 New Wharf Road, London N1 9RR
Basingstoke and Oxford
Associated companies throughout the world
www.panmacmillan.com

ISBN 978-93-89109-05-4

Typeset in Scala 11/15.5
by Manmohan Kumar
Printed and bound in India by
Gopsons Papers Ltd.

For Sadiq, Ayesha and Hisham ... Salman,
Sarosh and Billo

PART I
THE HINTERLAND

ONE

He lay at the back of the truck, scanning the terrain. He could feel the jostling and tossing of the recumbent bodies on either side of him as the truck went over bumps on the way uphill. The flap had been raised, letting in the cool night air. It offset the fetidness of humans, polyester foam and diesel fumes. He sat up rubbing his aching limbs, wiped the dust caked on his brow and blew it out of his nostrils. He could make out indistinct shapes rising up in the darkened horizon and approaching the truck.

The truck, carrying five youths and bales of cotton cloth from Karachi to Peshawar, had taken almost four days, including stops for refuelling, namaz, meals and calls of nature. They were being smuggled into the tribal area north-west of the Khyber Pakhtunkhwa province, formally referred to as the Federally Administered Tribal Areas or FATA.

He saw his fellow passengers for the first time in late summer while boarding the bus at the wholesale vegetable market in Karachi. They ranged from seventeen to twenty-three years of age, all strangers to each other, with little in common with him. One, older and taller than the rest, caught his eye. They looked at each other for a moment, then turned away. All five were travelling to the tribal area to join either a madrasa or a mujahideen outfit – or both.

They had been told, for purposes of concealment while crossing checkpoints, to lie still under the polyester foam packages. He dreaded being buried in that manner. He had almost given away their presence during a cargo inspection after the truck had crossed the Indus at Hyderabad.

While the inspectors poked and prodded, he gasped for air to keep from suffocating. The inspectors heard nothing. But when they had gone, the driver appeared, fists clenched.

'Which of you bastards was it?'

The boys emerged from their cover, dishevelled by the ordeal, and exchanged dazed glances.

He was about to own up when the lad he had noticed at the pickup point in Karachi admitted responsibility in Pashto, explaining that he was asthmatic.

When the journey resumed, he sat beside his saviour.

'Why did you take the blame?' he asked.

'Because he would have thrashed you had you owned up – in Urdu. He may even have thrown you out of the truck.'

'You mean he didn't hit you just because you spoke to him in Pashto?'

'Not just that. My Pashto was in the dialect spoken in his area.'

'My name is Akbar Ali,' he said, smiling as he extended his hand.

'Bairam Khan Afridi,' said his saviour, shaking his hand warmly.

Bairam and Akbar were the same age and looked remarkably alike. At six feet, Bairam was slightly taller than Akbar. His golden skin, slanting eyes and chiselled Grecian nose set him apart from the rest. He had tawny shoulder-length hair and the shadow of a beard. His Urdu was accented yet clear.

'You're different...not like the rest of us,' Bairam remarked. 'I noticed that at once. You have fair skin like a Pakhtun...like me...but seem to come from rich folk. Is that why you keep to yourself?'

'The difference doesn't matter...I keep to myself because I have too much to think about...the life I left behind...and what is to come.'

'I see.'

'You too, I noticed,' said Akbar, 'seem to keep much to yourself.'

'I can't make small talk,' Bairam said, 'and the other three are kids.'

Seizing the opening to chat, Akbar asked, 'Why are you taking this trip?'

There was a pause.

'I am going to serve Allah.'

'How?'

'By joining the mujahideen...what about you?'

'*Alhamdolillah*...I am finding my way to Him too...I'll be taking courses at a religious retreat.'

'So you will become an *Aalim-e-Deen*,' Bairam remarked.

'If I can absorb the learning...and you'll be a warrior... for faith.'

'Inshallah, I will go on jihad in His name,' Bairam said, reaching for his water bottle. It was almost empty.

'Here,' said Akbar, offering his thermos.

Bairam looked into Akbar's eyes, drinking deeply.

For the rest of the journey they sat together and slept side by side at night. Akbar was surprised by his quickening response to Bairam, especially to a stirring in his loins when their bodies touched.

Before leaving Karachi, he had resolved to avoid close human contact and had drawn away from family members.

Yet here he was, warming to Bairam. Until they met, Akbar had not felt the need for friends. He had not bonded with fellow students at school, being drawn more to his mentors instead. Kinship was confined to siblings, and personal rapport he associated instinctively with God.

Perhaps, it is His doing, he thought, smiling to himself.

As the truck lumbered across the length of Pakistan towards Khyber Pakhtunkhwa, they chatted easily. Bairam's curiosity was boundless. He had never come across anyone like Akbar.

He wanted to know everything – about Akbar's home, family life, education and what it was like living on the right side of town. He listened closely when Akbar disclosed the circumstances that had led to him leaving home.

It was so different to the wretched life Bairam had led in Kati Pahari, an outlying Pakhtun suburb of Karachi. He was an orphan, living with an aunt and a brutish uncle who beat him viciously and forced him to do menial household chores.

Other than reading and writing connected with religious studies – taught by the imam of the local mosque – he had little education. The urge to become a mujahid came after hearing the speeches of a fiery cleric. He had never travelled out of Karachi. This was his first trip to the north-west of Pakistan. He was excited about visiting his ancestral land.

'If you haven't run away from home, why have you chosen this risky way of getting to Peshawar?' Bairam asked. 'You could have travelled by coach or train, then taken a truck ride to FATA.'

'That's what my uncle had planned, but I didn't want him to accompany me, so I made my own arrangements with a man from my madrasa. I wanted to travel with other madrasa-bound boys. So, on the day of departure I slipped away from home.'

'You didn't tell your parents?'

'Oh yes, I left a letter for them...I didn't want them to worry,' Akbar said, grinning.

'No one worried when I left...no one cared.' After a pause Bairam added, 'Tell me,' he said, 'what's it like to have a father...and a mother?'

The truck bumped along during a pause in the conversation.

'It's difficult for me to answer that,' Akbar said, 'I've always had parents. I can't imagine life without them.'

'And I can't imagine life with them,' Bairam said with a short laugh, 'nor with a brother or sister...no friend either... never had one...where I lived, it was not possible...it's different now...there is you.'

'In such a short while,' Akbar remarked.

'Yes, in such a short time,' Bairam murmured, 'I've found a friend...who has chosen a devout life in FATA, giving up home, family, an important city madrasa...all for faith. While I...I'm only running away from hell.'

'All of us in the truck are running away from something.'

'No Akbar, not everyone, you're special.'

'Come on Bairam, I don't see that.'

'Look, it's not just about having a family and home. You also have your education, your professor uncle, the imam and the tutor at Beyt-as-Salah who were your guides.'

'But for now, there are only our destinations in FATA...
that's all,' Akbar said with finality.

'Our destinations and our friendship...which we mustn't
forget. I need you as my friend. There is no one else.'

'I am your friend,' said Akbar.

The Peshawar stopover – where they stretched their stiff
limbs and dined on kebab and nan – was to be their last
encounter with a bustling city before the final leg of the journey.

On being allowed by the driver to move around the bazaar
after the meal, Akbar and Bairam wandered off, gazing at
shops, exploring alleys. To Akbar's surprise, Bairam kept
hold of his hand while they strolled. He took it as a sign
of friendship.

After the stopover, the truck left for FATA while it was still
dark. Their destination was Bajaur Agency, a region deep in
the mountainous tribal belt.

From his cramped seat beside the sleeping Bairam, Akbar
watched the sky above the distant peaks grow lighter. The
truck ascended to the top of a shallow pass, at which point
the driver applied the brakes and called out, 'Wake up you
slugs, it's time for *Fajar* namaz.'

The boys stumbled out, shivering in the chill morning air,
performed ablutions – with mountain soil, in the absence
of water – and assembled for prayer led by the driver. After
prayers, they bought tea and nan from a roadside shack.

The trip from Peshawar took an hour. The sun had risen
by the time they reached Shabqadar, a township midway
between the settled area and FATA.

The outpost of the Political Agent of Mohmand Agency,
which marked the entry into FATA, lay at some distance
from Shabqadar. The truck stopped there for inspection

by the Frontier Constabulary. It was inspected again some distance later within Bajaur Agency at a picket of the Pakistan Army Frontier Corps. Thereafter pickets appeared regularly at short intervals on the road.

A few miles into Bajaur Agency, the truck was once more stopped for inspection on an empty stretch of road, by three men who appeared suddenly, waving Kalashnikovs, their faces masked by turban wrapping.

The driver switched off the radio before getting down and greeting them deferentially. He showed them a special permit issued to him for ferrying cargo to FATA territories and answered their questions while pointing at the truck. They went round and checked the human cargo, looking closely at the boys. Then they let the truck pass.

'Taliban,' said Bairam.

Akbar shuddered involuntarily even though he had known that the journey would end in Taliban territory.

The terrain they now entered was different from the mix of desert, rivers and canals, ripening crops and bazaars of Sindh and Punjab they had passed earlier. The mounting oppressiveness in the wake of the monsoon of the plains – referred to as the 'sting in the summer's tail' – gave way to a dry briskness, scorching at midday and chilly as evening turned to night.

They faced mountains – dotted with maple, pine and juniper – temperate in summer and snowbound in winter. The ridges were interrupted by narrow, gorge-like valleys thousands of feet below, with occasional fruit trees, yellow-green crops and ribbon-like watercourses. Strips of step cultivation were visible in the valleys. Hawks, swallows and falcons swooped and wheeled across the sky.

The truck's route ran through settlements, mostly rundown little villages, except for the township of Nawagai which was larger, with single-storey concrete structures.

In the villages, the bazaar lay at the base of the surrounding mountains with villagers' homesteads ascending the slopes. The habitations were mud-plastered with slanting roofs which served as slides for winter snowfalls.

There was not much traffic. An occasional truck or bus came by. Cars and pickups appeared. Pedestrians were scarce. There were mostly men in the bazaars. The few women visible were working in the fields or tending to farm animals.

The truck stopped at some bazaars to offload bales of cloth.

The boys observed the village sights with interest. A village called Loysum stood out from the rest. It had been destroyed by a hard-fought operation between army regulars and Taliban fighters. All that remained were wrecked homes and a shell-like outpost of the Frontier Constabulary. 'Will you change places with me?' a pale-faced boy asked Akbar, 'I can't see what's out there.'

Akbar moved without a word. Except for Bairam, he had not spoken much to the others. Now it was time to part ways. The truck dropped them off, one by one, at various hamlets where they were met by armed representatives of the group they had come to join, some of whom were masked.

When the truck reached the village of Inayatkala, it was Bairam's turn to leave. The wrench of parting was felt by both men. They did not know whether they would see each other again. The uncertainty of what lay ahead hung menacingly over them. They embraced fiercely, parted silently.

Akbar sat with his back pressed against the steel side of

the truck. He watched as Bairam collected his kit and jumped off without a word, or a backward glance. He saw him shake hands with a surly-looking guide and take leave of the driver. Then he went off with his escort. They turned a corner and were out of sight.

Akbar was the last passenger. He was bound for the Dar-ul-Aman retreat in the village of Kitkot. Alone at last at the back of the truck, he gave full rein to thoughts he'd held back during the journey.

I need a clear head to face my destiny.

He mulled over the events that had led him there. *Home... and family...and Beyt-as-Salah, of course.*

Home and family meant the colonial sandstone house in Civil Lines, Karachi, residence of the Chief Justice of the Sind High Court, Javed Ali, and his wife Lilian Armstrong, daughter of Reverend Armstrong, vicar of Avebury, Wiltshire, England, who met and fell in love on a skiing holiday in Switzerland twenty-five years earlier – and their three children, Akbar, Aliya and Kamran. There was also Akbar's adopted godfather, his uncle Ahmed Ali.

TWO

'Lily,' Ahmed Ali said to his sister-in-law, 'you should think about making Akbar switch from 'O'levels to the International Baccalaureate. It will help him more in the future.'

'I know,' she said, 'I have no problem with that. The catalogue you gave me is quite informative. It's really up to Akbar.'

'I've given him some Bac course material. Has he discussed it?' Ahmed Ali asked.

'He's going through it. So far he hasn't mentioned it...I'll bring it up this evening.'

Ahmed Ali, the older of the Ali brothers, was childless and had been drawn to Akbar as to a son from the time of his birth. He took a keen interest in the boy's welfare. This had been encouraged by Akbar's father Javed Ali and his concern was accepted as a matter of course by Akbar.

Apart from his mother, his uncle was the one who had always been there for him. Akbar responded by following his advice – usually unquestioningly.

When Ahmed Ali first broached the subject, Lilian knew that the point about the Bac was as good as won. Ahmed Ali's views on education were given weight by the family partly because of his academic background. He was an ex-Cavendish scholar and visiting fellow of Trinity College, Cambridge.

No one was surprised at Akbar's reaction. He fell in readily with the plan. Ahmed Ali suggested that it was best for Akbar to enrol at College du Leman, Versoix. And he did. His grades at school more than sufficed. Ahmed Ali accompanied Akbar to Switzerland and stayed till he was satisfied that his nephew had settled in.

Akbar remained in Europe during the two-year course. He studied on campus – history, sociology, whatever came his way – toured the Continent and spent his holidays with his mother's family in England. He was visited twice by Ahmed Ali, and once by his parents.

A natural sportsman, Akbar played baseball, basketball, soccer and cricket. He was looked up to and even liked by his contemporaries, despite his faintly distant manner.

In his second year, Akbar was selected for a study programme for exceptional students, which required submission of a dissertation on a socio-political topic with international implications.

Trophies were to be awarded for the three best dissertations and the names of the authors entered on a roll of honour kept at the European Union Secretariat at Brussels.

Akbar chose to write on 'The Muslim Footprint in France,' starting with the invasion of southern France in 711 by Arab and Berber armies led by Tariq ibn Ziyad and culminating in the influx of Muslim immigrants to France, up to 9/11.

It was a large canvas. To research the Arab invasion, Akbar travelled from Narbonne to Poitiers, touring the Rhone valley, visiting Muslim occupation sites and unearthing original and later records of the Berber presence in France.

The second part of his research was conducted in Paris and Marseilles, where he interacted with Muslim settlers, visiting their homes, mosques and communal centres. He saw for himself the discrimination they had to face on a day-to-day basis.

The impressions would endure. His dissertation was the best of the three selected for the awards, but for Akbar, the experiences of the immigrants had a greater impact than the trophy.

He completed his Baccalaureate with honours by the time he was nineteen. Ahmed Ali was present at the graduation ceremony to cheer when Akbar received the diploma and citations for his performance.

Akbar returned to Karachi in a somewhat subdued frame of mind. For the first few days, the family basked in the pleasure of being together again. But in time they reverted to their routines – all except for Akbar, who seemed to drift.

Applications to foreign universities suggested by Ahmed Ali – two in England and two in the US – were forwarded, but Akbar did not react as expected at the prospect of joining either Harvard or Columbia, Cambridge or Edinburgh.

His mind was on other things – uncertainty about the future and a nagging awareness that decisions affecting his life were being made by his uncle. A growing desire to engage in something more significant than worldly success added to his frustration.

The depressing conditions prevailing in the country – lawlessness, extremism, and a compromised democracy – suggested the likelihood of people like him having to revise their priorities. Moreover, he had an enduring sense of guilt at having disappointed God when, aged nine, he had walked away from the task of memorizing the Quran. The breach in that relationship, brought about by the fearful encounter in the cellar under the imam's chamber, was taking its toll. At the time he had buried it in the recesses of his mind, but now, years later it had germinated into a sore that he could not talk about to anyone.

Lilian caught him twice pacing the upstairs veranda early in the morning. During the day, he avoided family members, preferring to loiter in the garden.

'What's the matter?' Kamran asked Lilian. 'He's changed so much.'

'He seems to be going through a phase,' Lilian replied, 'I'm sure he'll come out of it.'

'Have you tried talking to him?' Kamran asked.

'Of course I have. But he just mumbles and walks off.'

'I know. He does the same with me.'

One night, Lilian thought she heard the sound of sobbing from Akbar's room. Alarmed, she went in. The bed was empty. He seemed to be taking an extended shower. She decided to take up the matter at another time.

'What's bothering you, my love?' Lilian asked as they sat together for tea in the garden the following day.

'I'm just unwinding,' Akbar replied as a breeze swept through the old casuarina trees.

'No, that's not it. It's more...much more.'

'Mother, I've just got back. I'm trying to recover my bearings.'

'Why? You know exactly where you're heading academically.'

'I have no worries on that account. I think I can cope.'

'What is it then?'

He looked up as his sister Aliya joined them. She had recently come home for her vacations from an agricultural university in Punjab.

'Tell me, baba,' Lilian persisted.

'We are surrounded by so much negativity, Mother. The bad far outweighs the good,' Akbar finally burst out, unhappily. The remark took both Lilian and Aliya by surprise.

'What do you mean?'

'Look around,' he said, squinting slightly at the sun, 'do you see anything other than...rottenness?'

Aliya shot a quizzical glance at Lilian.

'Everything,' he continued, 'work, business...professions, industry, sport, entertainment, politics...even religion...is all a mess...and we have to deal with that...live with it.'

There was a fine sweat on Akbar's brow when he finished.

For a moment, no one spoke.

'Akbar,' Lilian said at last. 'Where does all this come from?'

'Can't you see Mother, it's around us.'

'I think I know what you're talking about, but I don't quite see why it should affect you so much.'

'This, and a lot else...I look at things differently after having seen how those in power treat ordinary people.'

'There's no need to be so holier-than-thou,' Aliya remarked. 'What do you expect us to do?'

'Darling,' Lilian said, 'the way I see it, if one is powerless to do anything about rottenness, survival with self-respect is all we can hope for.'

'That's what respectable people always say.'

'They're quite justified,' Lilian said, somewhat put out. 'If you have such concerns, deal with them by entering politics or leading a revolution. Frankly, my view is that for the present a university education is your best option even if you are...different.'

'Well said, Mother,' Aliya remarked as Lilian got up to go indoors. 'Bhaijan, are you sure the problem isn't personal? Something seems to be gnawing at you and I don't think it's the state of the country.'

Kamran was playing cricket in the spacious back compound of the colonial Gizri-stone house flanked by garages and staff quarters built along the walls on either side.

The players included sons and daughters of the servants employed at the Samandar and neighbouring homes. Wives and children squatted outside their quarters, cheering. Two boys, perched on the wooden gate at the back of the house, kept score.

Akbar appeared unexpectedly. Kamran bowled a yorker which was hit for a six. Kamran signalled to Akbar to join in, but he turned away.

'Come on bro,' Kamran yelled, 'just bowl an over to see how it feels.'

Akbar shook his head and was about to leave when some of those watching the game called out, 'We want Akbar Sahib. We want Akbar Sahib, Akbar Sahib.' They were joined by the players, 'Akbar Sahib, Akbar Sahib.' Akbar threw up his hands and stepped forward.

Every ball he bowled was greeted with clapping, cheering and whistling. Aliya watched from an upstairs window.

It pleased her to see Akbar bowling with abandon, face glistening, hair ruffled.

All at once she saw him stop in the middle of an over. He handed the ball to Kamran and walked away – without a word. The spectators fell silent, the game came to a halt.

After her chat with Akbar, Lilian could see a problem developing. She wanted her husband's advice on how best to handle it. So, as she had throughout their marriage, she waited for Javed Ali to wake up from his siesta. Whenever Lilian faced a crisis, she would wait for her husband, to return from court, the club, a bridge game or to wake up from his afternoon nap.

She had found that dealing with Akbar's issues was different from dealing with the other children. When he was born, Lilian had been taken aback on discovering the numbers 786 inscribed in blue on the left side of his chest.

Surprise had turned to awe when Javed Ali explained that the figures were traditionally taken to mean: 'In the name of Allah.'

As far as she knew, no one had ever told young Akbar about God, yet he seemed to be instinctively aware of Him. It was an inner realization – an instinctive acceptance – similar to drawing breath or drinking water when thirsty. God, to Akbar as a child, was imageless, like a fresh breeze, the smell of rain or the melody of birdsong.

He rarely spoke of this to anyone, even Lilian. But she suspected that he interfaced with a secret world. 'Godscenes' she would call them when, at the age of three or four, Akbar would come running, flying through the air, eyes shining, lips parted, hastening to share some of his wonder with her.

She recalled him examining objects such as a conch shell or a pine cone or a cobweb and declaring, '*He* designed that.'

'How do you know?' Lilian would ask.

'Because only *He* can do that,' would be the reply.

Looking at a flower on one occasion, he had whispered in Lilian's ear, 'That colour is Him...the smell is Him...every flower, nothing but Him,' and 'a mother's love is Him.' Sometimes he would tell her about laughter in the bushes, a humming in the trees or a whispering amongst leaves.

She was baffled by the changing shades of the 786 birthmark from its normal bluish hue to an angry pink when he was unwell, or mauve when worried, to skin-coloured paleness when he was deep in thought.

'Do you know who He is?' she asked when she felt that Akbar was old enough.

'He is...He is...' Akbar said, then stopped, at a loss to proceed further.

'He is Allah,' Lilian said.

'Allah?' Akbar echoed.

'Yes, Allah,' she said, explaining in simple terms what Allah meant while watching Akbar's wide grey-blue eyes.

'But He is not people?' Akbar queried.

'No, He is not people...we are.'

'He loves us?' he wanted to know.

'Yes, He does...because we are His people.'

Other unusual happenings during Akbar's childhood convinced his parents that he was different from his siblings. He could utter complex sentences and read by the age of three. He spoke Urdu, English and Sindhi. He could solve complex puzzles, problems and riddles – logical, mathematical or mechanical – that baffled adults.

His IQ was exceptionally high. He received ratings of 'genius' or 'extraordinary talent' through his school years. With Lilian's proclivity for languages, Akbar also learnt French, Italian and Spanish.

Despite Ahmed Ali's abiding interest in Akbar, it was Lilian who was his sole confidante and sharer of his other-worldly encounters. Her role in such situations was essentially reactive. She would on occasion chafe at her helplessness. Her life was centred around her concern for him. She was alive to the extraordinary nature of happenings he faced at times. Akbar suspected that his mother fretted over him. He felt less alone because of that.

Seeing his wife's strained expression, Javed Ali heard her out with the close attentiveness he reserved for complex court hearings.

'Lily,' he said finally, 'from what you tell me, I don't think that simply talking to Akbar will ease the situation. At the same time, communication is the only recourse. Ultimately he will have to come to terms with his concerns by himself.' After a pause, he added, 'When I talk to Akbar, I get the strange feeling that I am with someone far older...and wiser... it's quite unsettling.'

'So you think, we shouldn't discuss this with him?'

'No, no. Discuss with him by all means. It may help him but it is unlikely that his problems will go away.'

'Will *you* talk to him?'

'Yes, I shall...but any talking has to be done carefully, he's a sensitive boy.'

'Javed,' Lily remarked, eyebrows raised, 'try, for Heaven's sake...'

'Clearly, it is important to take him seriously. We can't be dismissive of his views and hope to achieve results.'

'You're making it sound complicated.'

'Look, I'm as worried about him as you are Lily but I've come across these situations before. That's why I'm pointing out the risks.'

Javed Ali and Ahmed Ali met for lunch at the Sind Club. The brothers were physically dissimilar. Javed Ali was tall, grey-haired, distinguished. He looked and behaved like a judge – unflappable, balanced and precise.

Ahmed Ali was homely in comparison. Shorter, plump and balding slightly, he was also devout and scholarly.

They chose a secluded corner in the dining hall under oversized paintings of Talpur rulers. The place was brimming with members, many of whom made it a point to greet the brothers.

'There may be,' Ahmed Ali observed, 'a solution.'

'All right...you tell me,' Javed Ali said.

'You have to believe in it – if it is to be successful,' Ahmed Ali said, looking at his brother. 'Take him back to religion... to Dars-e-Nizami studies.'

'How will that help? Don't forget he gave up on religious studies when he was nine.'

'We'll make him realize that he has a duty to God to complete what he left unfinished.'

'By reciting prayers he doesn't understand?'

'He'll read the Quran again and, if need be, learn its meaning. He'll be trained to recite, memorize and internalize... the word of God. That will give meaning to his life.'

'How and where do you intend to accomplish this?'

'I've discussed the matter with the imam of the Beyt-as-Salah mosque. He understands the problem and will provide a suitable instructor.'

'You've thought of everything except the one that counts,' Javed Ali said. 'Will Akbar agree to this arrangement? Remember, he left his studies at that mosque of his own accord.'

Ahmed Ali was silent for a moment.

'I believe he will,' he said at last. 'A part of him has been touched by God. It's something we've been aware of for years.'

'How much time will this take?' Javed Ali asked uneasily.

'I can't say. Let's make a start. We have to make him whole first. Other matters can be dealt with later even if it means that his studies abroad have to be shelved for the time being... Cambridge, Harvard and all that can wait. It won't hurt him.'

'In some respects you know him better than I.'

'I'm his uncle. I hope you have faith in my commitment to your son.'

'You mean, your soulmate,' Javed Ali said. 'Dear brother, how can one possibly doubt you? He may have been born to us but you seem to have made him the centre of your life, your sole concern...especially after the loss of your dear wife. He is fortunate to have you by his side.'

There were tears at the corners of Ahmed Ali's eyes.

THREE

Akbar listened with growing concern to Ahmed Ali on the veranda. His uncle was speaking about the importance of religious guidance prior to a university education.

'Why *now*, Uncle?' Akbar asked, frowning.

'You have the time. You want answers to questions that plague you. You need peace of mind. And you have been guilt-ridden ever since you stopped memorizing the Quran...'

There was a pause before Akbar spoke.

'Will I get that peace...through this course?'

'You will if you approach it properly. You claim you are close to Allah. He will help you.'

'I'm confused, Uncle.'

'When you were younger, you had no doubts.'

'I have no doubts now. But having walked away once, I wonder if I'm really cut out for a religious way of life.'

'You are required to study rules and principles that will channelize your thoughts. No one expects you to adopt a religious lifestyle.'

'I feel close to God. Isn't that enough?'

'Not quite,' Ahmed Ali said, 'feeling close to God is rare, but it's not the same as knowing Islam. Feelings relate to emotions, knowledge brings about intellectual awakening.'

'I completed the thirty *siparas* as a child. By the age of eight, I began to learn the Quran by heart...'

'And gave it up when you were nine,' Ahmed Ali said, interrupting him. 'Rote exercises including Arabic letters and syntax designed for children are not part of this course, but comprehension, correct recitation and internalizing the text are.'

Akbar gazed through the trellis at the gardener weeding the lawn.

Ahmed Ali asked softly, 'What happened to that youngster who followed me around in the mosque, prayed beside me and sat close to me during discussions?'

'He went away,' Akbar replied in a flat tone.

'What became of his classmates who squatted in rows and recited *sipara* texts, rocking back and forth, or played hide and seek when the ustad wasn't looking?' Ahmed Ali asked.

'All scattered, a while back,' Akbar replied.

After a pause, Ahmed Ali asked, 'Are you a believing Muslim?'

'I am,' Akbar murmured, taken aback.

'Well then, you are morally obliged to finish the study of the Quran which you haven't done.'

'I know...I know,' Akbar said.

'Then let me tell you this. If a believing Muslim – with your IQ and level of awareness – deliberately misses an opportunity to get to know Allah through study and prayer, he will be running afoul of God.'

'Does it have to be the...Beyt-as-Salah?' Akbar asked.

'The madrasa is situated in an adjacent building which is not part of the mosque...that you seem to dread,' Ahmed Ali said.

'Same thing,' Akbar commented. 'They are linked...why go there at all?'

'Why not?' Ahmed Ali responded, somewhat surprised. 'It's in your neighbourhood. It is where you studied the Book as a child.'

'Perhaps that's why,' Akbar remarked wearily.

'Your reactions are strange. I don't know what to make of them.' Ahmed Ali said.

'Never mind, Uncle...we're here now' he said, when they got to the mosque, so...let's get on with it.

'Akbar, this is a serious matter calling for a responsible approach,' Ahmed Ali chided. 'Don't be so casual about it,'

'I am committed Uncle, otherwise I wouldn't be here...I am yet to be convinced though. But as always, I have faith in your judgement.'

His bare feet felt the cool tiled floor of the courtyard as they had on his very first visit. Everything was as he remembered, the colonnaded galleries on either side of the courtyard, the washing section beyond, the stairs leading to the upper prayer terrace, the minarets, the rounded dome – now touched by the rays of the setting sun – and the arched prayer chamber. It was as if time had not moved.

'He's too young,' Lilian had remarked, leading four-and-a-half year old Akbar downstairs to the veranda where Javed Ali and Ahmed Ali waited.

'Too young for what?' Javed Ali asked.

'For the mosque,' she said. 'His *Bismillah* ceremony took place just three months ago, and he has been learning the Arabic alphabet and conjugation every day since. Isn't that enough for the time being?'

The brothers exchanged glances.

'I went to the mosque at the age of three, and my brother here,' Javed Ali said, 'went on his fourth birthday.'

'How will he cope with Karachi Grammar School *and* the madrasa?' Lilian asked.

'As his uncle and I did,' Javed Ali said.

Lilian realized that further resistance would be futile, so she handed her son over to Ahmed Ali and saw them off – Javed Ali to his chambers and Ahmed Ali, with Akbar, to the mosque.

It was Friday. The muezzin had given the call for midday prayer. Holding Akbar's hand, Ahmed Ali led him to an empty space in the rows of worshippers in the terraced courtyard. Akbar sat close to his uncle, observing the proceedings.

After the sermon and recitation from the Quran, the congregation got up for the namaz. Ahmed Ali told Akbar to sit quietly between him and his neighbour during the prayer.

An air of regimented masculinity prevailed, as suggested by the rows of barefooted men standing side by side performing the rites in unison. The poised feet reminded Akbar of smooth-skinned puppies poised for a race. Midway through the prayer, when the worshippers were standing upright, Akbar looked to his right down the row of legs extending like posts, in a straight line from where he sat, to the edge of the courtyard.

Then he looked to his left and noticed a boy his age sitting in the same row a short distance away, pulling faces at him. Akbar responded in kind. When he wearied of that, he lay on his back and observed the faces of the worshippers arrayed above. Ignoring Ahmed Ali's look of disapproval, Akbar turned towards the boy who had been making funny faces.

As he watched, the boy began to crawl over the worshippers' feet down the row towards Akbar. Not to be outdone, Akbar too crawled in the boy's direction alongside worshippers bowing in obeisance, like a surfboarder tunnelling through a giant breaker towards God, until he came face-to-face with the other crawler. They chuckled and exchanged high fives, much to the consternation of the looming worshippers.

On the way back, Akbar missed Ahmed Ali's feet and crawled on till he reached the end of the row. By that time the congregation was squatting on its haunches for the final part of the prayer, leaving no space for crawling back. Finding his path blocked by squatting bodies, Akbar panicked, reacting the only way he could. His cries were heard over the imam's closing prayer.

'*Masha'Allah*,' the imam said, embracing Akbar, 'you have become a young man. I recall a curly-haired eight-year-old who couldn't get through lessons fast enough before scooting off with his classmates to play cricket.'

Voice dropping slightly, he added, 'I also remember a nine-year-old who broke his trust with Allah by failing to memorize the Quran.'

Ahmed Ali and Akbar were on a courtesy call at the imam's chambers. Akbar stopped short at the imam's last remark but was urged on by Ahmed Ali. The imam led them to a carpeted alcove cushioned with bolsters, where they sat cross-legged.

'Where have you been all these years?' the imam asked

Akbar mumbled something about school and travel.

The face is the same, somewhat weatherbeaten – the dark, piercing eyes that could look through objects, more hooded now – the beard, graying and wispier than before – the same tapering fingers – the voice, sometimes stentorian, at times rasping or playful, just as before – the same long white robe and head cloth – the frame, shrunken, more emaciated.

'Daydreaming,' the imam called out as he passed young Akbar squatting at his desk in the gallery, fretting about a game of cricket that had been disrupted by the rain.

'Daydreaming again,' said the imam to Akbar, now staring out of a window in the imam's chamber – as if eleven years had not elapsed.

'Sorry, Imam Sahib, I was just...'

'You haven't given up the old habit from your cricketing days,' the imam said, interrupting Akbar.

'We're here to learn about the Dars-e-Nizami curriculum that you recommended for Akbar when we last met,' Ahmed Ali said.

'I know why you've come, Ahmed Ali Sahib,' the imam said dryly.

An attendant came in with green tea.

'Some *qahwa*, before we talk,' the imam suggested.

Between sips, the imam said, 'We'll start with Arabic lessons. First there is grammar comprising *sarf* and *nahw*, then *Arabi adab* which is literature. Then there is *balaghat* or rhetoric. The next part – *tarjuma* and *tafseer* – involves translation and explanation of religious texts.'

There was a pause during which the imam looked solicitously at Akbar and said, 'This sounds forbidding, I know. I hope you aren't afraid of hard work.'

Ahmed Ali answered for him. 'It's all right. Go on, Imam Sahib.'

'Very well...this will be followed by a study of the Hadith, containing the traditions of the Prophet and the six canonical books from Imam Bokhari to Tirmizi. Then there is fiqh or Islamic law, followed by *usool-e-fiqh* or jurisprudence. Next, *mantiq* or logic, and finally *aqaid* or *usool-e-deen* discourses on Islamic theology and dogma.'

Peering at Akbar, he said. 'Are you prepared to undertake such a course?'

Akbar murmured, 'I can only...try.'

'Why the hesitation?' the imam asked, 'you should be familiar with some of the subjects. They were part of your syllabus when you attended lessons in your earlier days at the mosque.'

'Yes, I recall,' Akbar said, feebly.

'But of course, you never completed the course. You left midway, all of a sudden,' the imam said. 'I've often wondered what made you do that.'

Akbar gazed out of the window instead of looking at the imam.

'The increasing pressure of school studies in all probability,' Ahmed Ali said lamely.

'Ah, yes,' the imam said, 'Western education always comes first with the well-to-do. But I wouldn't have thought the dual workload would have deterred Akbar from Quranic studies. A less dedicated student may have been put off but not Akbar. Anyway, now you're back.'

He continued, 'I've put you in the session that starts well before midday prayers and finishes by 5 pm. An instructor has been appointed exclusively for you. He will teach you the Hadith, fiqh, *usool-e-fiqh, mantiq* and *aqaid.* To qualify as a Munshi Fazil one must complete the Wafaq-al-Madaris syllabus. I cannot see you completing it in one go. The entire programme is very long, and successive exams are taken as a rule.'

Akbar tried to focus on the imam's remarks.

'You'll be taught exclusive topics at the mosque by your instructor. For the general subjects, you'll attend classes at the madrasa according to the timetable followed there.'

He pattered on about workday timings, duration of classes and textbooks. When he had finished, he leant back against a bolster, breathless, his hooded eyes half-closed. The interview was over.

In his first year, Akbar, barely five, attended class twice a week at the madrasa's nursery section. His uncle would bring him to the mosque, returning when it was time to take him home. The nursery class was taught the Arabic alphabet with the help of painted blocks or slides. The children also practised reciting the first prayer in unison.

There is no God except Allah,
And Mohammad is the messenger of Allah.

Two new prayers were memorized every week.

Akbar liked story time more than his other classes. His imagination would enter a world peopled with characters involved in extraordinary situations.

On the night of his fifth birthday, he dreamt of the Prophet hiding from his enemies in a cave. He escaped discovery because after he entered the cave, a spider rapidly spun a web across the entrance and a bird built a nest at the base of the entrance, and in the twinkling of an eye, laid eggs in it. The intact cobweb and the undisturbed nest fooled the enemy into assuming that no one had entered the cave – despite the presence of a pesky chameleon, that kept bobbing its head pointing to the Prophet's hiding place.

Having just turned twenty, Akbar found it awkward to attend Arabic language classes alongside a mix of very young boys and some older ones. He was anxious to move on.

Introductory lessons were all that he needed to come to grips with the Dars-e-Nizami programme. He was a hard-working pupil supported by a skilled instructor.

Akbar found his instructor intriguing. The thirty-two-year-old Austro-Hungarian had converted to Islam eight years earlier and was now known by the Muslim name of Abdulla Saleh. Religious research on Islam had taken him to several Muslim countries. He came to Karachi after a six-month stint in FATA, north-west of Khyber Pakhtunkhwa. He was married to a woman from Sind and had two children with her.

His Gothic features, pointed beard and darting eyes topped by arched eyebrows gave him a quizzical look. In a salwar that ended well above his ankles, long flapping kameez and bright green turban, he looked like an extra from a *1001 Nights* Hollywood film.

He communicated with Akbar in Urdu and English. His teaching focused on the jihadi aspects of religious conduct which he viewed as a prerequisite for a correct understanding of Islam.

His fiqh classes on obligations and prohibitions dwelt on laws governing conduct in warfare. In the Hadith classes, he emphasized the traditions laid down during hostilities. The examples and explanations he cited as points of reference in classes on *tafseer* and *usool-e-deen* related to the Battles of Badr and Uhud and other armed conflicts.

Akbar's aversion to the mosque lessened as the studies progressed. Unlike other day scholars, he found it more convenient to spend lunch break at the mosque. He preferred homemade sandwiches and fruit to the food served at the madrasa mess. He ate alone, either in a breezy section of the gallery or on the terrace upstairs. Lunch hour was also a time for introspection – for reviewing morning lessons, going over obscure concepts taught earlier, distilling information. There was a growing new awareness.

He was in an enquiring frame of mind one day when he was drawn, inexplicably, to the prayer chamber. Finding it empty, he sat down in a dark section. His eyes wandered over the frescoes on the wall – *ayats* in Kufic script bordered by floral panels – gleaming pieces of mosaic bearing the names of Allah panelling the inner surface of the vaulted dome.

Why haven't I noticed these before?

Just then a boy ran breathlessly into the prayer chamber and hid beside the imam's lectern. In a short while, another boy came in, looking for him. The memories came flooding back.

It was here...it started here...that afternoon the mosque was empty... everyone seemed to have left...we were on the terrace...we decided to play hide and seek...just the two of us...Imran and I...we tossed a coin to play hide and seek. I chose heads for hiding...and heads it was... Imran closed his eyes and started the countdown...I ran downstairs... making for the washing section...I couldn't find a nook to hide in...the alley behind the imam's chambers was a good spot...but there was no escape route in case he caught me there...the minarets...of course... two birthday candles...with winding stairs...going up...up...up...to the top of Karachi...the best place for hiding...but what if he picked the minaret I had chosen...the galleries were too exposed...but the prayer chamber was dark and cavernous...I hid by the lectern and waited...he came in looking for me...I held my breath...

I heard him approach...then he seized me and placed a foul-smelling cloth over my nose and mouth...when I woke up I found myself in a dark, dank room...on a cot covered by a filthy quilt... after a while a door opened somewhere above...daylight fell on steps leading down into the room...darkness again when the door closed...it was not Imran who came down the steps and turned on a portable lamp...the light from it fell on stacks of weapons that caught my eye...I saw a tall, black-bearded man with a pock-marked face...it was one of the attendants...he spoke to me...I kept silent...I was afraid...he offered me water...I did not take it...he came up to me...picked me up and held me close...I struggled and kicked ...he held me fast and bit my ear...I cried out and struck his face...he laughed...and put me down saying he wanted something...I could not guess what he wanted...until...he tried to undo my salwar...sweaty, stinking beast...I screamed at the top of my voice...and lashed out, hitting his nose...it started to bleed...he let me go...then placed a dagger on the cot...threatening to punish me for striking him...he retreated to a tap...washed his nose...I ran blindly towards the steps...leapt on them and made for the door...the latch was stuck...leaving the tap running, he bounded after me...I hurled myself against the door...the latch gave way...I ran out in the sunshine from that cellar under the imam's chambers...I kept running all the way home.

FOUR

'You belong here as much as you do there. You should spend
more time with us before we go away...'

The words moved Lilian. The remaining phrases conveyed
news about the family and the parish. She put the letter
from her father on the escritoire and smiled, recalling his
preference for letters over emails.

His remarks were justified. She had neglected her parents,
paying them fleeting visits over the last few years. They
were fairly old now. Her mother had survived cancer after
a difficult struggle. They deserved more of her time. She
decided to spend several weeks with them in the summer
now that Akbar seemed more at ease.

Initially she had reservations about him taking up
religious studies. But now, despite lingering doubts about the
effect of such a course on Akbar, she felt it could help him.
She was uneasy about religion. There were issues that defied
explanation, whether in Islam or in Christianity. Esotericism
was one such subject.

Aliya saw her mother seated at the Queen Anne bureau
she had brought with her at the time of her marriage.
She looked strangely fragile, her features framed by high
cheekbones, touched by deflected light, chestnut-coloured

hair piled high, grey eyes, reflective. Aliya watched a while before walking across to kiss the top of her head.

'I've had a letter from your grandfather.'

'All well?'

Lilian nodded.

'I plan to visit them.'

'Great, may I go with you?'

Their conversation was interrupted by a phone call from one of Aliya's friends. She came back smiling.

'What is it Alee?' Lilian asked.

'It was Simeen...she's arranged an evening at the French Beach on Saturday...barbecue...the works.'

'Who'll be there?' Lilian asked

'The old A-level gang,' Aliya said

'Will Teymour be there?'

'Of course...he's part of the gang,' Aliya said.

'You remember what I said?'

'Yes Mother...don't worry.'

'So when will you be back?' Lilian asked.

'It's an all-nighter, Mother.' Aliya said.

Lilian sat up. The tone of her voice changed.

'There's no question of you spending the night out,' she said.

'Mother please...Simeen's aunt will be there,' Aliya said.

'I don't care if her parents are there. You're not spending the night at the beach. Your father wouldn't approve. Besides it isn't safe.'

'Akbar will be there too and Kamran. Isn't that enough?'

'Akbar?' Lilian exclaimed, 'It's not his sort of thing. Are you sure he's going?'

'He doesn't know yet but Simeen has asked both of them.'

'You'll be lucky if you can persuade him. In any case, Akbar or no Akbar, you're coming home by midnight. Or you're not going at all. Make your choice.'

When Akbar got home from the mosque, Aliya told him about the invitation from Simeen.

'At the beach,' he remarked, 'no Alee, I don't think so...'

'Why not Bhaijan? It'll be fun. You need a break.'

'Alee, I don't see myself fitting in. It's not my kind of fun. What's more, I don't know your friends well.'

'Come on bro,' Kamran added, 'It'll do you some good to get out and be with young people.'

'Please Bhaijan,' Aliya pleaded, 'do this for me. We haven't been out together in ages. Even if you don't know my friends, isn't communicating with others something religion encourages?'

Akbar smiled.

'At least, I managed to get a smile out of you.'

Finally Akbar gave in, 'All right. I'll come.'

Four air-conditioned SUVs carrying twenty young people, Simeen's aunt, two servants, a dog and iceboxes packed with food and beverages, sped in a convoy on a fine Saturday evening towards the French Beach.

Akbar sat silently in one of the SUVs among the chattering passengers. They were in branded sportswear, he in his salwar kameez. The convoy moved swiftly over newly constructed flyovers.

'More billboards,' Akbar mumbled as they passed some giant hoardings.

'Did you say something?' a girl next to him asked.

'Not really. I was commenting on the billboards.'

'You're Aliya's brother, Akbar?' she asked.

Akbar nodded. He noticed that she was a trifle thin and angular but had a curious charm.

'I'm Tooba Shirazi, Aliya's friend,' she said with a dimpled smile.

'Hello.'

She asked about his work. He told her what he was studying. She wanted to know more. He had little experience of women. His responses were brief and to the point. When asked what his aim was, he replied somewhat self-consciously that he wanted to specialize in theology.

'Fascinating,' she said, 'I've never come across anyone doing something so unusual.'

'Well, now you have. And it's really not unusual. There are Islamic scholars all over,' Akbar said, opening up.

'I meant someone involved in...such meaningful work.' After a pause, she continued. 'What I do seems trite by comparison.'

'Work is never trite,' he said. 'What do you do?'

'I'm a model...I model clothes.'

'You mean high fashion?' he asked. 'Like the girls on the hoardings ...draped in lawn.'

'That kind of thing...but it's more a catwalk thing than photographs...and with fancy designer wear...'

'Well, it's still work, isn't it?'

They were passing through a suburb which served as a stopover point for trucks.

'In your opinion...' Tooba asked uneasily, 'does my kind of work...seem questionable?'

Akbar was reluctant to respond but the face turned towards him demanded an answer.

'Islam,' he finally said, 'disallows public display of a woman's body. But in your case we have to consider whether modelling is acceptable in our society.'

'Is it?'

'That's something for the concerned person to decide. In my view many things take place that are more questionable than modelling.'

'Such as...?'

'Just look at any newspaper. There's rape, target killings, *karo kari*, child molestation. Shall I go on?'

'No, no, I see what you mean,' she said, placing a hand on his arm.

'There's one more, which to my mind is the mother of all evils,' he said, 'and that's lawbreaking...whether it's a violation of the Constitution or a traffic offence.'

'Quite a list!' she said.

'In comparison modelling comes off as downright respectable,' he said with a smile. 'Even at its worst it's unlikely to damage the state.'

'You should smile more often,' she said. 'It lights up your face.'

Leaving the outskirts of the city, they crossed a terrain that was once windswept and open. Now it was cluttered with low-cost houses.

Tooba's attention was drawn to a roadside hoarding that showed a girl in a hijab displaying cosmetics to a customer with a niqab. It was captioned:

Welcome to the realm of Islamic beauty products. We offer Shikakai shampoo, Aritha hair conditioner and Lobaan hair spray for glorious hair. Ubtan cleanser for soft, fair skin. Kajal eyeliner and mascara for dreamy eyes. Miswak for white teeth and red lips. Ittar perfumes for a fragrant presence. Plus a whole range of Islamic cosmetics for beautifying the Begum.

A diagonally printed banner read:

For the perfect image use Islamic body products. Add your beauty to the World of Islam.

'What do you think of that?' she asked.

'That's pure commercialization...it's not about Islam.'

'It's gross. Shouldn't be allowed,' she said wrinkling her nose.

'Call it what you like. It's an example of free trade. Anything goes'.

'You sound like a wise old man.'

'I'm lucky to have someone who guides me...he's helped open me up...you know what I mean...' then, murmuring under his breath, 'even though his religious orthodoxy is at times a pain in the neck.'

She gave him a quizzical look.

'It's too long to explain. You see, I don't just study the Quran and Hadith and current affairs, but I also look at other scriptures and philosophy – Plato, Kant, Marx and Rousseau,' his voice trailed off.

'You really do know it all,' she said.

'Not quite,' he said, noticing her dimples.

'Isn't it...?'

'Boring? No, it isn't...actually it's fascinating. You see it's helped me learn German. And at the risk of sounding big-headed, I should add – Arabic, Persian and a working knowledge of Latin.'

A corner of her Nike scarf had slipped from her shoulder on to his knee.

'Tell me,' she said after a pause, 'is there more?'

'Yes,' he said sheepishly.

'What?'

'Religious studies require some familiarity with historical scripts, Aramaic, Kufic, Devnagari, cuneiform.'

'Wow...'

She was distracted by the others singing along with a number playing on the SUV's stereo system. By the time they reached the last Makrani settlement the day was ending. At the muezzin's call to prayer, Akbar joined the congregation at the settlement mosque.

The stopover was good for the dog too. It got to run around in the open air. On his return, Akbar became aware of the pointed glances from some at the party. Word had evidently spread about his tête-à-tête with Tooba.

For the final lap they travelled on gravelled roads leading to the beach. Simeen's beach hut was located on a rocky promontory. A sloping path led from the hut to the beach. Barbed wire ran across the landward side of the hut. It was manned by armed guards.

The hut had a spacious entertainment area which opened onto a covered veranda facing the sea. There were two tiny bedrooms and bathrooms at the rear. Electricity was provided by a generator.

Crabs, crayfish and prawns were being grilled on a barbecue pit when the party reached. The sun had set, leaving a reddish glow reflected by the sea. Some swimmers ran out towards the waves, with the dog giving chase. Simeen's aunt retired to one of the bedrooms. The young people assembled at a bar in the entertainment area. Music was switched on, drowning out the sound of the sea. The hut was soon overflowing with voices and laughter – and alcohol.

Akbar found it oppressive. He went down to the beach and sat on a sandbank, content to be alone. Sometime later he heard a strange buzzing in his ears. He was overcome by dizziness and a sudden surge of nausea. He broke out in a sweat and wondered what was happening. He tried to get back to the hut but was unable to move. A violent shudder ran down his spine, causing his eyes to roll and his limbs to flail. The fit lasted for some minutes. When the trembling abated, a sensation of peace started from his toes and flowed like a fresh water stream through his body. As the haze cleared, he had an intense urge to express in words all that he had felt.

For the stars appearing in the darkening sky as pinpoints of light, he involuntarily intoned: *We have indeed decked / The lower heaven with beauty / In the stars.*

A breeze whispering sea-secrets passed by him murmuring: *And He it is who sends / The winds as heralds / Of glad tidings...*

The waves in constant motion, surging and crashing, affirming the force of nature, resounded: *It is He who has made / The sea subject.*

As the trance subsided, his body stilled, savouring the experience. The sandbank had been churned up by the thrashing convulsions of his arms and legs. He lay in a shallow pit burrowed in the sand.

His sense of wonder was disrupted by rock music blaring through the night air. The young people in the hut gyrating to the metallic beat could be seen by passing fisherfolk. Two couples nestled on the beach, entwined, oblivious of time, place and occasion.

Nothing they do, he thought, *fits in with the order of things... or the needs of the land beyond – they are not real.*

Akbar shut his eyes, drifting into a deep, dreamless sleep. He heard Aliya's voice calling out, 'Bhaijan, Bhaijan, where are you?' Then it receded into the distance. Suddenly, he felt someone shaking his shoulder. Jarred, he opened his eyes and saw Kamran bending over him. 'How long have you been asleep?' Kamran asked.

'I don't know,' Akbar said, sitting up. 'Everyone's asking about you,' Kamran said. 'Really?' Akbar remarked. 'Food's been laid out for ages...come back to the hut...you're probably famished...' 'I'm okay,' Akbar said, getting up. 'What have you been up to while I slept?' 'We danced, played games on the beach, sang songs...you know...the usual.'

'Sounds like fun,' Akbar remarked as they headed back. When they neared the hut, Aliya left her place beside Teymour on the steps and ran towards them. She threw her arms around Akbar, chided him for disappearing, then led him in. The music was quieter. The whole party was there, seated in groups or pairs. They greeted Akbar like an old friend. Some of the men got up and embraced him. He could smell alcohol on them. Aliya brought him a plate of food. He found a place to sit beside Kamran.

'Tell us Akbar, what's it like being in a madrasa?' a boy called Mansoor asked. Startled, Akbar replied, 'It's like being at school or in college, depending on the level of studies.' 'But there must be something special about it since someone like you with honours in the IB has chosen to go there,' Mansoor slurred. 'Leave him alone, Mansoor,' Tooba said. 'He went there because he wanted to. It doesn't concern you.' 'Yes, it does,' said another, called Rajab. 'He wants to know, as do I, the advantages of a madrasa education. Who knows, it may suit us.' They were not going to be put off.

Akbar pondered for what seemed like ages then said, 'There are four major advantages – learning one's religion, learning Arabic, and learning in an environment in which Urdu is the medium of instruction...and where all students are treated alike, despite differences in class or ability.' 'You mean an *awami* set up...like for the masses,' Rajab said. 'Whatever,' Akbar remarked. 'Great,' said Mansoor raising his voice, 'but what about the special courses?' 'What special courses?' Akbar asked. 'Come on yaar,' Rajab said, 'stop being cagey.' 'I've no idea what you're talking about,' Akbar said. 'I'll tell you then,' Mansoor said, 'courses on what is the one and only correct Muslim faith...instructions on how to destroy non-conformists.' 'How to become a suicide bomber,' Rajab added. 'Stop asking stupid questions,' Teymour said, 'he's already told you what you wanted to know.' 'Butt out, Teymour,' Rajab mumbled, 'you're siding with him because of Aliya.' 'You're being offensive,' Aliya said sharply. 'Sorry Alee,' Mansoor said, swaying as he spoke, 'but we want to know about fundoism because sooner or later we'll have to deal with it. Since there is a Talib in our midst, he should be able to answer...' He was interrupted by Kamran, who stood up, hands balled into fists, face contorted with anger. 'Who are you calling a Talib... what's all this shit about fundos?' he raged. He moved towards Mansoor but Akbar leapt up to hold him back.

The speed at which the situation had escalated from light needling to full-blown threats took the onlookers by surprise. At first they all watched silently, hoping Mansoor would stop badgering Akbar but after the reference to 'fundoism' and 'Talib' they sensed that the matter was heading elsewhere.

Alarmed at the prospect of real violence, they tried to get both sides to cool down. Some suggested that Mansoor should apologize to Akbar. Others felt that it was best to pack up and go home.

While this was going on, Akbar decided to confront his detractors. 'I don't know why you said those things,' he said, 'but you should know that the madrasa I attend is free from such influences like many other madrasas that are exclusively academic.' 'So you're saying that you know nothing about such matters,' Rajab remarked. 'I've already told you about my study course,' Akbar said. 'I forgot to mention though that madrasa students work hard and conduct themselves correctly, as you'd expect of...of *awami* folk...something which seems to be missing from the conduct of better-off young people.' 'What does that mean?' Mansoor asked. 'What it sounds like,' Akbar replied. 'Are you saying that your behaviour is civilized and ours is not?' Mansoor said, his voice rising, 'Are you insulting us?' Akbar was silent. 'That's exactly what a fundo would say. That's what you are...a bloody fundo.' The word 'fundo' was heard by a hulk called Nasir who was emerging from an alcoholic stupor. Some months earlier, he had lost his twin brother in a suicide bombing. 'I heard the word fundo...who is the fundo here?' he shouted. His eyes fell on Akbar. 'It must be that bearded bastard over there,' he roared and lunged at him. Akbar stepped aside. Nasir hurtled ahead, missing Akbar, and fell heavily on the floor. He got up shaking his head like a bull clearing cobwebs, and rushed back at Akbar.

By then Kamran had joined the fray. Akbar tried to push him out of the way. Mansoor stepped up to engage Kamran. The brothers stood back to back, Akbar exchanging blows with Nasir and Kamran with Mansoor. Teymour jumped in too when he saw Rajab moving towards them.

Some of the others tried to separate the combatants and hold them back, but they managed to break loose and get back in the fray. Glasses were smashed, bottles tipped over, furniture overturned, and obscenities hurled as the fighting raged. The scene drew spectators. The servants and passing fishermen watched the fighters swinging blows, grappling and knocking down opponents, while the dog leapt about excitedly, barking furiously.

Simeen called out to her guards for help. Their intervention finally brought the scuffle to an end.

Six bruised, battered and bleeding contestants, some distraught onlookers, an overexcited dog and an unruffled aunt – who had slept through the evening – sat grimly in the SUVs on the way home.

FIVE

Akbar went bandaged to the class at the mosque the next morning. The imam was conducting a *hjfz* lesson.

He looked at Akbar searchingly and murmured, 'Been grappling with the devil, have you?'

'Something like that, Imam Sahib.'

'Hope you won,' the imam said.

'Wouldn't be here otherwise, would I?'

Later during the tutorial session Abdulla Saleh asked, 'What happened?'

Akbar told him.

'Fight only for right causes...and then fight to win,' Abdulla Saleh advised.

'Having been attacked, you were right to fight. You were defending yourself. But you would have been justified even if you had attacked first. They made fun of your religious studies and abused you.'

'Hadn't thought of it that way,' Akbar said. 'It happened so fast that we were drawn in before we knew what was happening...once in, we slugged away reflexively.'

'Remember what I said,' Abdulla Saleh reiterated, 'when you fight, fight to win.'

'I don't know who won. I'd say we were pretty evenly matched except that they suffered more injuries. There was a dislocated jaw and a fractured arm.'

After a while, Abdulla Saleh said, 'You should make it a point to stick to devout and right-thinking persons.'

Akbar blinked, wondering what had prompted such a remark. He asked, 'By devout, I suppose you mean someone who is...*ameen?*'

'I'm referring to pious Muslims, not the kind you went with to the beach.'

'Ustad, what do you have against them?' Akbar asked.

'They consumed alcohol, didn't they?' Abdulla Saleh said with disgust.

Akbar fell silent but was not ready to let go.

'Why should one only seek out Muslims? What's wrong with good Christians or Buddhists?'

'Perhaps, those who are *ahle-Kitaab* – people of the Book – such as Jews and Christians are exceptions. All others are Kaffir or non-believers. They should be excluded from one's circle of friends.' Abdulla Saleh said with a sly smile.

'Being good isn't confined to Muslims,' Akbar said, 'there are good people in all faiths.'

'I mention what is prescribed. You don't have to look beyond that,' Abdulla Saleh said with finality.

'That's a little difficult. I don't know of any Muslim society that shuts out the rest of the world. Some interaction with others is unavoidable...'

'Associating with non-Muslims for legitimate reasons is not forbidden.'

'That means we also have to allow for closer ties. How can we separate the extent of involvement?'

'I pointed out in last week's lessons on behaviour that *kalaam*, also known as speculative discourse on the ordained rules of conduct – which is what you are indulging in now – is prohibited. It falls in the same category as *bidah*... or innovation.'

Akbar fell silent though he was not convinced.

After the Friday prayer that week Akbar was invited by the imam for lunch at his chambers. Other guests included two senior students from his class – Mehrab Khan and Sirajuddin, deputies of the imam – and two strangers wearing belted fatigue jackets over salwar kameez.

The imam introduced the strangers, referring to them as 'emissaries from distant seminaries', then said that the lunch was being held in honour of Mehrab Khan and Sirajuddin. Akbar was puzzled by this. He was also curious about the seminarians. There was something disturbing about them.

The imam invited his guests to a *dastarkhan* laid out on the carpeted floor. Food was served on large trays laden with spit-roasted lamb stuffed with pulao rice, herbs and raisins, yogurt sauce with diced greens, curried quails, *seekh* kebabs, tandoori nan and buttermilk.

The imam tore apart the roasted lamb and distributed severed pieces to the guests. It was a sign for the guests to help themselves. Akbar started on his meal with a spoon but switched to fingers on noticing the others eating by hand. Fruit was served after the meal, followed by cardamom-flavoured green tea.

Mehrab Khan and Sirajuddin sat with downcast eyes, picking at the food. They seemed under some kind of pressure. The imam picked choice pieces from the trays and placed them on their plates. He spoke in Pashto to the seminarians. Akbar was familiar with the tongue. It was commonly used by the Pakhtun attendants at the mosque.

'This one,' the imam said sotto voce, indicating Akbar by a flicker of his eye, 'is special.'

'How so?' asked one of the seminarians.

'He is one of the most intelligent pupils I have come across in all my years of dealing with students...highly capable in all respects...a brilliant mind in a young body.'

'Can we use him for our cause?' asked the other.

'He can become a leading authority in any field he chooses. Properly guided, he can be moulded into a powerhouse for us.'

'*Jazak'Allah*,' they murmured looking sideways at Akbar.

Akbar leant back against a bolster sipping tea. He did not want them to guess that he could understand what they were saying.

When lunch was over the imam announced that the time had come to bid farewell to Mehrab Khan and Sirajuddin who were setting out for the tribal region north-west of Khyber Pakhtunkhwa province to join the seminaries from which the emissaries had come. The news came as a surprise. Akbar was not aware that the madrasa arranged cross-country educational stints for students.

A mixed group had gathered at the entrance to see the boys off. The near-blind mother of Mehrab Khan was there, guided by a small girl. A ragged middle-aged couple – the parents of Sirajuddin – stood close by. One could tell by their appearance how poor they were. Some attendants looked on.

Mehrab Khan and Sirajuddin, with carrier bags slung over their shoulders, waited at the entrance with fixed expressions, anxious to get on with the departure. The imam, accompanied by his guests, joined the group.

When Mehrab Khan took leave of his mother, she wailed, 'I don't know if I'll be alive when you return.'

He held her close whispering words of comfort in her ear. Sirajuddin's mother wept unabashedly, while his father faced the moment with stoicism.

After their farewells, the boys kissed the imam's hand. He embraced them, kissed their foreheads and made them pass under the Quran.

The taxi taking the boys and seminarians to the coach terminus drove off just as the heavens opened and the monsoon rain came crashing down.

The imam stepped back into the mosque leaning on his walking stick, saying, 'Your ways, dear God, are Your ways. After months without a drop, water enough to meet Karachi's needs comes in a flash and vanishes after turning the city into a watery waste. *Wah! Wah!* Your ways are indeed Your ways!'

Despite being drenched, he managed to hand a sealed envelope to each of the boys' parents. Akbar learnt later that the envelopes contained a portion of the price paid by the seminarians to the imam for the students. The sum represented compensation for parents who gave up their sons to the religious order. The remainder was deposited in a special account for Islamic causes.

Eight months after rejoining the madrasa, Akbar's memorizing of the Quran had gone far beyond the sura at which he had stopped earlier. He told Abdulla Saleh that he finally felt free – 'like Sinbad when the old man slipped off his back' – of the burden of guilt borne for eleven years. His exhilaration was catching.

The imam was pleased too. He felt that Akbar's return had erased a blemish from the mosque's record. In commemoration of the event he decided that Akbar should practice reciting the azan.

'Me a muezzin?' Akbar exclaimed.

'Why ever not?' Abdulla Saleh said.

Akbar was intrigued by the idea of calling the faithful to prayer. So he started his first azan one Friday afternoon from the top of a minaret.

When his voice rang out with, '*Allah hu Akbar, Allah hu Akbar*,' many were struck by the beauty of the delivery. Such an azan coming from Beyt-as-Salah was a revelation. Some were drawn to the prayer merely because of the haunting effect of the call. When the sound reached the imam's chambers, tears clouded the old man's eyes.

His attendants heard him murmur, '*Subhan'Allah*, we have a muezzin befitting our mosque...Allah has at last given Beyt-as-Salah a voice.'

After a while, he was heard to murmur, 'Worshippers who were used to hearing my Friday sermon, will now rejoice on hearing Akbar recite the azan.'

Akbar's involvement with Beyt-as-Salah began to increase beyond that of a mere student's. The teaching staff at the madrasa treated him as an intern. Students looked upon him as a sort of leader. Everyone, down to the attendants and cleaners, sensed he was 'special'.

He taught biweekly classes for boys under ten besides giving special lessons to minor girls in the imam's chambers. Academic proficiency had opened doors for participation in mosque and madrasa panel discussions on Islam and modernism and seminars with interfaith committees.

Akbar's responsibilities also included teaching slum children and distributing alms, food, medicine and clothing to the needy. The Beyt-as-Salah Foundation had appointed him group leader for these activities. This gave him access to other Foundation madrasas in the city.

During Ramadan he was kept unusually busy monitoring activities from the provision of food to overseeing the month-long practice of *aeteqaaf* observed by devotees on retreat at the mosque for prayer and meditation.

He was also a member of a committee that organized religious and social functions at the mosque throughout the year, including the Eid-ul-Azha sacrifice and distribution of meat.

'Beyt-as-Salah is more your home than this is,' Aliya once remarked bitterly.

'He has no life...no involvement...other than the mosque or madrasa,' Kamran complained to Ahmed Ali.

Akbar became aware of the extent of his commitment when he was assigned the task of preparing biographical data of the four hundred *tulaba* enrolled in the madrasa. Most of them were boarders. Many came from rural areas. Some were from orphanages, some had been abandoned. A large number of the better-off boys belonged to the Memon business community. There was however, only one Akbar.

At times during the year, Akbar noticed strange faces among the familiar ones in daily congregations – faces not only belonging to strangers but also strange-looking.

Many had Mongolian features suggesting regional differences. Others with light eyes and fair hair were clearly from the West. The heavy-browed ones with Semitic features were unmistakably Middle Eastern. There were also South East Asians from Indonesia and Malaysia.

They spoke in their native tongues, moved in tightly knit groups and kept largely to themselves. They were billeted in the mosque for temporary stay, sleeping in bedding rolls kept in the galleries and taking meals in the imam's chambers. After a few days they were not to be seen at all. Abdulla Saleh explained their presence as stopovers of Islamic scholars travelling through Pakistan. After the third or fourth such occurrence, Akbar presumed that facilitating touring Islamic scholars was an additional service undertaken by the administration.

Extra-curricular activities at the madrasa included a weekly question and answer session on social and religious matters. During one such session, a sixteen-year-old called Tariq Rafiq voiced concern about the 'obscure' nature of some of the citations.

'Which ones?' enquired Abdulla Saleh who was acting as moderator.

'*Ayat* number 125...I think...in sura VI,' Tariq said after a while.

'Sura VI, the one which is titled *An'am* or The Cattle.' Abdulla Saleh asked, 'is that the one?'

'Yes, that's it,' Tariq said.

'Read out the passage from the sura that is posing a problem,' Abdulla Saleh said.

Tariq hesitated before reading self-consciously from a Quran lying nearby:

'Those whom Allah (in His Plan) / Willeth to guide – He openeth / Their breast to Islam; / Those whom He Willeth / To leave straying – He Maketh / Their breast close and constricted / As if they had to climb / Up to the skies: thus / Doth Allah (lay) the penalty / On those who refuse to believe.'

'Well?' Abdulla Saleh remarked, lips fixed in a half smile.

'This suggests that God intends to let some people take the wrong course and then makes it difficult for them to take corrective steps,' Tariq said.

Abdulla Saleh glanced at the students on the panel before deciding who should answer the question.

'Akbar,' he said finally, 'you take this one.'

Akbar sat up, looked around, scrutinized the text and after a long pause, said, 'I think this passage should be construed in the light of the last portion which mentions that God penalizes those who refuse to believe. So the person to whom this is addressed is a disbeliever. If a man refuses faith, each step takes him downward, making recovery that much more difficult...'

Abdulla Saleh pondered over Akbar's explanation before asking Tariq, 'Does that clarify the matter?'

Tariq nodded.

'What else bothers you, Tariq?' Abdulla Saleh asked.

'Ustad, the need to fear Allah is a little confusing. Why is that a requirement? Why is fear brought into it?'

'Let's find a passage that mentions fear,' Abdulla Saleh said, turning the pages of the Quran. 'Here's an appropriate one. *Ayat* 102 of sura III, *Al-i-Imran*, "The Family of Imran".'

Abdulla Saleh read out the text in recitative:

'O ye who believe! / Fear Allah as He should be / Feared, and die not / Except in a state / of Islam.'

'Anyone prepared to deal with the reference to fear?' Abdulla Saleh asked turning to the boys seated in a semicircle. None volunteered.

'It seems I'll have to ask Akbar again to help give an answer.'

Akbar read the passage, and said, 'The word "fear" as used here, doesn't mean fear in the sense of being frightened. The equivalent Arabic word *uttaku* can be used in different contexts to mean different things but in most non-Arabic languages only the synonym "fear" is available as a substitute for *uttaku*. The mention of "fear" in this translation does not represent the connotation intended by the use of the Arabic *uttaku* in the original. The translation is restricted to one specific meaning. In the passage and elsewhere in the Quran, *uttaku* refers to a reverence which is like love, which fears to do anything not pleasing to the object of love...a fear of losing the beloved. Also, fear may be equated with concern, that is, a concern for the well-being of the beloved.'

'Bravo Akbar,' Abdulla Saleh said, 'I don't think I could have put it so well.'

Winding up the discussion, Abdulla Saleh stated that belief in God was a basic requirement for a Muslim.

'When your mind is sufficiently attuned to the notion of an all-powerful governing entity, then you must strive to equate that notion with Allah.'

'Surely, one must have some information about Allah before one can grasp the notion,' one of the boys remarked.

'That awareness is instilled in every Muslim child by the time he learns to toddle,' Abdulla Saleh said.

'What if one is not told about God until much later?' asked another.

'That's not possible in a Muslim community,' Abdulla Saleh said testily, 'so let's focus on realities.'

'But Ustad,' Akbar said, 'such a thing *could* happen. What then?'

'Then you are absolved until you are given your first lesson about God,' Abdulla Saleh said.

'Like the aborigines and heathen tribes...who were regarded as innocent until they came to the faith,' said a twelve-year-old boy.

'No one told me about God when I was a toddler,' Akbar murmured,

Abdulla Saleh heard him and retorted sharply.

'So how did you get to believe in Him?'

'He was within me,' Akbar replied.

Taken aback, Abdulla Saleh said, 'What do you mean?'

'I was always aware of Him...with my entire being. I felt Him there, like a part of me. I even played hide-and-seek with Him as a baby when I crawled and later when I could walk. It was not until my third year that my mother – and as I grew older, my uncle – spoke of God...giving me a sense of Him.'

Silence followed Akbar's revelation. Some boys shuffled uneasily. Others exchanged glances and looked furtively at Akbar. Abdulla Saleh was at a loss to deal with the situation. To end the proceedings, he got up from his chair saying, 'That's truly remarkable...I suppose,' then somewhat lamely, 'that's what it takes to be a Muslim.'

'Why only a Muslim?' Akbar retorted.

'What do you mean?' Abdulla Saleh asked ruffled.

'I mean...I think that...I would probably have God in me even if I'd been born in a home that followed some religion other than Islam.'

'What are you trying to get at?'

There was astonishment in Abdulla Saleh's voice.

'That closeness to God is not restricted to Muslims...He is God for everyone.'

SIX

Chief Justice Javed Ali had taken his children to view some accommodation by the sea, being constructed for underprivileged law students from Sind, sponsored by him and two other judges. On the way back he elaborated, to the silent amusement of his children, on the wonders of British Indian Karachi. 'It was not grand like Bombay or Calcutta. It was neither a feudal, nor a rich man-poor man city. It was not just for the white man or the native, nor for a single nationality or a sect. It was a gentle city, a communal city, with moderate, breezy summers and mild chilly winters requiring occasional fireplace-heating. Perhaps the cleanest subcontinental city, devoid of mosquitoes, flies or pye-dogs, where the streets were hosed down nightly, serviced by silent tramcars, traffic-rules-compliant vehicles and horse-drawn victorias. Muslims, Hindus, Parsis, Christians, Jews and even theosophists shared the city and mosques, temples, *agyaris,* churches and *jamaat khanas* were hallowed places of worship. Citizens participated in all religious festivals, moving freely, unmolested, unharmed. Gates of homes remained open, front doors unbolted, and no security guard was seen. The only bombs heard were those exploding in World War II newsreels. It was a peaceful city by the sea belonging to all, whether it be Frere Hall, Sind Madrasa, Jehangir Kothari Parade, the Hindu Gymkhana, Grammar School or St. Patrick's Cathedral. When we turned our backs on all that and drove the original Karachites away, we set foot on the path that has led to this.'

'To...what, Papa?' Aliya asked.

'This fearful urban jungle, noisome and brutalized.'

'Such bitterness, Papa...it's quite unlike you,' said Kamran.

Ahmed Ali was waiting for them at home.

'I have some news for you, young man,' he said, passing a typed letter to Akbar, 'You've got admission to Cambridge... yet again.'

Akbar was uncertain about how to react. Ahmed Ali had been applying for admission on his behalf every year since Akbar's enrolment in the seminary.

'That's great,' Aliya said, beaming.

'Very gratifying,' Javed Ali remarked hesitantly.

Kamran looked searchingly at his brother, 'Isn't that what you wanted bro?'

'Yes...yes...of course,' was Akbar's reaction, 'I'm just a bit surprised.'

Tea, savouries and cake were laid out on a wrought-iron table in the veranda. Lilian, recently back from a visit to her parents in Wiltshire, came down to pour, adding a breath of lavender.

She was pleased to hear about Akbar's admission to Cambridge.

'What subjects are you down for?' she asked.

'As before, Economics in Part I of the Tripos and Philosophy in Part II,' Akbar replied.

'Which college?' she asked

'Trinity,' Akbar said, 'Uncle's college.'

'Does that mean you'll have to wrap up your madrasa programme?' she asked.

'At some point I suppose,' he replied offhandedly.

'There's plenty of time for that,' Ahmed Ali said. 'You're not due at Cambridge until October.'

The news from Cambridge made Akbar uneasy. It was part of the dilemma he had been grappling with the last two years. Joining a foreign university was no longer his primary concern. His involvement with the Dars-e-Nizami course was so intensive now that he had scant time for other matters. He would delve deep into each subject and struggle until he felt at one with it. This continued with successive Wafaq-al-Madaris exams.

There was something more...glimmerings of a faith larger than academe, reaching out towards a communality beyond the Dars-e-Nizami course...a hint of something that lingered like fragrance.

He mentioned this to Lilian. She was saddened by his news but wise enough to point out, 'Akbar, you must do what you consider best...I suggest you think this over carefully... You're unlikely to get more offers from Cambridge or other universities in the face of repeated refusals. So make your decision with care.'

Later at night she expressed her disappointment to her husband. He too was at a loss to understand why Akbar preferred madrasa studies to Cambridge. Lilian felt she knew her son better. She sensed that it was more than just a matter of making a choice between alternative courses of study. Akbar's commitment to the madrasa arose from some force that was drawing him away from the type of life he was born into.

Offers from three other universities also came through, but the situation remained unchanged. Akbar insisted that he would be ready to consider such offers only when he had completed enough of the Dars-e-Nizami curriculum to justify giving it up. In any case, he planned to revert to theological studies after graduation, possibly on a permanent basis.

'Why would he do a thing like that again?' Ahmed Ali remarked in dismay.

'You'll have to ask him,' Javed Ali replied.

'But...it's so unlike him, to walk away repeatedly from such opportunities...he knows of the credibility of a Cambridge degree.'

'Talk to him. I've tried. It's like arguing with a wise old man who knows his mind and is probably capable of convincing even you that he may be right. He says he can't drop theological studies until he has achieved some measure of mastery. He won't be moved. You know how tenacious he can be.'

'But it will take him a while to complete that curriculum,' Ahmed Ali said, shaking his head.

'He's not planning to do the complete course,' Javed Ali explained. 'He goes on about "a level of awareness"...whatever that means. He doesn't want a revival of the guilt that he felt when he gave up the *Hafiz-e-Quran* programme. He says that is no longer an option...he calls it a bottomless pit.'

Ahmed Ali tried to persuade Akbar to reconsider his decision but Akbar was resolute. He would follow what he felt was the right course of action no matter what reasoning his uncle put forth.

Although the outcome was not what she had hoped for, Lilian viewed the crack in the bond between uncle and nephew with some satisfaction. It suggested that Akbar was now making decisions about his life on his own.

Aliya and Kamran were used to Akbar's idiosyncrasies. This time however, Kamran felt that Akbar was overdoing it. 'It's weird,' he remarked, 'what can he be thinking of?'

'Try to look at it from his point of view,' Aliya said.

'I can't,' Kamran replied shaking his head, 'his mind works abnormally...there's no comparison between Cambridge and a madrasa in Karachi...The point is Alee, where will this take him? Does he want to become a mullah?'

'Well,' Aliya said, 'if he does, it'll be the way of life he would have chosen. Look, the family has always known that he was born with a...strong spiritual bent but on account of some misplaced sense of shame he never had the guts to admit it. It's almost a part of his physical being...like...a heart valve. The point is, can one pluck *that* out of him?'

After Friday prayers, Ahmed Ali called on the imam. He wanted the old man's support to persuade Akbar to accept the Cambridge offer. 'I'll look into the matter,' the imam said, 'and advise on what I regard best for Akbar.'

Ahmed Ali suspected that the imam would not be an impartial arbiter. The imam advised Akbar to settle for the educational programme that he felt suited him better. Such a choice had, the imam emphasized, been put in Akbar's way by Providence.

'Bear in mind,' he said, 'that it is you who will have to live with the consequences of your decision. May Allah guide you in this.'

Akbar reviewed his options but came to the same conclusion. The Munshi Fazil study course should be completed before he attempted anything new. It was not a matter of gaining more knowledge but of attaining the first objective.

'There is no going back now,' Ahmed Ali told Akbar's parents ruefully. 'Perhaps later, there will be other openings.'

Abdulla Saleh felt vindicated by Akbar's decision to continue with him in preference to other options. By exercising his discretion Akbar showed capability to resolve such issues without recourse to mentors.

Abdulla Saleh sensed that his coming of age was due in large part to religious discipline. He firmly believed that if Akbar decided to specialize in theology, he would ultimately do well in any field – from academic research to politics. Given the growing importance of Islam in the world, he felt it was only a matter of time before Akbar became a name to be reckoned with.

Abdulla Saleh saw this as a demand for a more concentrated and purposive form of guidance and sought the imam's prior approval for such a plan. The imam pondered over the scheme, wondering if he should inform Ahmed Ali about it, then decided against it. He cautioned Abdulla Saleh to use tact if ever called upon by Ahmed Ali, Akbar or anyone else, to explain the purpose of the revised programme.

Abdulla Saleh pored over books and papers in the madrasa library, selecting authoritative works containing views he wanted Akbar to imbibe. Some of the texts were not available at Beyt-as-Salah.

Those he borrowed from the well-stocked bookshelves of the Binori madrasa at Teen Hatti. DVDs of talks by Dr. Israr, Maulana Shafi Okarvi, Maulana Taqi Usmani and other notable speakers, were also added.

Observing him dart about like a roadrunner, the imam remarked, 'You may lose him, if you bludgeon him with such fervour!'

Abdulla Saleh nodded his head respectfully but was undaunted.

'That boy,' the imam said, 'is a bookworm...it's quite abnormal.'

'That's probably why he is able to cover the Dars-e-Nizami curriculum with such speed,' Abdulla Saleh murmured.

'His parents aren't happy with the situation,' the imam remarked, 'so they must not suspect that much greater output is expected from him.' At their next class, Abdulla Saleh told Akbar with a sly smile that the programme had been reorganized, with a special focus on certain topics.

'I've stated my intention of completing the Dars-e-Nizami curriculum instead of going to Cambridge, so why the change?' asked Akbar, puzzled.

'I know, I know,' Abdulla Saleh said reassuringly, 'but at the speed with which you're gobbling up the curriculum, I wouldn't be surprised if you were to complete the Dars-e-Nizami course earlier. So I thought it best – after conferring with Imam Sahib – to extend your workload to more specialized fields of study and research.'

'I'm familiar with the Binori and Dar-ul-Uloom dissertations,' Akbar said, 'as well as accessing coded or classified information online in chats with Muslim and non-Muslim scholars, worldwide.'

Abdulla Saleh flinched at the mention of non-Muslim scholars. '*My* sources,' he remarked fervently, 'are rare discourses on duties and observances for the enlightened.'

In his tiny study Abdulla Saleh pulled out one rare publication after another – like a magician. Akbar regarded the books with silent awe. Some he recognized. Others he had come across in footnotes. The works included eighth-, thirteenth-, fourteenth- and eighteenth-century compilations, preserved in varying stages of fragility, and some sturdier latter-day works. Akbar noted the thirteenth-century *Kitabul Waasityyah* of Ibn Taymiyyah juxtaposed with the eighteenth-century *Kitabul Tawhid* by Sheikh Abdul Wahab; two eighth-century works, a tackily bound publication of 'Introduction to the Law of Nations' by Imam al-Shaybani and some incomplete Al-Awazi texts. There was also some historical material – major twentieth-century publications –works of Hassan-al-Banna, founder of the Muslim Brotherhood of Egypt; Syed Qutb, best known member of the Brotherhood; and Maulana Maudoodi, founder of the Jammat-e-Islami in British India, later Pakistan.

Akbar leafed through the books for almost an hour. When he had finished, he stood up, stretched his almost-six-feet self and gazed at a favourite sight – the sun drawing closer to the dome of the mosque.

He recalled a prank he had played on Aliya when she was only six and he was all of seven about the sun kissing a dome.

'Why the smile?' Abdulla Saleh asked Akbar. 'Just reliving a memory,' Akbar said. 'Smiling's good for you. It's catching', Abdulla Saleh said smiling. For the next few weeks, Akbar concentrated on the new material, following the sequence laid down by Abdulla Saleh. Selecting extracts from different scholars and setting written assignments, Abdulla Saleh skipped nimbly from one topic to another.

Gradually a pattern began to emerge from which the thrust of the exercise became discernible. The earmarked texts propounded a step-by-step approach to a specific form of Islam.

The course also included discussions held at radically inclined madrasas attended by ulema from Yemen, Mali, Indonesia and even the US. Akbar found them strangely aloof but put this down to the age difference between them and him. Abdulla Saleh indicated a different cause.

'These ulema regard themselves as red-blooded Islamists,' he observed with a smile.

'So what?' Akbar remarked. 'Our faith is probably as good.'

'Not if you're a European or a Pakistani...for them we are akin to... non-Arabs or *ajamis* as in the *ajami/watani* Arab nationalist analogy.'

'Surely the *ajami* stigma applies only in the Arab world to non-Arabs.' 'By some strange logic they've extended the qualification to scholars at large,' Abdulla Saleh said with a snigger. 'Some animals are more equal than others...I'm afraid, we aren't quite halal enough.'

Akbar's sense of discomfort with the direction of the course grew till, late one evening, he finally brought it up with Abdulla Saleh. The discussion turned to a heated argument. Suddenly they were surprised to hear the tapping of the imam's walking stick. He rarely visited Abdulla Saleh's study but echoes of the altercation had brought him there. A moment later, they looked up to see the old man with long wispy beard and drooping lids peering through the door.

'What's the matter? You both look so grim...' the imam glanced from red-faced Abdulla Saleh to wild-eyed Akbar. Abdulla Saleh stood up deferentially. Akbar remained where he was.

'We were discussing my concerns about the study method Ustad wants me to follow,' he said, ignoring the warning look Abdulla Saleh shot at him.

Noting the exchange, the imam asked, 'What method?'

Abdulla Saleh cleared his throat to respond but was forestalled by Akbar, 'First, Ustad selects passages from the works of Islamic scholars he rates highly...I study them in class...when I get home, I research them some more...next day we discuss the findings...then I write a paper on the lead topic assigned by him for assessment.'

'So,' the old man said with a touch of impatience, 'what's the problem?'

'Ustad leaves out large chunks of text that are essential for one to understand the author's line of thought. I am told to focus strictly on pieces of information about remote practices in preference to the main argument. So I miss out on a full appreciation of scholarly thought, ending up instead with one-sided declamations on obscure aspects of dogma.'

In the pause that filled the room, time stood still. The imam – canny enough to gauge undercurrents – sensed that the measures for inducting Akbar into the sectarian creed of the Beyt-as-Salah Foundation had been mishandled. He clutched his walking stick and suggested casually that they continue the discussion in his chambers – over a cup of qahwa.

'Your Ustad's selection of authorities,' the imam said, after they were seated in his chambers, 'includes eminent scholars. What's wrong with that?'

'True,' Akbar said, 'Ibn Taymiyyah, for instance – his top preference – is one of the greatest, but Ustad makes me focus on his outlandish forays such as his bad-mouthing of the Sufi order or his dismissal of Ibn Arabi as a heretic ...'

'Those are important references in the context of the fourteenth century,' Abdulla Saleh interrupted.

'As I suppose is his fatwa for jihad against the Mongols... making it a duty to wipe them out despite their conversion to Sunni Islam,' Akbar snapped.

'Yes,' the imam said gently, 'that development was relevant too.'

'What is one to make of his denunciation of Christians and Jews as non-believers or his opposition to the observance of the Prophet's birthday...or even for not honouring sites such as the Aqsa Mosque?'

'Akbar,' the imam cautioned, 'such emotionalism is unworthy. Draw on your reasoning power and it will all start to make sense. Negative practices including some of those you mention should be rooted out.'

'Imam Sahib,' Akbar said, determined not to be put down, 'Ibn Taymiyyah did great service when he took on scholars of his age for blindly following early jurists without reference to the Quran or Sunnah. He saw them as encouraging *taqlid* – imitation – leading to stagnation in religion. He single-handedly reversed the trend. Aren't those services to Islam notable? Why then keep them out of the course?'

The imam and Abdulla Saleh said nothing. While sensing unspoken disapproval in the two men, Akbar went on about Ibn Taymiyyah's promotion of Arabic literature, lexicography, mathematics, calligraphy, secular and religious sciences and his distinction as a jurist of the Hanbali School of Law.

'He was honoured,' Akbar added, 'with the title of Shaikh al Islam for believing that God had created the best of all possible worlds. These factors are not highlighted in my course or given the same importance as his other controversial discourses.'

'Of course, you should know these things,' Abdulla Saleh said, fidgeting, 'but a balance must be maintained between all aspects.'

'What aspects?' Akbar burst out, 'his off-the-cuff observations as compared to the substance of his teachings... that's not right...it's offensive...to deny homage to a giant among scholars. Any impartial scholar would have reservations about such a course.'

'Reservations!' Abdulla Saleh exclaimed indignantly, 'I prefer certain aspects of the work of some scholars over the rest. The texts guide one to an acceptable approach... to faith...'

'With respect Ustad,' Akbar said firmly, 'they contain points of view which are essentially individual interpretations of Islamic ways.' 'They are the best views in our scholarship,' Abdulla Saleh insisted.

'Then why is Imam Ghazali omitted? He contributed to recognition of Sufism and its integration in mainstream Islam,' Akbar persisted.

'Sufism, Sufism. Young people and liberals talk of Sufism without knowing its content,' Abdulla Saleh said scornfully.

'Apart from Sufism, there are other lessons to be learnt from him.'

'And I suppose you're going to tell me about them.'

'Ghazali was responsible for the revival of Islamic sciences that form part of our Dars-e-Nizami syllabus. His influence was lauded even by St. Thomas Aquinas.'

'Enough, enough,' Abdulla Saleh said, 'you refer to one who claimed truth is attainable in an ecstatic state and not by reason.'

'So? His claim was affirmed by the experiences of Rumi. He too is excluded from your selection. Instead, you promote the Al Shaybani/ Al-Awazi collection – which is of course the earliest documentation on the law of jihad.'

'Imam al Shaybani's eighth-century publication, *Introduction to the Law of Nations*, is a major work,' Abdulla Saleh stated pompously.

'Agreed Ustad,' Akbar said, 'but the book is more a treatise on public and private international law than on jihad.'

'There are comprehensive guidelines on jihad as well.'

'Yes, yes' Akbar affirmed, 'but they are less on justified killing and more about responsibilities arising during war such as the protection of women, non-combatants and children, treatment of prisoners of war, rights of asylum, truce, peace treaties, diplomacy and so on.'

Fearing that the situation had got out of hand, the imam interceded with unexpected sharpness, 'Get a hold of yourself Akbar.'

Taken aback, Akbar murmured, 'I'm sorry Imam Sahib.'

'The apology is owed to your Ustad who has laboured over your study with the care of a mother tending a special child,' the imam said.

'Sorry Ustad ...truly, truly sorry,' Akbar said, unrepentant and unbowed.

SEVEN

It was the death of Ahmed Ali's wife that first brought Akbar face to face with the loss of human life, reflected in images of a broken Ahmed Ali and the statue-like stillness of his parents and the shadowy mourners ranged behind them. The sight of tears coursing down his uncle's face had a paralyzing effect on the four-year-old. At first, he was appalled, recoiling and turning away. Then, drawn by echoing sobs and candles around a prostrate object covered by a white sheet, he crept back on all fours wanting to know – as was his nature – the reason for the tableau. Reaching the object unnoticed, he extended his fingers to raise the sheet. There was a gasp from a female relative and a startled cry of, 'What are you doing child?' just as the rough hand of a man grasped his wrist.

Akbar cowered, shrinking back in panic. The silence was broken by Javed Ali's stentorian tones, 'Let him see what he wants to see.'

The cover was drawn and Akbar saw the look of death – stone still, expressionless, frozen in time – quite unlike the silently reposing birds, butterflies and goldfish that he had seen before.

Later that night he lay beside Ahmed Ali, little hands dabbing his tears with tissues, whispering, 'Allah *mian* will take care of her in His wonderland in the sky.'

Years later, there was loss of a different nature when Aliya left the Samandar home following her marriage to Teymour.

As the family was getting ready for the upcoming celebrations, Lilian complained to Ahmed Ali about Akbar's prolonged absences from home. 'We see little enough of him. It's either the mosque or the madrasa or some function or other that never seems to end.'

'I have talked to him about it,' Ahmed Ali muttered lamely.

'Much good that has done...he's never here...he has no idea about what's going on in the family...Aliya's engagement is coming up ... and where is her dear brother? Chasing some good cause or other.'

'Lily, I had no idea it was as bad as that,' Ahmed Ali said, trying to mollify her.

'Dear Brother Ahmed,' she said, not to be fobbed off, 'you know exactly how it is...this is as much your home as anyone elses...you *do* know what goes on.'

Ahmed Ali took up the matter with Akbar in Abdulla Saleh's presence. He explained that commitment to religious studies did not justify ignoring family ties. If there have to be temporary absences on account of study and meditation, these should be compensated by Akbar spending commensurate time with the family.

'A *momin*,' he said, 'is obliged as long as he draws breath to live in the world while also fulfilling his spiritual obligations. That is why we have been given feelings and emotions...unlike animals who rely on instinct. Wouldn't you agree, Abdulla Saleh?'

Abdulla Saleh mumbled a 'Yes,' not wishing to be drawn into the conversation.

'Having feelings of love for parents, siblings, wives and children is quite normal. Wouldn't you say so, Abdulla Saleh?'

'Quite normal, quite normal,' Abdulla Saleh was obliged to concur.

Ahmed Ali continued, 'Falling in love – loving a member of the opposite sex – these are special faculties granted to us.'

Abdulla Saleh's eyes popped. Akbar suppressed a smile.

'Akbar's complete absorption in Beyt-as-Salah has caused much resentment at home,' Ahmed Ali pointed out.

'I know, I know,' Akbar replied, I'll just have to make up for it.'

'It may not be that easy...time has gone by...and you were just not there when needed. These are duties too you know.'

'All I can do Uncle is try.' Then, as an afterthought, 'I don't recall being told that interacting with family is part of prescribed conduct.'

'Well, you should have been told,' Ahmed Ali said, glancing at a distinctly uneasy Abdulla Saleh.

Aliya's engagement was brief. Her wedding followed soon after as her groom, the faithful Teymour, was on a tight schedule to take up an engineering post at a solar power project in Canada before the next winter.

'A hit-and-run affair,' Akbar joked, 'is what you've made of marriage to my sister. What makes you think we'll let you take off with her?'

Akbar was sad at the prospect of Aliya leaving home. He had been neglectful and tried to make up by reaching out to her in the remaining time. He took leave of absence from madrasa activities. It was comforting to be at home.

'Like a schoolboy on vacation,' Javed Ali remarked.

When it was time for the newly-weds to leave, brother and sister clung together, aware that their shared existence at home had come to an end, recalling things left unsaid, moments not shared.

With Aliya gone, visitors to the house sensed the difference, as did the family and domestic staff. Lilian experienced loneliness for the first time. Kamran felt deprived of the shelter Aliya had provided after Akbar adopted the madrasa. Javed Ali tried to remain stoic but could not help missing his favourite child.

Weeks after her departure, the Samandars faced a trial of a different nature. While lecturing at the university, Ahmed Ali suffered a cardiac arrest. He wavered between life and death for a while. Stabilization was hampered by an unexpected coma. Bypass surgery followed, leading – eventually – to recuperation. His physical condition prompted his retirement from university.

The changed circumstances brought Akbar closer to the family. After the altercation with the imam and Abdulla Saleh, he spent less time at Beyt-as-Salah. Instead, he studied at home for the final stage of the Wafaq-al-Madaris exams. He felt that it was now time to finish the Dars-e-Nizami course after almost three years.

By the time Akbar qualified as a Munshi Fazil, information about his profile as a new generation Islamist had been circulating for a while on the mosque/madrasa circuit.

It was eventually picked up by a media agent on the lookout for material for a story. He was among those who had been drawn to the Beyt-as-Salah Friday prayers by Akbar's azan. Sensing a big story in the making, he traded his findings with a major TV network.

Shaista Sabzwari had become executive producer of the network due to her uncanny knack for launching programmes that often went on to become countrywide hits.

She put together a pilot programme, splicing clips of Akbar's public appearances, sermons and azan recitals along with snippets involving his family and academic highlights. The pilot succeeded in projecting the image of an up-and-coming Islamist with movie-star looks, charisma and a progressive world view.

'It's a daring idea,' remarked Daud Panwala, managing director of the network.

'So daring in fact that no one will *dare* question our right to expose Islam for a righteous cause,' Shaista said.

She felt that general viewers who were besieged by rightist propaganda would benefit from the message of the series.

'Our cameras will roam in and out of madrasas, libraries, living quarters, lecture halls and quadrangles. We'll show students at work and leisure, engaged in sports, charitable activities...all as part of normal existence in recognizable surroundings.'

'And you propose to use Akbar Ali Samandar as the host,' Daud Panwala remarked.

'The important thing, Daud Sahib, is that he'll popularize Islam not by gimmicks like other popular hosts, but by leading from the front with his actions, achievements and his life at the Beyt-as-Salah complex.'

'He'll arouse a lot of female interest,' Daud Panwala said drily.

'That's okay so long as he can also get young people to fall in love with Islam. It's the best thing this show will do. It will lead the young towards faith without coercion, terror tactics or fear of hellfire. Nobody can object – neither the government, nor the politicians, nor the mullahs.'

Shaista's plans suffered a setback when Akbar declined to take part in the series. He was appalled at the extent of self-exposure involved.

'Hosting a programme for a worthy cause is different from being an object on display. Why do you need such extensive coverage of me?' he asked.

'Your life, your activities, your views will inspire our youth,' Shaista explained. 'Besides you're doing good work that should be aired.'

'Popularizing Islam is a good idea,' Akbar said, 'but I have reservations about the way you intend to go about it – not about the merits of the scheme, but the extensive personalization. My role as a host is possibly okay but as a... sort of leading character...it is not.'

'Audio-visual messages impact much better if the messenger is an effective medium,' Shaista pointed out.

'But all that personal stuff...it's not in good taste...it's too flamboyant...besides it's a little...intrusive.'

'There's a purpose, Akbar Sahib. You lead by the examples you set...just as the holy Prophet did...'

'*La houl wala*...surely you're not comparing my performance with His?' Akbar exclaimed, shocked.

'I was merely illustrating a point.'

After a pause, Akbar said, 'I'm prepared to consider helping in the promotion of Islam, provided the programme content is acceptable and not focused on me...'

Used to having her own way, Shaista decided to force the issue by telecasting the pilot in the hope that the interest generated by it would impress Akbar. But her winning instinct failed this time.

The programme was aired, and did have the reaction she anticipated, but it also implicated the network in a civil action initiated by Akbar, for a stay order and damages for invasion of privacy.

The case was ultimately settled out of court by the network having to pay substantial damages which were diverted to charitable causes nominated by Akbar. It was his first brush with ambition, greed, exploitation and the power of the media.

Shaista's error of judgment also precipitated a situation Akbar wished to avoid. The exposure he feared had overtaken him. He was now a celebrity in the public domain.

He was tagged, twittered and blogged about, and was the subject of comments, proposals and offers that were laudatory, lucrative or suggestive – from both sexes. It was also the first time since he faced the attack at the age of nine that he had been made an object of sexual fantasy. He felt violated.

EIGHT

The imam's speech at a ceremony held to honour the Munshi Fazil graduates included a reference to Akbar. It created a stir among the founders of the Beyt-as-Salah trust. It also touched a nerve, bringing tears to the eyes of Ahmed Ali and Akbar. In his closing remarks the imam said, 'Akbar Ali Samandar will inshallah, achieve much success wherever he goes, but he will always belong as much to us as we to him. Every time I pass by a young scholar, I see the little boy who has gone on to become the highest scoring Munshi Fazil in the annals of the Wafaq-al-Madaris...' There was a break in his voice that caused him to turn away and clear his throat.

'This, *Alhamdolillah*, is his gift to Beyt-as-Salah and Beyt-as-Salah's legacy to him, as willed by Allah,' concluded the frail old man in white robes, tapping his way off the podium.

After the evening prayer, Akbar visited Abdulla Saleh's office intending to mend fences. He found the usual warmth missing.

Abdulla Saleh was upset more for having failed to win Akbar over to his cause than for the defiance Akbar had shown in the imam's chamber.

'Now that you've become a celebrity,' Abdulla Saleh said frostily, 'I don't suppose you'll be interested in continuing with the course.'

'Ustad,' Akbar said, 'most of what I know has been taught by you and that will remain with me always.'

While they were talking, it had turned dark. The mosque lights had been on for a while. It was almost time for the *Isha* congregation. Akbar got up, prompted by a sudden urge to commune with God. After a few words with the mosque's muezzin, he ascended – vaulted rather – to the top of a minaret. When the moment came, he stood upright and filling his lungs with air, raised his hands to his ears and exhaled,

'*Allah hu Akbar...Allah hu Akbar,*' the words rang out, filling the night sky.

'Hush,' the imam said to his visitors, placing a finger on his lips, 'listen to that call...'

And they listened to Akbar's call to prayer. When it was over, Maulana Fazal Deen, who headed a seminary in Bahawalpur, stroked his beard and said, 'We've heard it called one of the wonders of your mosque...I now see why.'

The Maulana was one of four prominent guests who had stayed over from the graduates' function for discussing matters of common interest with the imam. The other three, a crafty-looking founder called Seth Abid Ali Memon, a clean-shaven Saudi diplomat and Mullah Usman, a turbaned cleric from the Kunar province in Afghanistan, swathed in yards of fabric, nodded in agreement. All four were in their mid-fifties.

'I didn't know Akbar was still here,' the imam said, pleased at the prospect of bringing him before them. 'I'll introduce him to you after the *Isha* prayers.'

'Good,' said Mullah Usman, exchanging glances with Seth Abid and the Saudi diplomat, 'it will give us an opportunity to check whether he will be suitable for the youth programmes we have in mind.'

Noticing the imam's enquiring look, he said, 'You know of course, that we four are senior policy members of the Youth Council reform movement.'

The imam nodded, his curiosity aroused.

'We are always on the lookout for good workers,' Seth Abid explained, 'and this young man has impressive credentials.'

The group reassembled in the imam's chambers after prayers. Akbar and Abdulla Saleh sat facing the visitors. The imam had briefed them in private on the visitors' role in the Beyt-as-Salah management. Green tea was served with dates and nuts.

'Tell me, Akbar,' Seth Abid asked, 'what are your future plans?'

Before Akbar could respond, Abdulla Saleh declared, 'He is already involved in research on the works of our most eminent scholars.'

Unsettled by the remark, the imam cast a hooded glance at Abdulla Saleh as a warning to speak sparingly.

'I *was* doing such a course,' Akbar said quietly, 'but won't be continuing with it for the time being.'

'Why is that Syed Akbar?' the Saudi diplomat asked.

The imam seemed distinctly uncomfortable. He cursed Abdulla Saleh under his breath for raising the issue. Abdulla Saleh appeared to be shrinking into himself.

'There is no simple explanation,' Akbar said.

'For an elective research programme, it shouldn't be compulsory for a researcher to have to study one prescribed text as opposed to another. He should be given the opportunity to use his discretion in selecting texts under some form of supervisory guidance.'

There was silence.

'Academic research is not like ordained practice,' he continued, 'that *must* be performed in a particular way. It's more like individual effort...that a scholar undertakes on a discretionary basis on selected topics.'

How masterful he is, the imam thought, *in sidestepping quicksands...*

The matter was turned on its head when Mullah Usman – a renowned scholar and linguist – asked Abdulla Saleh for the bibliography he had drawn up for the course. Abdulla Saleh gave him names and titles. Where he faltered Akbar filled in the gaps.

The imam cringed at the mention of certain authors. When the exercise came to an end, the Saudi diplomat and Mullah Usman exchanged glances not missed by the imam. There was no doubt about the fundamentalist nature of the course.

After another round of qahwa and dates, Mullah Usman asked Akbar, 'Was it the extreme nature of the writings that turned you off?'

'No sir,' Akbar said, 'I was frustrated at being restricted to studying a particular perspective of Islam. Not having recourse to counter points of view on the prescribed subjects prevented me from reaching a balanced assessment.'

Dreading the direction the discussion was taking, the imam suggested that the importance of the matter in discussion and the late hour called for the talks to be adjourned to the next day.

Ignoring him, the smooth-faced Saudi said, 'Syed Akbar, we can understand why you withdrew from what is probably dogmatic study material, but what are your views about the scholarship of the last 250 years?'

Abdulla Saleh bit his lower lip in anxiety. Akbar knew that the spotlight was on him.

This is surely a day of reckoning, he thought. *First, the remarks about me in the imam's speech...then mending fences with Ustad...and now this...this...tribunal...was this planned...or has it just come about by chance...they want to assess my worth...I want to know about myself too...so many words...so much praise... how worthy am I?*

'Among latter-day Islamists,' Akbar said, his eyes level with theirs, 'I would rank Syed Qutb as a great scholar who identified the issues Muslims should focus on.' He searched among his papers for a reference by two Western scholars.

'It was Syed Qutb,' he read, 'who fused the core elements of modern Islam: the Kharajites' takfir, Ibn Taymiyyah's fatwas and policy prescriptions, Rashid Rida's Salafism, Maudoodi's concept of the contemporary *jahaliya* and Hasan-al-Banna's political activism.'

'Do you agree with that assessment?' Mullah Usman asked.

'I agree with the view generally held even today that Syed Qutb, Hasan-al-Banna, Maulana Maudoodi...and...Ruhollah Khomeini are the most influential Muslim thinkers and activists of the modern era.'

Mention of Khomeini's name drew a chorus of protests, '*La houl wala quwat Allah illah billah hil aliuiazeem.*'

'So you do accept the truth of some of what you've read,' Seth Abid said.

'Of course, these are leading authorities,' Akbar said, 'Hasan al-Banna founded the Muslim Brotherhood which dominates the Middle East today. Syed Qutb was a leading intellectual of the Brotherhood. Ayman Al Zwahiri of Al-Qaeda was greatly influenced by the views of Al-Banna. Maulana Maudoodi's Deobandism is on the rise in the Indo-Pakistan subcontinent. Khomeini ignited the Iranian revolution and has since led Shi'ism in Iran, the Lebanon and elsewhere.'

'What do you know of Shaikh Abd-al-Wahab?' the Saudi asked quietly.

'He was perhaps the earliest "modern" reformer – paradoxically urging a return to the fundamentalist, literalist Islamic movement that prevails today. He had a pragmatic impact – in conjunction with the dialectical influences of the others – for promoting the Wahabi practice in Saudi Arabia and neighbouring areas. Wahabism, as you know, is a forerunner of Salafism which the pan-Islamists – who aspire to conquer the world – regard as the only true religion.'

'Since you know so much, why the reluctance to proceed further?' Mullah Usman asked.

Both the imam and Abdulla Saleh held their breath.

'I wanted to look at the other side of the picture without being confined to political Islam.'

'What does that mean?' Maulana Fazal Deen joined in.

'Well, we are currently swimming in a wave of political Islam,' Akbar started to say.

'Currently?' Maulana Fazal Deen asked, raising his eyebrows.

'By currently,' Akbar said, 'I mean the last one hundred and fifty years or so...the period during which many of these movements surfaced.'

'Why do you use the label political Islam?' Seth Abid inquired.

'They were reactionary movements opposed to the Western invasion of Middle and Near Eastern territories through colonization.'

'Are you suggesting that the Islamic movement of the last two hundred years came into being only as a form of protest against Western culture?' Maulana Fazal Deen enquired.

'Well, the Western presence posed a threat to the local way of life,' Akbar said. 'The movements were part of the reaction to that presence. Falling back on faith and tradition helps bring people under threat together.'

'That's a cynical observation,' Seth Abid said.

'It's a historical reality, sir.'

The Saudi diplomat and Mullah Usman exchanged glances, tacitly acknowledging that Akbar was no ordinary student.

'In your opinion, Syed Akbar,' the Saudi diplomat asked, 'do the political undertones affecting them take away from the religious merit of these movements?'

Akbar paused before replying.

'Can't say, but it does seem that instead of being a cause and effect rationale for the actual event, the explanation put forth for such movements usually turns out to be an "afterthought justification" – worked out by latter-day scholars some time *after* the occurrence of the central event.'

Masterful, thought the imam, *he has them in hand...they may not agree with his views...but they will hear him out...he speaks fearlessly.*

Mullah Usman took a different line, 'In a word, how would you describe the attitude of Western powers towards countries like Pakistan and Afghanistan?'

'Exploitative,' Akbar said.

There was laughter.

'Seriously sir, the West is driven by self-interest but that's nature's way of keeping the earth controlled and manageable. Exploitation has to do with survival. That's why we exploited the Bengalis.'

'Don't go there Akbar,' cautioned Seth Abid.

'Doesn't that mean we should refashion our views about the glory of the West?' Mullah Usman enquired.

Akbar took a deep breath before resuming.

'Unlike the early Islamic civilizational centres which provided the base for the cultural liberation of Europe, the Western Renaissance powers that followed gave much to far-flung regions of the world, but also took much away from them by pursuing self-interest. That is the way their power worked. Now several hundred years later, a strange desperation is in the air, in part, probably because we have acknowledged the reality of nature's role in the world: Natural systems are being eroded. We are slowly being poisoned. The world faces the possibility of destruction. So we are looking closely at all aspects of the story of mankind.'

Everyone in the room, including Abdulla Saleh, listened intently. The imam sensed a change from the inquisitorial mood. Reassured by Akbar's reasoning, he felt a sense of ease.

I have not given him the recognition he deserved. Despite having this huma bird in our midst, I have kept silent about it. Why have I held back?

'You're implying that the Western powers are *not* to be blamed,' Seth Abid said scathingly.

'Of course they are. I blame them for collateral damage worldwide. They are also guilty of criminal greed. Above all, they have ignored the demands of the spirit.'

Akbar stopped when – at that moment – his assuredness was touched by doubt.

'Akbar Sahib, are you really just twenty-three years old?'

'Twenty-three or two hundred and thirty...only the wise can express such views,' Maulana Fazal Deen remarked.

Seth Abid was somewhat less enthusiastic.

'Even if the curriculum you have been studying has political implications, it doesn't mean that it is not the correct approach,' he said.

'No sir, it doesn't,' Akbar said, 'but it does suggest that the form of faith being taught me was conditioned more by political factors than by...enlightened transparence.'

'Is that why you have reservations about accepting it?' Mullah Usman asked.

'I need to be convinced by study, research and comparative analysis or a flash of enlightenment.'

I wonder whether they are capable of absorbing his explanations, the imam thought.

'What makes you different to other scholars who have accepted it as the true faith?' Seth Abid asked

'Scholars differ,' Akbar said bluntly.

'Wasn't the study material sufficiently persuasive to convince you?' Seth Abid persisted.

'Sir, I am a scholar, not a preacher. My intellect is trained to question, research and reason before reaching a conclusion.

The study material was clearly not persuasive enough...so I could not conclude...as other scholars may have...that the approach discussed in it represents the true Islam.'

'It *is* the correct way,' Seth Abid said tapping his knee.

'But that is what other Islamists also claim for their beliefs,' Akbar pointed out.

'They are wrong and will be damned as infidels,' Seth Abid bristled.

'They don't see themselves as infidels. All of them subscribe to the oneness of God, the finality of the Prophet, the sanctity of the Quran and Sunna and the hereafter,' Akbar blurted out.

The atmosphere had become highly charged.

'Do you see yourself among the "anything goes" liberal believers?' Seth Abid demanded.

'Abid Sahib, I am a practising Muslim with what I believe is a Muslim awareness. For these last few years I have been seeking the way to Allah.'

'So you would not at this stage discredit any of the other so-called Islamic modes of worship?' Mullah Usman asked.

'How can I, unless I'm convinced of their wrongness through study, research or divine inspiration?'

'And if you were convinced they are wrong would you then condemn their practitioners?' Mullah Usman asked.

'Such eventualities are provided for in the Quran,' Akbar said. 'Several passages declare that God will punish those who distort faith. So it's best to leave the condemnation and punishment to Him. We aren't equipped to do so. There are too many fatwas and blasphemy charges floating around.'

'Akbar Sahib,' Mullah Usman enquired, 'what if your study and research do not lead you to the ideal mode of Islamic practice?'

'Then...I will probably take on the mode of practice best suited to my temperament.'

'Like cocktail-party canapés,' Seth Abid remarked sneeringly.

'Abid Sahib, belief in Islam is the key. People, regions, climates and cultures vary. What matters is that faith and essential duties should be observed. Allah is unlikely to hold us to account for following different time-honoured practices. The last line of *Al-Kafirun* sums up our discussion: For you is your faith and for me mine.'

'La kum deene kum wale ud deen,' intoned the imam reciting the Quranic version.

NINE

Sounds of women's voices and laughter drifted into the veranda. Lilian was strolling in the garden with someone Akbar could not identify through the lattice. He decided to leave and get out of their way.

'Akbar,' a voice called out before he reached the door. Looking back, he saw a familiar face from the get-together at French Beach.

'Tooba Shirazi,' he exclaimed, '*Assalam alaikum.*'

'Salaam, salaam, to you too,' Tooba said, coming forward to greet him with a kiss which he managed to avoid by holding out his hand.

It must be that celibacy-until-marriage thing they teach, Lilian told herself.

Tooba shook Akbar's hand warmly. This came as a surprise to Lilian. She was not aware of their earlier acquaintance.

Tooba had just got back from Canada after visiting Aliya and Teymour at a solar power project base. She returned with stories, digital snaps and gifts from Aliya.

'Are we going to sit,' Lilian said, 'or continue...waiting for a bus?'

When they had settled down, she said, 'You two chat...I'm going to get some tea.'

Left alone, Akbar asked Tooba how she was doing in modelling.

'So you do remember, Akbar Ali Samandar,' Tooba remarked, 'the way you greeted me just now, I thought you had forgotten who I was.'

She laughed – a clear sound – which Akbar recalled from the drive to the beach. 'I gave up modelling a while ago,' she said wrinkling her nose, 'it seemed a bit too girlie-wirlie... besides, it didn't make sense...dabbling in pricey fashion wear in this screwed-up place.'

'So, do you do anything else instead?' Akbar asked.

'I work for an NGO rehabilitating the rejects of society.'

'That's good work,' he said.

'It's more real anyway...sad and uplifting all in one,' she said.

'Must be hard,' he remarked.

'Can't afford to get too close,' she said. 'To do a good job, you have to keep things at arm's length.'

'That really sounds remarkable,' he said.

'No more remarkable than some of the things you've been doing, Azaan-e-Akbari,' she said, addressing him by the title given to his azan by the media.

'I was referring to your handling of human problems. That is remarkable. I have little experience of dealing with people,' he said self-consciously.

She reflected for a moment. 'That's because you are so absorbed with meditation. And teaching religion gives you little time for people. That's the way with scholars.'

'Is that what you think of me?' he asked, regretting the question the moment it was asked.

'Yes Akbar,' she said, 'you don't let people get close to you. I think I understand.'

'How can you say that?'

'Instinct, I suppose.'

She presented a challenge. He noticed the white cotton *angarkha* with chikan embroidery, the loosely knotted hair falling off her shoulders, the shell-pink toenails. He was being drawn into the conversation once again by the dimple on the cheek.

'Why aren't you married?' he asked, 'or are you?'

Startled, she said, 'I am single, because I haven't come across anyone I want to marry.'

'But most of Aliya's friends are married,' he said.

'Good for them, but that's no reason for me to jump into marriage ...even if I end up sitting on the shelf.'

'I didn't mean that,' he said, feeling he had been clumsy.

Lilian came in pushing a tea trolley.

'Sorry it took so long,' she said, 'I had to do it myself... it's everyone's day off.'

They jumped up to help her but she waved them off positioning the trolley in front of her chair, and poured the tea.

'Has Tooba been telling you about her visit to Aliya?' Lilian asked.

'I was just about to.'

'We were discussing work.'

'I had the time of my life,' Tooba remarked. 'We were living close to the forests of Ontario.'

Tooba's account of her trip was entertaining. She mentioned in passing that Aliya was newly pregnant.

Going through digital pictures, Akbar noticed shots of Tooba cavorting by a waterfall and in green meadows with a strapping Canadian. Noticing Akbar's interest, Lilian asked, 'Is that the lumberjack who chased you across the landscape?'

'Lumberjack, my eye,' Tooba remarked, 'he was a colleague of Teymour. He was fun to be with.'

'Not just fun from what Aliya said,' Lilian remarked.

'Aliya read things into the situation...he showed some interest...' Tooba mumbled.

'Aha!' said Lilian, 'here comes the truth.'

'Aunt Lilian, nothing came of it...when I told him that I did not reciprocate...he suggested a holiday liaison. Why am I telling you this?' Tooba blushed.

'Because you want to be absolved of the Canadian temptation,' Lilian said.

'I told him that if I hadn't known him better, I would have found the suggestion offensive.'

'But from what I understand,' Lilian said, 'he was not put off.'

'He said he wanted to...well...romance a Pakistani girl... find out what it was like,' Tooba continued awkwardly.

'Really. And then what?' Lilian asked, eyes wide open.

'I told him that we were like other girls – all sisters under de skin!'

They laughed.

'Sisters under de skin, except with regard to the casual sex part,' Tooba blushed.

'Stop blushing, darling,' Lilian said, 'I'm teasing. Aliya told me you were correct and firm but didn't spoil the friendly atmosphere. Good for you...except it hasn't helped it seems... because Aliya says he is coming after you.'

'No, really?' Tooba looked alarmed.

'Teasing, darling...just teasing,' Lilian reassured her with a smile.

Later that evening Lilian told Javed Ali about Tooba's visit. 'I was pleased by the way Akbar reacted to Tooba,' she said.

'What did you expect? He's like any red-blooded chap,' Javed Ali said.

'Well, I didn't know what to expect after all the years at the madrasa.' Lilian said.

'He's his father's son,' Javed Ali said.

'Heaven forbid,' said Lilian with mock alarm, 'another dirty old man in the making.'

'A gentleman down to his toenails,' said Javed Ali, 'a chip off the old block. You'll see Lil.'

A lull in the madrasa programme gave Akbar time to spend at home. This pleased Lilian even though it meant putting up with his various idiosyncrasies. His bedroom resembled a monastic cell. There was a bed, a durrie, a wall table and a floor desk from the madrasa for reading, writing or meditating while sitting on the floor. He ate sparingly, and with his hands, kept away from visitors, and showed little interest in TV.

Lilian had always felt that there was something unresolved in Akbar. She sensed, but had not been able to pinpoint the cause of the earlier rift with Beyt-as-Salah. She realized too that matters would not continue the way they were. She felt that sooner or later Akbar would either revert to religious studies in earnest or start working at something else like other young men of his age. Her concern prompted her to spend as much time as she could with her son. It was now possible for them to sit together on their own during the evenings.

They spoke of 'Godscenes' – which were less frequent now – having changed from fantasy to more credible, if momentary, glimmerings. They chatted in a variety of tongues, switching from one to another amidst laughter.

Many of Lilian's misgivings about religion were laid to rest. Such exchanges had till then been confined to Akbar's talks with Ahmed Ali. Now Lilian was privy to them.

'Doesn't your upbringing...create a handicap in your dealings with people who have been raised differently?' Lilian asked.

'Adaptability, Mother, is the key.'

'How about...Arabs?' asked Lilian, 'don't they claim to have an edge over other Muslims?'

'One does not have to be born a Bedouin to be a true Muslim. Islam was devised as a global culture, not to be a colonizing power.'

Gradually, Akbar's life at home crystallized into a busy schedule of study, research, meditation, online exchanges, welfare work and teaching. There were also occasional interactions with Tooba. She found these meetings fluid, variable and unresolved.

'Will it always be like this – coming and going and catching up in between?'

'We'll meet when our paths cross...if they're meant to,' Akbar replied. 'Otherwise you must follow your course and I'll go with mine.'

With Kamran away in university, Akbar felt duty-bound to play backyard cricket with the young people of the neighbourhood. Everyone, it seemed, wanted a piece of him, but there was never enough to go around.

When asked about his future course of action, Akbar would reply, 'Allah has a plan for everyone...which dovetails with His master plan for the world. I will wait until I get a sign. It will come...'

One night, well past *Isha* prayers, Akbar decided to go to Beyt-as-Salah to look for Arabic and Persian dictionaries. When he got to the mosque, he found the doors of the entrance locked. This was unusual. Unruffled, he skirted the mosque's perimeter to get to a narrow street-level access which was used by the cleaning staff for removing debris, and eased his way in.

Finding the courtyard and cloisters in darkness, he made for Abdulla Saleh's study and located the books. On his way out, he was waylaid by two figures who emerged from the darkness. He almost dropped the books while preparing to face the intruders, until one of them spoke, 'Ustad Akbar, take it easy, it's only us, Tariq Rafiq and Khadim Shah.'

'What are you doing here?' Akbar asked.

They looked at each other sheepishly. 'It was our turn to clean the minarets, but they forgot about us when they were bolting the doors,' Tariq Rafiq explained.

'We've been trying to get out for quite a while,' Khadim Shah said.

'Apart from the unclean sweepers' opening, the only route open to our homes at this time passes through the outer gate of the imam's quarters,' Tariq Rafiq said.

'Well, why don't you use it?' Akbar asked.

The boys exchanged glances.

'What's the problem?' Akbar asked.

'Strange things are happening there,' Khadim Shah muttered.

'Strange things?' Akbar asked, 'what do you mean?'

'Ustad, promise you won't tell anyone about what we tell you.'

'You haven't told me anything,' Akbar said.

'Then go and see for yourself,' Tariq Rafiq said.

Before Akbar could get to the stairs Khadim Shah said,

'You mustn't be seen. Come with us and watch from the upper gallery.'

They moved stealthily along the upper terrace, crossing over from one side of the dome to the other until they reached a galleried section adjacent to the imam's chambers. From a crouching position behind the parapet they had a clear view of the scene.

Light was provided by dimmed lamps. The cellar door beneath the imam's chambers was open and men with covered faces moved in and out carrying weapons to trucks parked in shadows outside the mosque.

Before loading, each weapon was identified by a sharp voice: 'Kalashnikov, sub-machine gun, TT pistol, repeater, rocket-propelled grenade, anti-aircraft gun,' and entered on a roster. Armoured carriers bristling with rangers lurked in the alleys. They appeared to be keeping watch over the proceedings.

The latest batch of foreign visitors to the mosque were carrying food packs and knapsacks and boarding the trucks, in coordination with a roll-call conducted by Abdulla Saleh.

A Mercedes-Benz emerged from a dark side street across the road, stopping in front of the imam's gate. The smooth-faced Saudi diplomat stepped out carrying two briefcases, looked around quickly and slipped into the imam's quarters.

Through an open window in the imam's chamber, he could be seen delivering the briefcases to the imam, shaking hands and walking back swiftly to the waiting car. The entire transaction took three minutes.

After he left, the imam opened the briefcases and took out what looked like dollar bills, which were then duly counted and rubber-banded. Elsewhere in the chamber, Seth Abid and Mullah Jalal were busy putting away separate bundles of currency in boxes marked in bold red with pound sterling, euro and yen signs.

Akbar watched for hours in cramped silence. The boys had dozed off, worn out with fear and excitement. Overcome by a sense of outrage, Akbar felt a knot of sickness and disgust in the pit of his stomach, gulping down tears, rage coursing through his system. What remained was an abyss of treachery. Beyt-as-Salah, which had lovingly nurtured him all these years, was now revealing its dark side.

When it was over and the conspirators had departed, the trucks bearing weapons and fugitives rumbled away, the complicit rangers vanished, their vigil complete. Akbar placed the dictionaries beside the sleeping boys and left Beyt-as-Salah once again, slipping back through the narrow rear exit out into the world.

PART II
THE HIGHLANDS

TEN

After a stopover at one of the hamlets for food, fuel and the midday prayer, the truck set out for the last lap. The road wound round crags and inlets along the mountainside. Akbar dozed off. The driver's assistant, relieved at the prospect of the journey's end, broke into song, praising the braided locks and dark eyes of his beloved.

The truck moved uphill at a strained pace, rolling over bumps and grooves. Suddenly there was a violent jolt and a resounding bang, and the truck shuddered and swerved. Akbar jumped up with a start, hearing the driver's curses as he struggled to control the lurching vehicle.

'You whore,' he said bringing his fist down on the dashboard, 'you've come all the way from Karachi swinging your butt, only to fart your guts out in FATA...'

'Get down numbskull,' he yelled at his assistant, 'and fix the puncture!'

Akbar squatted on the landward side of the road while the two replaced the burst tyre. He watched a man herding sheep down a slope from the road to the valley below. At a height of several thousand feet, the air felt fresh against his skin. The valley was aglow with the golden tints of afternoon sunlight. He could see far-off objects with clarity.

A truck painted in bright colours roared by, honking as it passed the stranded vehicle. A pickup coming from the opposite direction stopped beside the driver and his assistant, who waved it on. It sped away, leaving a trail of dust dispersed by the breeze. Falcons and plovers flew overhead.

So different to the world I left behind, Akbar thought, recalling his uncle's words.

After his experience at Beyt-as-Salah, a distraught Akbar had turned to his uncle, who, at Lilian's insistence, was recuperating at the Samandar home.

As a distraction, Ahmed Ali urged Akbar to visit his old friend, Jalal Baba, at his retreat in Kitkot village, in the Mamund tehsil of Bajaur,

'Jalal's company was reinvigorating and inspirational,' his uncle said, recalling his own trip to FATA several years ago. Jalal Baba was older than Ahmed Ali. He lectured on philosophy at Peshawar University. The friendship, initiated by correspondence on theosophy, had endured for many years.

'At that point in time I was desperate for guidance to restore some order to my life,' Ahmed Ali explained. 'He suggested that I accompany him on a trip to the north-west to visit the archaeological site of Nysa, an Alexandrian city linked by tradition to Dionysus. The trip was a turning point. It helped me focus on things that mattered...brought back some of my resolve...and gave me peace. Jalal went into retreat in a cave above Kitkot, one of the last FATA villages before the Afghan border.'

'Didn't he go back to the university?' Akbar asked.

'He gave up the world and stayed on at Kitkot. After several years of meditation and religious study, he set up the Dar-ul-Aman retreat for advanced studies.'

'I've heard of it,' Akbar remarked. 'Its library is famous. It has an exceptional collection of Qurans and other Oriental texts. It admits only seasoned scholars and learned ulema for research. They come from all over. It's far too advanced for the average madrasa student.'

'That's right.'

'Isn't it located in a war zone?'

'Mamund is in the crosshairs of both the Taliban and the Pakistan Army, but neither the Taliban shura nor the Army interfere with Dar-ul-Aman...Jalal Baba is highly respected as a Pakhtun icon somewhat in the tradition of Khushal Khan Khattak, Haji Saheb of Turangzai or even the Faqir of Ippi. I'll write to him about you.'

Jalal Baba agreed to admit Akbar to Dar-ul-Aman, and also forwarded instructions on how to get there along with payment particulars. Akbar was keen to go. But it was hard leaving the family. His parents were appalled at the idea of his venturing into Taliban territory. Assurances from Ahmed Ali failed to allay their concern but Akbar was adamant.

Javed Ali and Lilian realized that they would not be able to stop him. Lilian blamed Ahmed Ali and stopped talking to him. Kamran wept for the first time in years.

The truck rumbled into Kitkot by early evening. The stop was adjacent to a grain store. The bazaar comprised a handful of shops located on either side of the dirt track passing through the village.

They were single-room mud brick structures which opened on porticos covered with thatched sloping roofs supported by wooden columns. Merchandise was displayed in trough-like containers placed during the day in the porticos.

Apart from the grain store, there was a grocery, a vegetable and fruit shop, a hardware store and a tea shop. Wooded slopes rose on either side. The highlands were fairly green unlike the earlier rocky stretches.

Akbar jumped off the truck, knapsack on his back and went over to where the driver stood talking to a local. Some villagers came out of the shops and stared with curiosity. Akbar thanked the driver and his assistant and took his leave of them.

He was expecting to be met by Jalal Baba's representative. There was no one there. So he went to the tea shop which served as a waiting room for travellers.

He had barely ordered tea when two armed men with half their faces wrapped in turban cloth appeared. Unaffected by their hostile appearance, he answered their queries in Pashto and explained the reason for his presence in the village. They mumbled brief instructions to the tea-shop owner, who dispatched his son to Dar-ul-Aman with news of Akbar's arrival.

Almost an hour later, Akbar observed a man with a limp emerging from a grove of trees opposite the tea shop. He was in his mid-thirties and had a hump on his back. He came up to Akbar and addressed him by name. Akbar nodded in response. They shook hands.

'My name is Janbaz Khan. I've been sent by Jalal Baba to fetch you,' he said.

Akbar picked up his knapsack and followed him to a path that led upward from the grove. They wound their way round rocks as they ascended. Pine needles crunched underfoot. The air was heavy with resin.

The path lay through a patchwork of sunlight and shade – cool and dark where the trees were abundant and dazzlingly bright where the sun shone through. The silence was broken by bird call, rustling leaves, scampering creatures, distant gunfire and now the footsteps of the two men.

When a buzzing noise drifted through the trees, Janbaz told Akbar to stand still.

'Why?' Akbar asked.

'Wild honey bees,' Janbaz said, 'the woods are full of them. When they sound like that, they're on the warpath. Something has disturbed their hive. If they see movement, they will attack.'

They waited, motionless, until the dark swarm had passed, then moved on.

Despite relishing the exercise after four days of confinement in the truck, Akbar found it difficult to exert his stiff limbs in the new terrain. Yet he somehow managed to keep up with Janbaz.

They chatted fitfully. Janbaz was curious but Akbar's replies were brief and to the point. Janbaz was more forthcoming. He said that Jalal Baba had been expecting Akbar for the last two days.

Jalal Baba lived with his family in a cottage, a short distance from Dar-ul-Aman. Akbar also learnt that there were seven scholars residing at the retreat, two from Uzbekistan, one from Turkmenistan, one from Malaysia, a Kazakh, an Indonesian and a Chinese imam.

The sun's intensity lessened as they climbed. The air became cool and strains of the azan filtered down from somewhere above.

Janbaz said, 'Time for the *Asar* prayer.'

He edged off the path towards a rocky ledge with a level base. It provided a view of the lowlands against a backdrop of mountain ranges among which one peak, higher than the rest, demanded attention.

'What is that?' Akbar asked, awestruck.

'Koh-i-Mor, the highest mountain in the borderland between Pakistan and Afghanistan,' Janbaz said.

'You can perform your ablutions there,' he said to Akbar pointing to a trickle of water flowing down a rock. Akbar found the water refreshingly cold.

They said their prayers facing the valley. When they got back to the path, the ascent was steeper, requiring greater effort.

'How much further?' Akbar asked, a trifle breathlessly.

'Not much more...we'll be there shortly...that azan you heard was from Dar-ul-Aman.'

A short while later they were at the clearing in which Dar-ul-Aman was located. It stood in a setting of trees against a rocky backdrop under a patch of open sky. The clearing was on a narrow ledge running horizontally along the mountain face. From its perch on the ledge, Dar-ul-Aman appeared to be clinging to the side of the mountain. The left façade of the structure stood above a section of the ledge that dropped down several thousand feet to the valley below. The mountain rose behind the complex with the trees giving way to bare rock. Some of the neighbouring peaks were snow-capped. The sight of Dar-ul-Aman in the evening light brought Akbar up short.

It was built on an elongated platform, three feet high and made of blocks hewn from rock. A colonnaded veranda fronted the structure, its roof supported by a wooden beam hewn from the trunk of a cedar tree running parallel to the veranda and extending on both ends by two feet.

Slimmer wooden columns rising at regular intervals from the veranda propped up the beam. A shingled roof, with sloping front and back sections subdivided by the hint of a ridge, covered the building.

The walls, made of mud and straw, were reinforced by embedded criss-crossing wooden staves and smoothed over by a coating of lime. The front door was of carved walnut.

Janbaz went up to a wooden post at the entrance of the clearing, from which was suspended a bronze bell with a greenish patina.

He pushed the bell. The peals announced the presence of visitors. Janbaz, with Akbar a step behind, walked towards the building. Just as they reached the stone steps leading to the platform, the front door swung open.

Jalal Baba stepped out. He was in his seventies. Unlike the imam, he was tall and straight. The flowing hair and beard were silvery white. He wore his years with grace.

'Akbar Ali Samandar,' he said with a welcoming smile, as Akbar climbed the steps, unsure of how to greet him. Jalal Baba outstretched his arms, drawing him into an embrace. As they came together, a current of recognition passed between, catching them by surprise.

'So you are Ahmed Ali's son by choice,' Jalal Baba said in Pashto, then stopped, 'Do you prefer conversing in Farsi, Urdu or English?'

'Anything will do,' Akbar replied.

'Good, we can choose whichever suits our mood,' Jalal Baba said, taking Akbar through the main door to a passage which led to a courtyard open to the sky. A pillared veranda ran around the courtyard, fronting rooms on all four sides.

The east and west wings of the veranda led on to an adjoining courtyard behind the first quadrangle which housed the kitchen alongside storage and washroom facilities.

Holding Akbar's hand, Jalal Baba took him to a door in the north wing facing the entrance. They removed their shoes and went in. It was the *hujra* – the room used for guests.

Floor seating consisted of *sandali* or upholstered benches without legs, running along the walls of the carpeted room. A square table, one foot high, was placed within the *sandali*. Quilted material was spread over the table, falling over the edges onto the laps of people seated around the *sandali*, their legs extended under the table. During the bitter cold winter months an oil stove under the table warmed their outstretched legs, keeping the chill at bay.

The table served as a surface for meals, paperwork and conferences. A second door, facing the one through which they had come in, opened on the second courtyard.

The *hujra* was a large room with seating space at the table for twenty-five persons. The ceiling was supported by wooden beams, with windows in the walls parallel to both the courtyard verandas. A stone fireplace was built into one of the walls. The room was lit by two oil lamps. The army had installed electric wiring in the main building (in anticipation of the eventual supply of electricity) and gifted Dar-ul-Aman some of its surplus generators – which were used sparingly because Jalal Baba preferred the traditional form of lighting.

An attendant served tea and dried fruit. Jalal Baba and Akbar sat at the *sandali*, the former propped against the bench backrest, legs stretched straight under the table, Akbar beside him cross-legged.

'Your uncle has written about the difficult time you went through. Do you want to talk about it?' Jalal Baba asked, his dark eyes observing Akbar intently from under his thick white brows.

Akbar paused before replying.

'How much do you know?' he asked.

'Well, I know about your involvement with Beyt-as-Salah and your exceptional academic record. I also know of your interest in religious studies. Ahmed Ali mentioned something about a deep depression caused by events at the madrasa. I am not clear about this.'

Akbar described his relationship with the imam and Abdulla Saleh in level tones. But some of his anxiety returned when he got around to narrating the events of his last night at the mosque,.

'Muslim politics based on strong beliefs are on the rise,' Jalal Baba said after hearing Akbar's story. 'You must view the nocturnal events at Beyt-as-Salah in that light.'

'That does not justify using the mosque or the madrasa as a screen for their agenda.'

'How else can covert groups operate except behind an acceptable facade?'

'I should have been told,' Akbar burst out.

'Why?' Jalal Baba asked. 'Were you indoctrinated enough to be part of their political agenda?'

'I was part of Beyt-as-Salah...I regarded it as...as a... sanctuary... holy and enlightened.'

'But surely, they had a bigger commitment to their cause than to you. Did you give them reason to believe in you?'

'They wanted me to go through an indoctrination process about which I had raised some queries.'

'That's interesting. Tell me about it.'

Akbar described the study programme devised by Abdulla Saleh. Jalal Baba listened with interest until they were interrupted by the azan for *Maghrib* prayers.

Jalal Baba called for an attendant, who guided Akbar to a hammam for ablutions, then escorted him to a mosque at a short distance from the main building.

Tucked away amidst tall trees, at a level higher than the main building, the mosque was a long single chamber of stone and wood with an alcove in the wall facing west for the prayer leader.

A twenty-foot high mud-brick watchtower stood next to it. The tower had a square base that was tapered at the top. A spiral staircase within led to the summit from where the azan was called.

Jalal Baba led the prayer. Residents of Dar-ul-Aman stood in two rows behind him. Akbar caught a glimpse of the visitors dressed in native wear. This included long robes and variations of the salwar worn with short jackets or calf length tunics topped by capped or turbaned headgear.

Darkness had descended and enveloped the woods by the time the prayer was over. The drop in temperature sent a shiver through Akbar.

Lanterns were lit for the walk back. Jalal Baba introduced Akbar to the visitors. Some of them returned to the main building. Others stayed on at the mosque reading the Quran until it was time for *Isha* prayers. Persian was the language of communication since many seemed familiar with it. Akbar also met two Pakhtun ulema who were instructors at Dar-ul-Aman.

Those who left retired to the *hujra* for the short wait between *Maghrib* and *Isha* prayers. In the highlands night set in on the heels of sunset.

Qahwa and bowls of dried apricots and walnuts were served in the *hujra*. *Isha* prayers were followed by a recital of the Quran by one of the visitors. Later all of them assembled in the *hujra* for the evening meal. They were served *aash* – a mutton broth, stewed lentils, spinach fried with onions, rice and nan bread.

The conversation focused on the events of the day and the latest reports on the Taliban and the Pakistan army in the area.

When the meal was over, Jalal Baba led Akbar to one of the rooms in the courtyard,

'This is where you'll stay,' he said, opening the door to a medium-sized room with a cot, a table and chair, a mirrored chest of drawers, a wall lined with bookshelves and a window looking over the ledge to the valley below.

'You'll have to turn this off before going to sleep,' Jalal Baba said pointing to an oil stove. 'It's unhealthy to keep it on all night.'

'Now get some rest,' he said, 'you must be worn out. We'll talk tomorrow. God keep you.'

As the door shut, Akbar turned off the stove and the oil lamp and fell on the cot. His knapsack lay unopened in a corner. He snuggled into the thick quilt, grateful for its warm comfort.

He thought briefly of Bairam Khan and wondered how he was faring. A sense of belonging – more intimate than it was at Beyt-as-Salah – swept over him, mingled with sleep.

ELEVEN

He kicked and hit out to avoid being dragged from the truck. Bairam Khan, the truck driver and his assistant were lined up on the road facing a firing squad. The young boys had been shot – their bodies lay by the roadside. Akbar had managed to evade the assailants until they discovered his hiding place behind a bale of cotton cloth. They were now on to him. Taliban hands, highway rangers' hands, customs inspector's hands, the imam's hands, Abdulla Saleh's hands – all reached out, grabbed him and tugged with all their might. He felt himself being drawn in different directions, his body pulled apart. He wanted to scream but no sound came. His eyes opened suddenly to find Janbaz Khan shaking his shoulder.

'Waking you is no easy task...' he said, 'get up now. It's time for the *Fajar* namaz...you'll have to hurry if you want to catch the congregation.'

Akbar took a moment to recall his surroundings, then jumped out of bed, grabbed a fresh set of clothes and rushed out in the darkness of the pre-dawn cold to the hammam.

He bathed hurriedly with warm water from a bucket and got to the mosque while the initial invocation was underway.

After breakfast Akbar accompanied Jalal Baba on a tour of the Dar-ul-Aman complex.

'I see a smile this morning in place of the wide-eyed look of yesterday,' Jalal remarked. 'Smile more often, your face comes alive.'

'This is for you,' he said, handing him a heavy woollen shawl 'It'll keep you warm. You will also need a pair of boots.'

They visited a succession of study chambers in the east wing of the front courtyard, fitted with floor desks, blackboards, pictures of mosques and holy sites and windows in the outer wall, bright with the morning sunlight.

In one of the rooms, Arabic studies were under way for the visiting scholars. The west wing, in which Akbar's room was located, contained the bedchambers. Their windows looked out over the ledge to the valley thousands of feet below.

Jalal Baba's study in the north wing lay on one side of the *hujra*. The library was on the other side with a small prayer chamber next to it.

In the second courtyard the cook was busy in the kitchen preparing the afternoon meal, while his assistant baked nan in a clay oven.

Akbar saw Janbaz watering plants in a shrubbery of greens and herbs in the centre of the second courtyard. Next to the kitchen there was a larder for food, medication and household provisions, and a storeroom for furnishings, linen, hardware and stationery. The attendants shared rooms in one wing. Staff family accommodation was situated in separate residential quarters lining the periphery of the property.

There were three hammams and three toilets in the seminary. Water came in buckets filled at a well located behind the seminary. Next to it there was a stone tank for laundering clothes with an enclosed platform and clothes lines. A large boiler for heating water stood nearby.

At a short distance there were sheds for cows, buffaloes and two donkeys and an enclosure for poultry strutting in the open, pecking at the dust. In another enclosure goats and sheep were being herded off for pasturing. The herdsmen raised their hands in salutation to Jalal Baba.

'You've thought of every need,' Akbar said admiringly.

'I've been here long enough to know what is required,' Jalal Baba said, 'but we still need the shops in the bazaar for odd items. We get some major requirements from Peshawar. Our published material comes on order.' After a pause, he observed, 'We manage to deal with cuts, bruises and minor ailments here or we may send for the village apothecary. Serious health problems are referred to Peshawar.'

They walked in the direction of the mosque with the watchtower. Akbar picked up a pine cone and turned it around in his hands.

'Only He could have designed such a marvel,' he murmured.

Jalal Baba stopped in his tracks, 'What did you say?' he asked.

Akbar blushed, 'Something I used to say to my mother... when I was little.'

'*Jazak'Allah*...you live with awareness of the Almighty.'

'I feel Him around me,' Akbar said, 'as spontaneously as I inhale the air, listen to bird call and see the sunlight break between the leaves of trees.'

Jalal Baba looked long and hard at Akbar and said, 'Come with me.'

He led him up the rocky path for close to an hour. Akbar was panting as he tried to keep pace with Jalal Baba who clambered up like a mountain goat.

When they reached a level where the trees were sparse and the rocks profuse, Jalal Baba led the way to a cave near which water spouted from an outlet in the stones, into a stream flowing down a rocky bed.

'I know this place,' Akbar said, before Jalal Baba could speak, 'this was the site of meditation at which you decided to found Dar-ul-Aman.'

'How do you know of this?' Jalal Baba asked.

'This is what the site tells me,' Akbar murmured.

'I searched the mountain seven times, climbing up to the top before finding this spot,' Jalal Baba said as he entered the cave. 'When I discovered it, I knew at once that this was what I was looking for. I went in as if drawn by an invisible force. I put down the nan I was carrying and sat here,' he said pointing to a niche in a rock wall. 'Then I thanked Allah for guiding me here and entreated Him to help me achieve my aim. After a while, I fell asleep. When I awoke, I was thirsty, but had no water with me. Moments later, I heard a hissing, bubbling sound and before my eyes a trickle of muddy water appeared from these rocks. Gradually it turned into a spout of clear water which flowed downhill. I stared at it, unable to move for a long time. Finally my thirst drew me to it. I tasted pure ice-cold water. Then I used the water for ablutions and prayed in gratitude to Allah.'

As he spoke, Jalal Baba dipped his hands in a shallow pool in which the water eddied before flowing downstream.

'In a few days the water had etched its course down the mountainside as you see it now,' he said.

Akbar squatted beside the stream sipping handfuls of water and wetting his face.

'I have never felt like sharing this with anyone before,' Jalal Baba said placing his hands on Akbar's shoulders, 'but down there when you spoke of Him, I felt I had to bring you here.'

Back at the *hujra*, Jalal Baba and Akbar barely spoke during the midday meal. While sipping qahwa Jalal Baba asked Akbar to follow him to his study.

'Your Munshi Fazil is equivalent to a Master's degree, so you can apply for a research project to – say Al-Azhar – for a thesis on a topic of your choice acceptable to them,' Jalal Baba said. 'You can also specialize in the subjects on offer here that are usually of interest to our visiting ulema.'

'I prefer subjects,' came Akbar's reply, 'that provide source material for discussion and dissertations for sharpening the mind, but Baba I'm done with Islamic studies devoid of human considerations. I feel religion should be a pulsating objective for living, breathing people, not something confined to the cold reasoning and arid discourse of academics. More than anything I want to be in touch with humanity...' he recalled his conversation with Tooba with surprise, 'like community programmes in education or welfare.'

Jalal Baba paused before speaking.

'I'll draw up a suitable programme of studies. If you are inclined towards meaningful discussion and exchange of practical data, the two-year Wafaq-al-Madaris programme for muftis may be a better option.'

'Jalal Baba, am I right in assuming that a mufti is an authority on Islam?'

'He is a sort of reference point,' Jalal Baba said. 'He is someone who resolves problems concerning textual interpretation. His opinion may also be sought on issues that are unclear or make little sense or have more than one meaning or give rise to a conflict of interest.'

'That sounds formidable...perhaps too grand for me.'

'Not at all, Akbar. In my opinion, you're the just the person for this. It would be neglectful not to put you down for it. As regards your need for community projects, welfare work in these areas is rare. People resent strangers interfering in their affairs. Your uncle has informed me of your academic achievements and your skills as an educator and social worker. We will try to make use of these.'

During an evening walk along the periphery of the ledge, Jalal Baba wanted to know why Akbar had decided not to continue with research. Akbar explained that he had spent enough time on research at Beyt-as-Salah, preferring now to interact with people.

'Your choice makes good sense,' Jalal Baba remarked. 'If you have already found a way to God, then you are right in giving time to serve His people. Usually when one is occupied with social work, there is little time for researching the ways of God. Yet research is essential for serious scholarship. You may of course discover God by research and get close to Him through prayer and meditation. You may also find Him in service to humanity but you cannot...uncover Him. No one has ever been able to do that.'

'My mother,' Akbar said, 'told us that by declaring that there is no God other than Allah, and Mohammad is His messenger, the first prayer links God with man. The Prophet who symbolizes mankind is the one God has chosen to associate with.'

'Your mother is a wise lady. You live an incomplete life if you spend all your time in meditation. You live a full life if you meditate and also live among people. Living in this world is one of the purposes for which we were created. Worshipping can only be done by those who have the energy to do so.' After a while Jalal Baba added, 'You serve God, when you serve mankind...so you don't have to look far for Him.'

Jalal Baba's remarks should be taken down, thought Akbar, *otherwise, like dewdrops, they will evaporate.*

Five times a day – early morning, midday, evening, dusk and night time – the occupants of Dar-ul-Aman prayed in congregation at the mosque. Akbar settled into the routine of the retreat. Until the start of the course work for the mufti study programme, his mornings were spent with the texts Jalal Baba had earmarked for him. Most of them complemented those he had studied under Abdulla Saleh.

They made for a heady collection of Greek philosophy, dialectics, the Bhagawadgita, the Vedas, Buddhist tantras, Taoism and Confucianism. To counterbalance the unipolar works considered imperative by Abdulla Saleh, Al-Ghazali and Jalaludin Rumi were included among the Muslim authorities.

The afternoons were taken up with discussions amongst the ulema on matters of faith and religious philosophy. In the evening Akbar went for a walk alone or accompanied by one or more of the ulema. During the walks he often wondered about Bairam Khan's whereabouts. He wanted to see him again.

Akbar gradually became a creature of Dar-ul-Aman. His movements became fluid, his mind more receptive, responses spontaneous. Jalal Baba's reliance on Akbar added to his confidence. The growing affinity between them was comforting when Akbar felt homesick – when he thought of Lilian.

Once a month, Jalal Baba made it a point to call on the village notables. His visits served to reassure them during the phase of militancy prevailing in Mamund. Akbar looked forward to these visits.

A few weeks after Akbar's arrival, they set off for the village after the Friday midday prayer. Despite the afternoon sun, the autumn air was cool. The foliage was tinted coppery brown or rusty red. Fallen leaves on the mountain paths crackled underfoot; there was wood smoke in the air.

So different from my first hike through these trees...Autumn is not a season for Karachi.

Passers-by in the village streets greeted Jalal Baba respectfully. Some shook hands with him, others acknowledged him with a salaam. A few women scurried by draped in chador, eyes downcast, faces averted. Little boys and girls played outside some homes.

Their first call was at the tea shop, where the plaintive tones of a female bemoaning the loss of her lover wafted through a transistor. Jalal Baba greeted the owner, who placed milk-brewed tea and *baqarkhani* biscuits before them. Jalal Baba enquired about local news, while Akbar waved off flies circling the tea.

The mood in the tea shop changed when the owner's son rushed in announcing the arrival of two militants. On spotting their half-covered faces approaching the tea-shop, the owner switched to a shortwave band broadcasting a religious programme.

They came in, scrutinized the customers and acknowledged Jalal Baba with a nod. A look of puzzlement passed between them and Akbar. Then they left without a word.

'We call them holy wraiths. They appear and disappear without warning,' the owner's son said.

Word of Jalal Baba's presence in the village had spread. When he got to the home of the village elder, Malik Abdul Ghaffar Khan, he was ushered into a *hujra* set with tea, dried fruit and nutty brown sugar rolls.

Jalal Baba's calls on the imam of the village mosque, the apothecary, the largest landholder, the chief trader and the administrator of the local madrasa were met with the same courtesies. Local matters were aired, spliced with gossip.

Taliban developments were reported in hushed tones. Although the village and surrounding areas were part of Pakistani territory, ostensibly under the administrative eye of the Political Agent of Bajaur Agency, one of the many splinter groups of the Taliban exercised control over it under a Commander stationed at an outpost some distance from the village. Village affairs continued to be overseen by the Malik under guidelines set by the Commander. Religious matters and judicial decisions of the jirga had to conform to Taliban edicts. The edicts were based on Taliban interpretations of the Pakhtun tribal code in conjunction with the Salafist *takifiri* doctrines of Al-Qaeda.

The village buzzed with the news of how the Commander's newly appointed deputy, Tarrar Khan, had terrorized the area by executing six locals in a neighbouring village on charges of spying for the Pakistan army. Four were shot dead while two were beheaded.

The news had a marked effect on Akbar. The forlorn droop of his shoulders prompted Jalal Baba to enquire from the madrasa administrator about the possibility of extending the teaching programme to include Dars-e-Nizami subjects – which were not provided for in the madrasa timetable – along with lessons on mathematics, geography, sciences and English.

'And where am I to get the teachers, textbooks and funds for these subjects?' the administrator moaned.

'Why, Akbar Ali Samandar here,' Jalal Baba said, placing a hand on Akbar's shoulder, 'is qualified to teach some or all of them...and he will do it without charge as a service to the village. As for textbooks, I will send for them along with duplications from Peshawar.'

The administrator looked from Jalal Baba to Akbar in disbelief. Akbar looked at Jalal Baba in astonishment.

'Tell me your decision after you've given the matter thought,' Jalal Baba said. 'Akbar is a Munshi Fazil formally qualified in all the subjects mentioned.'

'Yes, yes...of course,' the administrator said, anxious to take advantage of the offer before it was withdrawn. 'I would be very happy to consider your proposal. I will discuss it with my colleagues and send my answer tomorrow.'

'If it suits you,' Jalal Baba observed, 'we'll work out a programme which will allow Akbar to study at Dar-ul-Aman and also teach at your madrasa.'

Dearest Lilian had written, *I can't tell how long this letter will take to reach you.* It had taken over six weeks. On returning to Dar-ul-Aman, Akbar recognized the handwriting awaiting him on the *hujra* table. Elsewhere she had written, *I do wish*

we could communicate online. At least it would be instant,
but I suppose we must live with the limitations imposed by the
remoteness of Dar-ul-Aman.

The letter contained news of Aliya's growing family in
Canada, Kamran's activities, the grandparents in England,
Javed Ali's despair at Akbar's absence, passing references to
Ahmed Ali. She did not write of her own feelings but Akbar
could discern a hidden sadness. One remark said as much:
not the presence so much as other things that went with it – the
mysterious powers – the aura – the grey-blue gaze that looked
through to what lay beyond.

There was more.

We don't know where you are. I don't suppose you will tell
us, but at least let us know how you are. To the One that guides
you, I say, help him find whatever he is looking for. Let him come
back to us or at least let him be within reach.

TWELVE

'There is a new instructor at the village madrasa,' the rookie Talib informed the Commander.

'What do you know about him?' the Commander asked, tugging his beard.

'Some Munshi Fazil from Dar-ul-Aman in Karachi.'

'Has he been told about not teaching anything which conflicts with our code?'

'I think Jalal Baba would have instructed him about such matters.'

After a pause, the Commander said, 'Keep an eye on him for the next few weeks and report back on any irregularities.'

Akbar came from Dar-ul-Aman five mornings a week to teach at the madrasa. He was assigned two groups of students – children aged eight to twelve, and teenagers aged thirteen to eighteen.

He conducted preliminary lessons for the younger students, and introductory courses of the Dars-e-Nizami for the older group. He found them keen to learn but lacking in the rudimentary skills of reading, writing and numbers.

He returned to Dar-ul-Aman in time for the midday prayer. The afternoon was spent studying. Discussions with the ulema now took place in the evenings, followed by a stroll before the *Maghrib* prayer.

Often, the discussions continued during the evening meal. Issues that the participants had come across during the course of study usually came up. The topics ranged from philosophy to sectarianism, from Quranic verses to scholarly commentaries. On one occasion, Akbar's query on Salafi practices was addressed by one of the visiting ulema. 'The Salafi approach has the merit of being literalist.'

'Does that mean that it is the preferred approach for the study of scriptures?' Akbar asked.

'The literal meaning of a text *is* of primary importance, but for this purpose the reader should have mastered the Arabic language, which has mathematical precision, combined with specialized formatting and highly developed structurals. So, a single word in Arabic can have more than one meaning, some rendering others ambiguous, thus affecting the thrust of what a phrase means. In such cases, the meaning may be derived from the context of the passage. Meaning may also be derived from the historical events if any – to which the text relates. Tradition too plays a part...the literalist approach is only one aspect of the exercise.'

'That implies that the word by itself is not necessarily the criterion of what a phrase stands for,' Akbar remarked.

'The Salafist teaching your instructors subjected you to,' Jalal Baba said, 'was merely a teaching exercise. There is nothing misguiding about that as there is nothing wrong with the queries raised by you. It seems though that after you had expressed your objections no one pressured you to continue. So why the protest?'

'Their insistence on a single creed, the denunciation of other approaches, the recourse to militancy to strike out dissent...surely, these are causes for concern,' Akbar said.

'Such things have political connotations,' another of the ulema explained, 'there is little religious substance to them. They are not treated as matters of faith, but regrettably in some cases regarded as instances of practice.'

'Islamic history is replete with this sort of thing,' said another. 'The Sunni-Shia divide was a political event. Later, there were the Kharajites and the Assassins and their histories of violence and warfare. Today there are Al-Qaeda and ISIS...as in the case of all militant movements, the agenda is often political.'

'Dispatching the foreign militants and weapons that you saw at Beyt-as-Saleh,' Jalal Baba pointed out, 'was part of the strategy of your instructors to further their cause...it should not have unsettled you.'

'It was anti-state, an act of betrayal. It furthered the prospect of bloodshed under the slogan of *takfir*,' Akbar said indignantly.

'Perhaps it was all those things but it is also what they believed in.'

'Does that make it right?' Akbar asked incredulously.

'It is not a question of right and wrong,' Jalal Baba said, 'I would not have done it but they believe in it and whichever way you view it that is justification enough...for them.'

Sometimes, while studying, Akbar's level of absorption was so intense that the room, the desk, the books and other objects would seem to vanish. Time would cease to exist.

Consciousness would spiral upward, dizzyingly. By the end, Akbar faced some difficulty in coming back.

The experience was different from similar incidents in the past, yet the terrain was familiar. There was the same exhilaration, the same disconnect with the body. The symptoms were discernible.

When a tingling sensation heralded the onset of such an episode, he gave in to it. He found the experience so irresistible that he tried occasionally to bring it on by intensive meditation. But it did not happen.

He spoke of it to Jalal Baba, detailing all his trials and errors. Jalal Baba strove to dissuade him from such experimentation. 'Don't discuss the indescribable,' he said. 'Words describing human experiences are inappropriate for gauging other-worldly phenomena. Language can't express what is felt by the spirit.'

After a pause, Jalal Baba continued, 'You are among the few lucky ones, Akbar. Most believers – even devout ones – do not have the experiences that you are privy to. You are the recipient of something extraordinary but don't...I repeat, don't try to induce the sensation. It is not an intoxicant that you can turn to at will. You must wait for it to happen. It is triggered by a special magnetic force between you and the power of the universe, not by any device accessible to you.'

Akbar listened intently.

'You have been blessed with the Sufi experience.' Jalal Baba said. 'This happens to a person after intensive practice under the guidance of a Sheikh or Sufi teacher, not to an unschooled novice.'

'How should I deal with it?' Akbar asked, with a trace of confusion.

'Look, the event has already taken place, so it's impractical to seek a Sufi master as spiritual guide at this stage. But you will still need formal guidance. If you agree, I will be your guide. We don't need to go through the traditional ceremony of initiation...with you becoming my *mureed* and me your *murshid*. Perhaps that is why you came here.'

'I feel privileged...specially so on becoming your disciple,' Akbar said, much relieved.

'You are blessed,' Jalal Baba corrected gravely, 'but no more privileged than others who reach the plane either by means of religious formats such as Islam, Buddhism, Christianity, Taoism, Judaism, Hinduistic faiths or shamanic and tribal practices or those who attain it through dialectics. There are different ways towards the ultimate truth. The process is invariably an individual's singular journey requiring one element that is common for all...submission.'

Before the advent of Ramadan, most of the foreign ulema returned to their homes. The few who stayed on were busy with treatises scheduled for publication. Other ulema were expected to take up residence later in the year. The rotation of religious scholars at Dar-ul-Aman was a regular occurrence.

The month of Ramadan coincided with the onset of colder weather. The days were given to fasting and to special prayer which continued for part of the night. Akbar's experience of the Ramadan schedule at Beyt-as-Salah helped.

Dar-ul-Aman's ragtag arrangements of the past were succeeded by a new orderliness. Jalal Baba noted that Akbar seemed to come into his own during Ramadan. This served to remind Jalal Baba that it was time the retreat was turned from a hand-to-mouth abode for religious scholars run by

Janbaz Khan into an efficiently run institution. Akbar's presence seemed providential.

For Akbar this was unchartered territory. He was conscious that Dar-ul-Aman, like Beyt-as-Salah, needed someone with financial and administrative skills to handle the operation successfully, but he had no experience in such matters.

Jalal Baba was unrelenting. He drew Akbar in bit by bit, plying him with data, accounts books and files that documented the setting up and workings of the seminary.

'Your spiritual faculties are sufficiently developed,' he remarked, 'it's time now to hone your skills in practical matters for the task of administering Dar-ul-Aman.'

'Having no experience, all I can do is try,' Akbar's said.

'Remember, economic well-being is a touchstone for physical survival,' Jalal Baba pointed out, 'and physical stability is a sound base for spiritual exercises.'

'I know, I know, Jalal Baba.'

'Just bear in mind that steadfastness in prayer and the special learning imparted by me are better served by a sound body, and the body is sound when its physical needs are satisfied. For fulfilment of such needs money is a prerequisite.'

'Inductive reasoning is far too convoluted, Baba, compared to Uncle Ahmed Ali's directness. He said that a man has to have a livelihood to stay alive, procreate and worship. Otherwise it's all over.'

Dar-ul-Aman finances primarily comprised central and provincial government subsidies along with grants from national and international entities. Akbar was surprised when he came upon Ahmed Ali's name in a donors' list, at which Jalal Baba commented, 'Now you know why we let you in.'

Akbar was in for another surprise when Jalal Baba announced that for his services as administrator of Dar-ul-Aman, he would be paid an appropriate salary. Akbar protested, wanting to work without pay.

'That is out of the question,' Jalal Baba said. 'If a manager is hired, he would have to be paid a salary...-so why shouldn't you be on salary too? Besides, it is haram to benefit from your effort without compensating you...I will not do it. You are of an age to earn your keep and I expect professional competence from you. I had also promised your uncle that I would look after your interests. I would be failing there if I made you work for nothing.'

When he had gone through the Dar-ul-Aman papers, Akbar suggested that a professional accountant from Peshawar be engaged temporarily to reorganize the accounts and introduce book-keeping systems that could be handled by a figures' clerk.

A week later, Janbaz Khan ushered in a jittery accountant, who had come up from Peshawar. His encounter with the 'holy wraiths' had unnerved him.

Akbar diverted him with a tour of the complex before setting to work. They went over the accounts for five days, bringing some semblance of order to the financial operations.

Another day, another dimension. On how many planes does one exist? Akbar wondered, *teaching...researching...administering... communing ...perhaps reality is prismatic...or perhaps it is as now, dispersed...*

Akbar's assumption of his multifaceted new role at Dar-ul-Aman entailed adopting the different personas that went with it. His actions moved from that premise, until he changed, chameleon-like, to another hue, then another and yet another, until the day was done.

The nights were different. The darkness was studded by imagery of the Samandar home, of Lilian, Kamran and Aliya, father and uncle –even Tooba – and of the little boy in the garden visited by unseen marvels.

The month of fasting ended in Eid celebrations. The nights turned colder before Eid, blanketing the terrain with frost in the mornings. Despite the slippery descent to the village, the residents of the seminary joined the congregational prayer on Eid morning at the village common adjacent to the mosque.

All able-bodied males over the age of three attended. The Taliban were conspicuous by their absence. After the prayer, everyone seemed to rush forward to exchange greetings with Jalal Baba. Those who missed doing so, called at the seminary. They kept coming until dark.

'I've had a surfeit of figures today,' Akbar protested after a three-hour struggle with financial matters on the day following Eid, 'balancing revenues with expenses...allocating funds for the maintenance of buildings, replacement of livestock, writing to donors, reviewing the returns on our saving certificates...'

'What should I say?...Well done,' Jalal Baba responded with a touch of irony.

'Accounts don't come easily to me,' Akbar said.

'Money has its importance...what if you had to earn your living?'

'Why then, I would do it...and do it well.'

'So do it now. Dar-ul-Aman must thrive. That's what you have to do.'

'I have a money-making scheme in mind,' Akbar said softly.

'Seriously?' Jalal Baba remarked with interest.

'I'm putting together a feasibility study for a honey bottling plant...it's doable because the forest is bursting with honeybee colonies. We can also put up an apiary with hives. We'll require expertise for extracting and bottling wild bee honey and for breeding domesticated bees.'

Jalal Baba looked at Akbar in wonder, 'You never cease to amaze me Akbar Ali Samandar...of course it's doable. Visiting ulema from Germany and Japan suggested such a scheme three years ago. They also offered to supply equipment and send experts – all paid for – to install aviaries, honey extraction and refinement systems and train local operators. It's certainly doable. I just needed someone here to tell me how it's to be done.'

'Put me in touch with those people,' Akbar said eagerly.

'Not now,' Jalal Baba said, 'You're tired. Now it's time for you to take your mind off money matters. Go to the cave for a spell.'

The prospect of visiting the cave was uplifting. Akbar put on hiking boots and set off. It was early afternoon. There was a chill in the air heralding the oncoming winter but the sun shone brightly. The morning frost had melted, leaving damp patches of earth. He felt lighter as he climbed, more sure-footed now.

He let his imagination wander. He thought of mountains in the scriptures, highlands on the moon. For a moment he thought he saw Bairam Khan among the trees, but it was a pair of hares that sped across his path.

By the time he reached the cave, the sun had moved westward, lighting up the sky, turning it pink, then red-streaked and illuminating the valley at the foot of a snow-covered Koh-i-Mor.

He knelt by the spring – gleaming at the edges with traceries of ice – and scooped water up to his lips. He heard rustling in the undergrowth and assumed it was a rabbit or a fox. Instead, an ewe came out of the thicket followed by a suckling lamb.

Curiosity about how they had got there was interrupted by a shrill call of 'Yi-ee-yi-ee' that seemed to be getting closer. Without thinking further, he made a dash for the cave, scaring the ewe into seeking cover in the thicket.

As he watched from the cave, a girl carrying a staff came into view. She could not have been more than eighteen. She was dressed in a tribal-style smock kurta embroidered in needlepoint and a voluminous salwar. A brightly coloured dupatta was slung over her shoulder. Tall and slender and – like most Pakhtun women – fair-skinned. Her hair was braided, reddish brown and gold-tinted when touched by the sun.

As she moved towards the cave she raised her hand, cupping her mouth, calling 'Yi-ee-yi-ee' repeatedly to her missing flock. At the spring she dipped a hand in icy water, placed it on the back of her neck and forehead and resumed the cries.

Akbar realized she did not know where the sheep might be. He stepped out of the cave to help, hoping also to get a closer look at her.

Seeing him, she retreated startled, tugging at the dupatta to cover her head. There was great beauty in her alarm – eyes set well apart with gold-flecked pupils, rosy lips parted.

Akbar drew his hands up to his chest, palms facing outward to ally her fears. In the best Pashto he could muster, he explained that he was from Dar-ul-Aman and had come across the sheep while hiking, pointing at the direction in which they had gone. He offered to help her find them. She shook her head, declining the offer and went off hastily.

Akbar watched. In a matter of minutes, she had come and gone, leaving him with a new awareness. He had not been close to a woman since he left Karachi, and now he had been close enough to touch her. Who was she? Where had she come from? How did she get to the cave? He was unlikely to find answers at Dar-ul-Aman. It would also be indiscreet to disclose the incident to anyone.

He dreamt of her that night. The shrill call rang in his ears. She was by the spring beside the cave. When he came out of the cave she was gone.

A letter from Tooba the following day reminded him of home. He tried writing one in response by steeling himself to think of other matters, but life in Karachi seemed far away.

Lapses in Akbar's attention during conversations at meals were noticed by Jalal Baba and some of the ulema.

'Perhaps there's too much for him to do,' remarked one.

'Meditation can become a drug,' said another.

'He is very young,' said a third, 'maybe he's struggling to find his way.'

'What is the matter Akbar?' Jalal Baba asked finally.

Akbar turned his grey-blue gaze on Jalal Baba, pausing for a moment before responding, 'I'm going through something...something indefinable...I'll talk about it when I can.'

THIRTEEN

It was the honey bottling programme that ultimately drew out Akbar. The torpidity of the environment had stirred him to consider schemes likely to benefit the area. He saw the honey bottling plant as a precursor to beeswax processing, fruit canning and bottling, dried fruit packaging and wood crafting.

'Despite the bulky fatigue jacket and shawl, I can't help but see entrepreneurial wings rising from your shoulders,' Jalal Baba teased. 'How many more guises will you adopt?'

'Why hadn't anyone thought along these lines earlier?' Akbar asked.

'There is a dearth of enlightened young people in the region,' Jalal Baba replied.

'The village notables are hardly capable of such thinking. Most young people leave home to seek work elsewhere on reaching their twenties.'

During the winter, Akbar corresponded with the German Islamists who had offered to assist with honey production. When the paperwork was done, Akbar approached government agencies in Peshawar to allot land in the woods to the Dar-ul-Aman Trust, and to sanction the installation of a plant and apiary and temporary power transmission.

Obtaining bank finance for the project required the skills of both Jalal Baba and Akbar. Since the equipment and expertise were to be supplied free of cost, approvals came through with minimal red tape.

It did not take long for word of Akbar's activities to reach the Taliban Commander. To forestall the likelihood of subversive developments, he sent a representative to find out the views of the villagers. The responses indicated that most people liked Akbar and appreciated his contribution to the madrasa. The reports made the Commander uneasy. The popularity of individuals not connected with their movement was frowned upon by the Taliban leadership. He deputed an astute subordinate to monitor Akbar's teaching.

One morning Akbar found a sharp-eyed Talib in his class. He had been allowed by the imam to attend the lesson. Akbar got busy with the *tarjuma* and *tafseer* course involving translation and explanation of religious texts.

Midway through the lesson the Talib questioned the authenticity of some explanations. Akbar explained that they were based on meanings derived from the translated text.

When the Talib challenged the accuracy of the translations, Akbar inquired about his competence in Arabic. The Talib countered by asking Akbar the same question. Akbar stated that he was a Munshi Fazil, conversant with both classical and modern Arabic. The Talib was at a loss.

'Since you don't know Arabic, how can you question the authenticity of a translation?'

'I know my prayers,' the man replied, reciting the *Sura-e-Ikhlas*.

When Akbar asked him for the meaning of the sura, he failed to respond.

'You should know the meaning of your prayers my friend,' Akbar said pointedly, rendering a Pashto translation of the verses.

The lull that followed was broken by sniggers in the class. Akbar raised his hand to silence the students. Stung at being shown up, the Talib got up.

'What is this course you are teaching the boys?' he asked.

'The Dars-e-Nizami designed by the Wafaq-al-Madaris,' Akbar said.

'Well, from tomorrow onwards, before your lesson, I will give a half-hour talk to your class on the duties and obligations of a Muslim. I have the imam's permission to do so...I want all the students to attend.'

He hoisted his weapon and left.

The following day, twenty-two out of thirty-seven students attended. They were subjected to a sermon on the appearance and conduct prescribed for Muslim men. The guidelines were Salafist and militant. The style of delivery was different from Akbar's inclusive approach based on reasoning and exposition.

The next morning only four students attended the Taliban lecture, which included readings from tracts published by fundamentalist Islamic groups such as the Jamaat-ud-Dawa and the Hizb-ul-Tahrir. The remaining students sidled in later for Akbar's lesson.

On the third day, no one came for the earlier session. The Talib waited for half an hour before leaving. He did not return to the madrasa.

A cold wave swept over the area during the last few weeks of the year. The days were shorter, the nights longer. The sky was overcast for most of the day. The gloom was relieved by intermittent snow but returned with spells of blinding rain. Winds sweeping down from mountains kept people indoors. Dar-ul-Aman was cut off from the village by snowdrifts. It was as a rule stocked with sufficient provisions for extended periods.

One morning in early February, as the sun broke through, Akbar heard high-pitched voices and laughter coming through a window. They belonged to little children playing in the snow.

There were two of them, a boy aged three and a girl of five. An attendant squatted close by. Janbaz told him that they were Jalal Baba's grandchildren who had come to watch the snow being swept off the Dar-ul-Aman roofs.

The children clapped their hands and jumped aside when snowy heaps were whooshed down the sloping roofs by massive brooms. After the excitement, they were treated to kheer, brown sugar candy and sweetened milk laced with almonds, nuts and raisins.

Akbar looked wistfully at the youngsters when Jalal Baba mentioned that they – and their baby brother – were the children of his only son who had been killed in a suicide bombing in Swabi bazaar.

They and their widowed mother lived at Jalal Baba's cottage. He also had four daughters older than the son, in different parts of Khyber Pakhtunkhwa. There were fifteen additional grandchildren and three great-grandchildren.

During his evening walk some weeks later, Akbar sensed a stirring in the air. He looked up at the skeletal branches of trees ranged against the blue sky. On some, bright green specks were breaking through the black bark. Little creatures scurried through the undergrowth at his approach. A pair of foxes crossed his path.

He felt the energy rising from the soles of his feet. It was the call of spring. His body had become hard and supple, the frame well-toned as a result of walking to and from Dar-ul-Aman. The jawline was firmer, the cheekbones more pronounced. It was a new awakening. A vision of the girl with the staff came to mind and wafted away like a hallucination. Akbar's azan that evening resounded through the trees.

Work on the bottling scheme intensified as the weather improved. Progress was assessed according to a detailed schedule of work forwarded by suppliers of the equipment. Honey extractors, pasteurizers and bottling plants were on the way from Germany. Beekeeping paraphernalia and an industrial power generator were being shipped from Japan. An apiarist and a honey packaging specialist from Germany had been smuggled into Dar-ul-Aman – with help from the army to avoid Taliban interference – for fieldwork and training. A local contractor was engaged for building works.

The labour came from Kitkot and neighbouring villages, the artisans from Peshawar. Janbaz Khan shuttled between Kitkot, Peshawar and Dar-ul-Aman, ferrying items ranging from mail to bottle samples and local requirements for the project.

On his return from teaching at the village madrasa, Akbar spent most of his time in the woods where work was in progress. Intrigued Dar-ul-Aman residents watched the men at work instead of attending to their chores.

The labourers were pleased to get work close to home. Villagers being trained for special tasks in honey processing regarded the opportunity as a windfall.

Trees chopped to clear the land were stripped and shaped to make beams for the roof of the shed and horizontal bars for fencing the site.

On the day the roof was to be laid, work was interrupted by a barrage of gunfire close to the site. Within moments a small company of soldiers with G3 rifles stationed nearby descended from somewhere above the shed.

'We're looking for militants on the run. They have blown up a bridge on the northern route,' the commanding officer said. 'Has anyone seen them?'

The workers were too startled to react. The officer looked around, exasperated.

'Who is in charge here?' he asked shortly.

The foreman came out of the shed. Janbaz Khan left his stool and approached the officer.

'This is the foreman,' Janbaz said pointing him out, 'and I represent Dar-ul-Aman.'

'Well, you should understand,' the officer said, 'there are militants around who are dangerous. There were five of them. We have got three, two dead, one wounded, but the other two managed to get away. They ran this way.'

'No one has come here,' Janbaz said, 'if we come across anything suspicious we'll send word to the picket.'

The officer directed his men to carry out a search. They fanned out, scouring the site, then proceeded to the sheep pen, the cattle and poultry sheds and the mosque.

At Dar-ul-Aman Jalal Baba led the officer through the premises. His men searched the rooms. The militants appeared to have found a way into the building and taken cover in the storeroom.

On hearing the soldiers close in, they dashed out shooting wildly. One of them ran across the courtyard towards the entrance. He bounded into the open but was caught in the back by a volley of bullets. The second one moved swiftly down the west wing and slunk unseen into a room. It was Akbar's.

Akbar was deep in meditation on a prayer mat, eyes shut, hands resting on his knees. He faced the window with his back to the door. The militant stopped when he saw Akbar. He approached him from behind, placed the tip of his gun next to his temple and said, 'Don't make a sound...and show me a hiding place.'

Akbar did not respond. He scarcely moved. He could not hear what the militant had said, nor was he aware of his presence. The militant cursed and prodded him with his gun. The continued silence bothered him.

He pushed hard at Akbar's shoulder but met with unexpected resistance. The body was rigid and unaffected by the pressure exerted. The militant suspected that something was amiss when he saw Akbar's eyes shut. At the sound of approaching boots he leapt towards the window, recoiling when he saw the drop to the valley below. In a panic, he ducked down beside the chest of drawers.

After a while the door was opened by Jalal Baba. The officer stood beside him. Noticing Akbar's state of meditation, Jalal Baba suggested that they should move on. The officer wanted to search the room but changed his mind on seeing its bareness.

As they turned to go, a bottle fell to the floor, knocked off the chest of drawers by the militant's fidgetiness. His presence would have remained unnoticed had he not moved.

Thinking he had been discovered, he fired at the door and clipped the officer's shoulder. The soldiers moved in instantly and sprayed him with head shots which reduced his face to pulp.

Akbar remained oblivious to all that took place.

In encounters involving Dar-ul-Aman, the Taliban invariably came off second best. They found themselves facing a prestigious place of learning recognized by the Islamic world where notable Muslim and non-Muslim scholars spent time in research or meditation. Jalal Baba's eminence as a leading Islamic academic, author and founder, lent credence to Dar-ul-Aman's fame. But it rankled as a challenge in their eyes. The rigidity and hieratic order of their madrasa culture was missing. Creeds other than the Salafist were accorded equal significance. Religions other than Islam also had a place in discussions. Art and culture were upheld as markers of civilization. Sufism was treated as an acceptable approach to God. Individual rights had sacramental significance. The concept of jihad was interpreted as a personal struggle for attaining faith, and warlike jihad as a means for preserving the sanctity of Islamic norms under threat of arms.

These practices were apostatical in the view of the Taliban, but they had been cautioned against issuing fatwas denouncing Dar-ul-Aman. Any such move would have raised protests from Afghanistan to the border of Punjab by people who were attuned – since long before the Taliban – to viewing

Jalal Baba as an enduring symbol of the Pakhtun people. It would also have turned off those foreign spigots showering money on the Taliban cause.

This uneasy state did not stop inquisitive or mischievous Talibs from showing up at Dar-ul-Aman. Jalal Baba always received such unexpected visitors courteously and opened up the complex to their nosy visitations.

To accommodate some of the younger Talibs who had shown an interest in the honeybee project, Jalal Baba allowed them to observe the honey collection forays of the harvesting team trained by the German apiarist. Akbar was assigned to keep an eye on them.

The team had been trying to locate a hive-intensive area that the villagers had been talking about for weeks. It was discovered by chance when two Talibs wandered off to relieve themselves in what they thought was a secluded spot within a grove of poplars, larch and juniper.

They had barely squatted down by some trees before they heard an angry buzzing overhead. Looking up, they saw several hives, two or three feet long, swarming with bees. Holding fast to their salwar drawstrings they scrambled back, blabbering in alarm.

It did not take long for the harvesters to don protective apparel and place tin boxes crammed with smouldering rags and straw under a group of hives. Dense plumes of smoke from vents in the boxes wound upward and into the hives causing a mass exodus of bees. The ones that remained in the hives lost consciousness.

Some twenty minutes later the harvesters detached the hives from their tree moorings by long poles and lowered them to the ground by means of metal hooks fixed to the poles. Some of the hives were then cut in sections by a sharp knife to extract accessible honeycombs.

The apiarist did not allow the cutting of those hives in which the honeycomb was likely to be damaged. Ultimately the honeycombs and intact hives were bound up in muslin and taken to the shed to be hung on bars for draining the honey into collection pans.

The Talibs were fascinated by the harvesting process. They chattered and giggled with child-like excitement that belied their gruff public stance. When the harvesting team was winding up for the day, the Talibs examined the equipment with interest.

One of them picked up a pole and sauntered into the grove holding it aloft. As he moved forward, the hook at the end of the pole grazed one of the treetop hives that had not been harvested.

Jarred by the impact, a stream of bees flew furiously down on the intruder, attacking the upper part of his body. He dropped the pole and ran back screaming. A black line of bees, swelling into a swarm, followed him.

The harvesting team and observers were caught by surprise. They scattered instinctively, running, leaping and diving for cover. Stray groups of bees chased them.

Akbar noticed the appalling state of the Talib who had disturbed the hive – writhing and moaning on the ground, beset by relentless attackers. Snatching a tarpaulin from the containers, he dashed into the centre of the attack to cover the poor wretch. He had barely got to the victim when his arms, neck and face were punctured by thorny thrusts. Searing pain engulfed him and spread through his limbs.

The shock was more than he could stand. He fell like a log on the contorted body of the Talib.

The apiarist who had been trying – unsuccessfully – from his hiding place behind rocks to make the team follow standard safety procedure, finally donned protective apparel and bludgeoned his way to the two inert bodies.

He wound the tarpaulin around them, bundling them like carpet rolls. On being denied access to their victims the marauding bees scattered and dispersed.

Except for Akbar and the Talib, most of the others had escaped serious harm. Some with the occasional sting were disturbed more by the experience than the pain. The Talib was badly stung but was not in danger. Akbar's condition was more serious.

Instead of being returned to his billet where there were no facilities for treatment, the Talib was kept back at Dar-ul-Aman. A few days later, he left Dar-ul-Aman grateful for the treatment he had received. He wanted to thank Akbar for saving him but was unable to do so on account of Akbar's more serious condition. His Commander, however, was constrained to acknowledge Jalal Baba's kindness in caring for the boy.

Akbar was allergic to bee venom which had entered his system, bloating his body and choking his lungs. Scores of embedded stings had to be removed. The 786 birthmark had turned a blazing scarlet. It was swollen and seemed ready to burst. The apiarist diagnosed his condition as anaphylactic shock which caused high fever and choking spells and sent him into a coma.

Jalal Baba was beside himself but had the presence of mind to establish contact, via the nearest picket, with his contacts in the army high command. The response was swift. An army air ambulance helicopter carrying medical paraphernalia landed within an hour. The captain in charge was accompanied by a specialist in venom-induced maladies, a paramedic and a male nursing attendant. The ambulance contained a stretcher bed along with antihistamine sera, cortisone and antivenom drugs, ointments, lotions and intravenous injectables.

Stormy weather conditions that evening caused a delay in the plan to move Akbar to an army hospital in Peshawar. The specialist decided to observe him overnight.

Next morning he concluded that moving him would cause great discomfort. Akbar could be fed and administered medication intravenously at Dar-ul-Aman by the paramedic. Pastes could be made locally from tobacco, salt or clay, garlic and ice and applied locally to the swollen parts of the body. The paramedic and nurse were directed to stay back to attend to Akbar.

The specialist planned to return in a few days to check Akbar's condition. He conferred by radio-telephone with the hospital and gave a status report to his superiors before flying back to Peshawar. Akbar needed constant attendance. As tending at the seminary would have presented a problem, Jalal Baba had him moved to his cottage.

He informed Ahmed Ali about the incident by a radio-phone call. A specialist in Karachi reaffirmed the military specialist's prognosis and treatment. Javed Ali and Ahmed Ali wanted to travel to Dar-ul-Aman to be with Akbar but were dissuaded by Jalal Baba from doing so because of the security risk. He assured them that he would advise them if his condition deteriorated. As Lilian was visiting her parents in England at the time, Javed Ali decided not to tell her unless it became necessary to do so.

FOURTEEN

Jalal Baba lived in a cottage made of wood and stone, built on a naturally formed terrace on the upper reaches of the mountain slope.

Akbar was placed in a small room made of roughly hewn logs, with a window overlooking trees. Stonework was confined to the fireplace. Toilet facilities consisted of a hot water samovar and a hammam, watered by a spring passing by the cottage..

Akbar was treated by the paramedic and tended by the nurse. Nourishment and medication were administered intravenously while he was in a coma. The specialist returned when the swelling had gone down. He could stir in bed and move his limbs but remained comatose.

When he finally came to, his mind reawakened by stages. At first, he saw flashes of colour – red, orange, yellow, stabbed by black spots. Then came distant honeycombs... growing closer until they became grillwork through which calligraphy was visible...Jalal Baba reciting the azan from the tower...Akbar's body rotating upward through space... chased by masked militants who push him off a minaret... falling down...down...down...Lilian in the garden where sheep grazed...watched by the girl on a hilltop holding a staff.

His eyes opened on leaves and branches framed by the window. Bird calls and the tangy smell of pine drifted in. Sunlit patches of the hillside were visible through the trees, dotted by mountain honeysuckle, rhododendron, mimosa and verbena.

The piping voices of children reciting Pashto nursery rhymes drifted into his consciousness. They were seated round a rock. Then he saw her...the girl with the staff. She stood on the rock. He blinked. She was still there.

He realized he was not dreaming when the paramedic came into the room. The nurse was seated next to his bed and drips were attached to his arms. The paramedic smiled. He examined Akbar's eyes, checked his vital signs then sat by the window and in response to his questioning look, told him all that had happened after he had lost consciousness.

News of Akbar's revival brought a tearful Jalal Baba to his bedside. Akbar tried to thank him for accommodating him at the cottage but was silenced by Jalal Baba.

Special food was served to Akbar – chicken soup with herbs followed by lamb stew with vegetables, ending with fresh fruit.

The food was served by the girl with the staff. She came in with her head covered. Jalal Baba introduced her as his daughter, Asmina Bibi. Akbar was dismayed on hearing this.

Those two – no three – youngsters must be her children, he thought. *Then she is widowed.*

The situation became clearer when the little boy put his head round the door.

'Tror,' he said, addressing Asmina, 'Bebe wants you in the kitchen.'

Akbar knew that *tror* meant aunt. Bebe, Jalal Baba explained was the children's mother, his daughter-in-law Ameera.

Jalal Baba's wife had been dead for some years, but his mother, who was almost ninety, still lived. She had henna-reddened hair and moved about with the help of a walking stick, tended by a maid who also doubled as the household cook. A twelve-year-old son of a sheep handler helped with chores at the cottage.

Bringing a strange man into the home and introducing him to the womenfolk was an extraordinary departure from the norm. Pakhtun culture ranked the sanctity of the home next to keeping faith.

But a stranger once admitted to the home was treated as part of the family. And so it was with Akbar. The children ran in and out of his room – playing rumble-tumble on his bed – when he was awake. They addressed him as Kaka and brought him wild flowers.

The houseboy took over the task of helping Akbar after the paramedic and the male nurse had left. The old lady appeared concerned every time she passed his door. His meals were served by one of the younger ladies. His medication was administered by Asmina. His room was dusted and cleaned by the maid. Jalal Baba sat with him morning and evening, discoursing on moot topics or chatting about lighter matters.

Akbar read until his eyes wearied, and prayed in bed. The cramps in his limbs made it difficult for him to get up.

Asmina approached his room with diffidence. When no one else was present a strange tension prevailed between them. They barely spoke to each other. She avoided his gaze and shied from physical contact when giving medication. The glimmerings of a bond were discernible.

Akbar had felt something after the first encounter which seemed to recede when he felt he had lost sight of her. Now he found himself faced with the reality. It was palpable... powerful...leaving him feeling like a diver coming up for air when she left the room.

It was more baffling for Asmina. The memory of the first meeting was imprinted on her but her approach to what lay ahead had to conform to the Pakhtun code of conduct for women. She knew that her fate lay in the hands of the male head of the family. She was overcome by emotion when she saw him in her home. She felt that fate had somehow conspired to bring him there. She had little control over her feelings. Something unusual was happening to her.

One morning when she was placing his capsules on the bedside table, Akbar held her wrist and asked, 'Did you find the missing sheep?'

She drew back, startled, turning to leave. At the door she looked back at him and laughed. It was Akbar's turn to look startled.

'I searched the hillside without finding them,' she said, 'when I came down I saw them with other sheep in the enclosure. They had found their way home without me but the keepers were so worried by my absence that they were about to send out a search party.'

With the ice broken they were hard put to revert to their earlier reserve. They spoke shyly at first about inconsequential matters – the weather, food, the children's escapades.

Gradually they began talking of personal matters. Akbar spoke about his family. Soon, when they came to know enough about each other, they were almost friends. They spoke of many things except for what was uppermost in their minds.

As Akbar's condition improved he would leave his bed and stand unaided for minutes. He even attempted a shaky step or two.

When feeling stronger, he was helped to a wooden bench lying in the spring sunshine facing Koh-i-Mor. During morning hours Jalal Baba's mother and Ameera's toddler, strapped into a baby chair, usually sat at a table beside the bench.

Day by day Akbar felt his strength return. He knew that he would have to leave the cottage shortly for Dar-ul-Aman. He fretted at the prospect of parting from Asmina, of not being able to see her.

Short of making a declaration of love, he had gone as far as he could. Additional moves might amount to a betrayal of Jalal Baba's trust and reduce something sublime to tawdriness. He felt that given his maturity and innate sense of responsibility, it was his call to set the course of the relationship.

Jalal Baba would have to be told, and the consequences faced. *But not as yet...not yet...There will be a right time...when both of us are ready for it.*

On his last evening the children were with him before going to bed. Their antics had brought laughter into his life. The older girl cried a little when he kissed and bade them good night.

When Asmina came with his medication he was by the window watching the sky darkening. She set down the tray and stood beside him dreading the prospect of his departure.

Akbar felt her shiver in the evening breeze. He placed an arm around her without thinking. There was no resistance. She seemed to merge with him. It was akin to the sense of recognition he had experienced on embracing Jalal Baba the first time.

'I love you,' he murmured, drawing her close, brushing the tip of her nose, cheeks and mouth with his lips. Whatever needed to be said was communicated in silence...

Akbar got back to work on his return to the seminary. He was gratified by the progress that had been made on the bottling plant in his absence. It seemed likely that Dar-ul-Aman honey would be available in supermarkets within weeks.

During his illness Dar-ul-Aman affairs had been looked after by Jalal Baba and the accountant. Some creases had appeared. He would have to fix them.

The madrasa students and administrator were beside themselves with joy at having him back. There had been poor attendance while he was away.

There were letters from home waiting for attention. He wrote replies. Work was what he needed most. The children visited him every day. He played ball games with them in the foreground of Dar-ul-Aman, joined frequently by the younger sons of Dar-ul-Aman workers.

On observing the youngsters' keenness, Akbar encouraged them to play cricket and football. He managed to train twelve youngsters who had a flair for sports, but finding a sufficient number of players to form two competing teams posed a problem. So he set about convincing the administrator of the village madrasa how field games would expose students to teamwork, sportsmanship and discipline.

Inevitably the teams of Dar-ul-Aman and the madrasa met for cricket and football matches, which were played, much to the delight of the villagers, on the oddly shaped village common adjacent to the mosque.

Eventually the land – which was also used for Eid prayers – came to be known as the cricket ground. Some preferred to call it the football field.

Despite the diverse activities, Asmina was never far from his mind. But he only got to hear about her when the children spoke of some incident that concerned her. His existence felt incomplete without her.

This awareness caught him by surprise. He had been born to faith and an abiding sense of extraordinary attributes that had led him towards transcendence. These factors had fulfilled his life – until this moment.

Now there was another need, a desire more compelling than any other felt before, different from what he had experienced, yet almost as demanding.

'The time will come,' Jalal Baba had said on one occasion, 'when you will want a mate.'

'Is that inevitable?' Akbar asked.

'Yes,' Jalal Baba said. 'It's Allah's way. The experience awaits you Akbar Ali Samandar.'

'I don't fully understand Baba...'

'You will...but remember there is more to marriage than just physical oneness.'

'What else?'

'You will experience emotional bonding. That too is part of the plan.'

The words came back to haunt Akbar...

Clandestine overtures were out of the question. Asmina's relationship to Jalal Baba called for transparency. It seemed the matter would begin or end with Jalal Baba. Timing was unresolved. How long could Akbar bear such an uncertain state of affairs?

Plans for launching Dar-ul-Aman honey in supermarkets at Peshawar and other urban centres gave little opportunity for broaching the subject with Jalal Baba. Akbar was kept busy with packaging and marketing requirements. He had to deal with purchasing agents coming from Peshawar and negotiate terms with wholesalers.

The promotion was successful. The honey gained popularity and the returns were encouraging. To deal with the increasing demand it became necessary to set up a management unit at the production site.

One afternoon, Akbar was invited to tea at the cottage to celebrate the toddler's birthday. He was excited at the prospect of seeing Asmina although he realized that he would not get a chance to be alone with her.

As he came up the slope, he was greeted by the children who clambered all over him. Tea was served outdoors beside the bench. It was bright in the sun. The snow-capped peaks of the Koh-i-Mor range stood out against a blue sky. A cool breeze stirred the air.

The old lady, wearing a bright red outfit, smiled and nodded at Akbar when he came over to kiss her hands. Ameera, who was laying the table, greeted Akbar warmly.

'Look how Bibi is dressed to welcome you,' she remarked. 'When she heard you were coming she couldn't stop fussing.'

Akbar blushed and murmured something about Bibi always dressing well.

'Not just her...the children too,' she said 'and the servants...all happy. Only Asmina she added glancing at Akbar, 'seems unmoved... not a word from her...'

Ameera was eight years older than Asmina. She was pleasant-looking but lacked Asmina's beauty. They had become more like sisters over the years.

Asmina and the maid brought out the remainder of the tea things just as Jalal Baba appeared at the top of the slope. Akbar took in Asmina's drawn face and her haunted look.

She had been troubled since Akbar went away. She did not doubt his love but was plagued with uncertainty. There had been no assurances or promises and there was nothing she could do about it. She suffered silently.

Ameera had noticed Asmina's decline after Akbar left. The old lady and the maid too had guessed what was going on but no one spoke about it. Asmina's appearance shocked Akbar. He decided there and then to talk to Jalal Baba. Later that evening Akbar made it a point to move to the bench next to Jalal Baba who was watching the sun go down over Koh-i-Mor.

'Baba,' he said finally, 'I want you to know that I care deeply for Asmina Bibi. I believe she also cares for me.'

Jalal Baba continued looking at Koh-i-Mor.

'So that is how it is,' he said after a while.

'I would have told you earlier...but it didn't seem right to do so till I was certain.'

'I'm glad you have spoken. I should have foreseen it...two young people...thrown together...a strange situation. It was bound to happen.'

'You're not upset?'

'Should I be upset? It is a natural occurrence...that's the way these things happen...I recall telling you so a while back... no, I'm not upset, but I am concerned.'

'I want to do the right thing...I want to make her my wife.'

'Patience, patience, Akbar,' Jalal Baba said, placing a restraining hand on Akbar's arm, 'we need to talk some more. I need to think this matter through before giving my views. It's not as easy as simply getting married.'

'I'll marry her with your blessing,' Akbar said.

'Before that happens some issues must be resolved,' Jalal Baba said, his brows creased. 'She is a Pakhtun whereas you are not. Your family's reaction to such a marriage is important. Where do you propose to live? How will you support a wife?'

Akbar was at a loss to respond to Jalal Baba's queries.

'Don't look so forlorn,' Jalal Baba said with a smile. 'I do understand that you are in love but there are things to be resolved before any steps can be taken. If, after thorough consideration, we come to the conclusion that it is not to be, then you must put Asmina out of your thoughts. She must be left to recover as best she can so that both of you are free to look elsewhere.'

'Are you saying I must stay away from her?'

'For the time being you must...until the matter is resolved in your favour... inshallah.'

'But what is it that must first be resolved?' Akbar asked nervously.

After a long pause, Jalal Baba said, 'Asmina has no blood ties with me. Her tribal family has to approve of the match before she can marry.'

FIFTEEN

Asmina was an Afridi from Khyber Agency in FATA. Her parents came from two feuding households of the Afridi clan. They had fallen in love and eloped and were hunted by pursuers from both households.

After weeks of dodging their pursuers all over FATA, they found refuge at Dar-ul-Aman where they felt relatively safe since Bajaur Agency was home to the Tarkhani and Uthmankhel tribes who were hostile to the Afridis.

As a precautionary step, Jalal Baba changed their names and found work for them – the man as mosque attendant and muezzin, and the woman as cook and cleaner at the cottage.

Some months later, a bullet killed the man in the tower while he was reciting the azan. Distressed at losing her partner, the woman gave birth prematurely to a baby girl. A few days later another bullet found her, while she was washing clothes at the cottage stream.

Jalal Baba placed the baby before the local jirga which gave him custody of the child. He was appointed her guardian for all matters affecting her life, except marriage.

According to the Pakhtun tradition, proposals of marriage were to be referred to her father's relatives. Decisions they reached consensually were to be adopted.

Jalal Baba thought over the matter of Akbar and Asmina for two days. He even discussed it with Ameera and the old lady. Both urged him to accept Akbar's proposal.

To drive her point home, the old lady recalled the frustration of one of her sisters after she was made to marry a man her family had chosen instead of the person of her choice. She finally went mad and killed herself.

'Do you want Asmina to go through that? You are wrong to assume that we women have no feelings because we don't talk about them. We feel as strongly as men do but learn to live with our disappointments.'

Jalal Baba eventually came to the conclusion that he had no right to stand between Akbar and Asmina.

Since it has come to pass, I must do what I can to help them, he thought. *Their families must be convinced and impediments tackled.*

He addressed a letter to the head of the family to which Asmina's father had belonged, explaining the situation and seeking his approval of the match.

Janbaz Khan was entrusted with delivering the letter to the family home in a village called Shinpokh. He also wrote to Ahmed Ali in the same vein and encouraged Akbar to communicate with his parents.

Asmina learnt of these moves from Ameera. It gave her hope.

The Samandar response came within ten days. Jalal Baba heard from Ahmed Ali, and Akbar from Lilian. Despite the fairly detailed reports given in the earlier letters, both replies were brimming with queries.

They suggested that Akbar should not get married in haste. Both counselled delay either by shifting the venue to Karachi or by waiting for Samandar family members to attend the wedding in FATA.

Lilian's letter betrayed other anxieties. She was concerned about the consequences of her son marrying a tribal bride from an entirely different culture. There was also the question of her compatibility with his family members. She pleaded with him to hold off the wedding until she met Asmina.

You have never ceased to surprise me, she wrote, *since the moment I saw 786 inscribed on your body. You have given me much joy and some sadness. You have brought wonder to my life by your inspired acts, and anxiety by your unpredictability. Even as I write, I know that in this matter, you will – as always – do what you feel has to be done.*

The Afridi response came six weeks later. It was heralded by the visit to Dar-ul-Aman of a representative of the local Taliban Commander.

Despite his apparent youthfulness he had an extended black beard and long hair. The lower half of his face was concealed by a bandana and his torso bristled with weapons. He was led to Jalal Baba's study where he removed the face covering. After qahwa was served, Jalal Baba enquired about the purpose of his visit.

'Our Commander, Tarrar Khan, will be calling on you about a letter you wrote to Haider Khan Afridi's family,' he said, brusquely.

'Tarrar Khan,' Jalal Baba repeated, a little surprised, 'isn't he a deputy to the Commander?'

'He was...but now he has taken over the post.'

'What is his interest in the letter?' Jalal Baba asked.

'You'll have to ask him when he comes.'

'When will he come?'

'Maybe tomorrow, or the day after.'

Jalal Baba waited for two days but Tarrar Khan did not come. For Akbar the wait seemed endless. On the third day the pealing of the bell at the periphery of Dar-ul-Aman announced the arrival of Tarrar Khan accompanied by seven Talibs.

All of them were bearded, long-haired, masked and armed. Three of them had the long-limbed grace of the Pakhtuns. The other four were shorter, sturdier and thick-bodied. They had the gait of bow-legged wrestlers. Tarrar Khan was taller than the rest. He wore dark glasses.

At Jalal Baba's invitation, he walked with a swagger into the *hujra*, accompanied by his men. They seated themselves on one side of the *sandali*, briskly removed their facial coverings – revealing the fair aquiline looks of the Pakhtun and the ruddy Caucasian features of the Uzbek, all camouflaged by bushy beards – and slurped the qahwa.

They were faced by Jalal Baba, Akbar and some of the ulema. Despite the dark glasses, Akbar could feel Tarrar Khan's eyes on him. He had been warned by Jalal Baba not to utter a word during discussions.

'All the talking will be done by me,' Jalal Baba had said.

The Uzbek ulema tried to talk in his native tongue to the Uzbek Talibs, but got no response.

'I have come, Jalal Baba,' Tarrar Khan said in level tones, 'to claim the Afridi girl who resides in your home.'

There was a gasp from Jalal Baba's side of the table.

'By what right do you make such a claim, Tarrar Khan?' Jalal Baba asked sternly.

'She is my kinswoman. I am an Afridi belonging to the family of Haider Khan, the girl's father.'

Akbar turned pale.

'I was informed by my relatives in Shinpokh of your letter,' Tarrar Khan continued. 'They were appalled at your suggestion of handing the girl to a non-Pakhtun. They have asked me to stop this disgraceful arrangement and retrieve the girl.'

'Where have your relatives been these last seventeen years since the girl's birth?' Jalal Baba asked angrily. 'No one came forward to claim her at the time, so the jirga gave her to me...My deceased wife and I cared for her and brought her up like our own. Everyone has come to know her as my daughter. She has known no other family and was not even aware until recently that she had been adopted by us.'

'I do not question the jirga's decision,' Tarrar Khan said, 'in giving her to you...and you have done well in treating her as your child...but your plan to marry her to a foreigner is contrary to *Pakhtunwali* and cannot be tolerated.'

Jalal Baba had known all along that among the Pakhtuns, the case for Akbar was unlikely to succeed under *Pakhtunwali* – the unwritten code of behavioural rules of Pakhtuns. But he was not prepared to let that override Akbar and Asmina's wishes.

'What will you do with the child after you take her away?'

'I will marry her myself, protect her and give her a home to make up for the one she will be giving up...I will not abandon her to other family members in Shinpokh,' Tarrar Khan replied in a level voice.

'Tarrar Khan, I see you want to do the right thing,' Jalal Baba said in conciliatory tones. 'I suggest we discuss this matter in privacy in my study...'

Tarrar Khan pondered over Jalal Baba's suggestion, then got up swiftly and said, 'Yes, talk about women should be held in private.'

The Uzbeks accompanying the Commander tried to follow him into the study but were ordered out, leaving him alone with Jalal Baba. Even Akbar had to stay away.

'What you are proposing to do is not right,' the Commander said at length.

'No Commander. What you're thinking of doing is not right.'

'I am observing Islamic rules,' the Commander said gruffly.

'In all my years of study, I have not come across such rules in Islam,' Jalal Baba said.

'Until her marriage,' the Commander observed, 'a female belongs to her father's family. There is no getting around that.'

'In name only – not by right – and that too is questionable if the family has not claimed her or provided for her survival...' Jalal Baba put in.

'Your plan to marry her to an outsider is against all norms,' the Commander said raising his voice.

'What norms?' Jalal Baba asked. 'There is nothing in the Quran that forbids marriage between two consenting Muslims within defined parameters, whatever their nationality, caste, appearance or age.'

'It is not normal for a Pakhtun woman to marry a non-Pakhtun,' the Commander insisted.

'Why not normal? Interracial marriages are not against nature,' Jalal Baba said quietly.

'It is against *Pakhtunwali*,' the Commander said.

'*Pakhtunwali*, you say?' Jalal Baba remarked.

'Yes, *Pakhtunwali*...a code that has come from our ancestors.'

'Rules made by men,' Jalal Baba pointed out, 'some of them go against nature; others have been imposed by men on what they claim has been revealed. Some rules run counter to normal family wedding traditions, some deny the truth of love between two people. Some lead to the forcible break-up of families, others legitimize marriages that have not been accepted by one of the partners. These are very strange rules.'

A long silence followed. It was broken by Akbar walking into the study, startling the Commander and Jalal Baba.

'What is it, Akbar?' Jalal Baba asked with concern.

'I apologize for this interruption. I've come to talk to the Commander,' Akbar said.

'We haven't finished our discussion,' Jalal Baba remarked, 'you will have to wait.'

'Let him talk Jalal Baba,' the Commander said, sizing Akbar up. 'Speak up...what is it you want to say?'

'I am the one who wishes to marry Jalal Baba's daughter...'

'You're talking out of turn, Akbar,' Jalal Baba said. 'You've no business to be here.'

'No, no, let him have his say,' the Commander said raising his hand. Then addressing Akbar, he said, 'I know who you are, Akbar Ali Samandar, and I know what you want. Tell me, what right do you have to marry a Pakhtun girl?'

'Before Allah, and according to my faith, a man is justified in marrying a woman he cares for,' Akbar replied.

'Your feelings count for nothing in a matter like this. Our rules forbid such a marriage.'

'What kind of rules are they that forbid what is halal?' Akbar asked with rising anger.

'By God, you are gutsy, talking to me in that tone...I say you have no right to marry her,' the Commander retorted, getting up to face Akbar.

'I have a better right than you to marry her,' Akbar shot back. 'What I want to do has her consent. What you intend, is a forced union against her wishes.'

'I'll show you, what I'm going to do.'

The Commander pushed open the door and ordered the Uzbeks to surround Jalal Baba's cottage and check anyone going in or out. He directed two of the Pakhtun Talibs to stay back and prevent Jalal Baba and Akbar from leaving the study.

'I'm going to your home to take the girl,' the Commander said.

'You have no right to violate my home,' Jalal Baba cried out in alarm.

'I'm not going to enter the premises. I'll call for her from outside.'

'That too is a violation. You can't take her without the jirga's consent,' Jalal Baba said.

'I don't care about the jirga. We have our own way of deciding matters.'

'You can't hold me here. No one from the Taliban has behaved in this way with me,' Jalal Baba said.

'I don't want to insult you, Jalal Baba but I urge you to stay here until we leave.'

With that he left, accompanied by the third Pakhtun Talib.

Akbar looked out the door. There were two guards standing outside, weapons in hand. One shut the door on Akbar's face.

Panicking, Akbar looked around, saw the window opening onto the second courtyard, and went towards it.

'Be careful Akbar,' Jalal Baba cautioned. 'You may get hurt.'

'We can't let them get away with this,' Akbar said with rising panic, 'we must protect the cottage.'

'I agree,' Jalal Baba said, 'we can't let them do this.'

Akbar opened the window and jumped into the veranda bordering the second courtyard.

'Go Akbar, go,' Jalal Baba waved him on, handing him a shotgun, 'I can't jump out of the window, but I'll find a way to get there.'

Akbar took a route that led from the mosque to the cottage. Some Dar ul-Aman attendants and workers, alarmed by the presence of the Taliban, had gathered in the backyard. Seeing Akbar dash by, armed with a shotgun, prompted them to collect whatever weapons they could and follow him up the wooded slope.

Approaching the cottage precincts stealthily, Akbar saw the Commander at the top of the slope, flanked by his guard.

Facing the cottage, the Commander called out to Asmina through a loudspeaker and asked her to come forward. Uzbek militants stood guard on either side of the cottage while Jalal Baba's family members were huddled in front, hemmed in by the two remaining Uzbeks.

A terror-struck Asmina took a faltering step forward. Ameera tried to hold on to her. The children clung to her legs, wailing. Without thinking, Akbar dashed forward, rushing past the Commander, shooting in the air, attempting to reach Asmina.

The shots startled everybody. The Uzbeks reacted automatically by shooting at Akbar. Bullets whizzed by and scattered around him as he ran forward. When he got close to Asmina, he stumbled and fell headlong. She screamed and flung herself onto his body, attempting to shield him.

The episode had an electrifying effect. The Commander shouted at the Uzbeks to stop firing. He marched across, followed by his guard, to where Akbar lay, face down. Ameera ran forward, to disengage Asmina.

Hearing the gunfire, the Dar-ul-Aman workers rushed up the slope. Jalal Baba, thoroughly alarmed, managed to persuade his guards to let him get to the cottage.

When the Commander reached Akbar, Asmina was sobbing in Ameera's arms. As he knelt beside Akbar, his guard laid his weapon on the ground, joined his palms together and begged him to spare Akbar.

'He saved my life by placing himself in danger when the bees attacked me.'

The Commander placed his hand on Akbar's arm. After a while, Akbar sat up. He had been grazed in the leg by a bullet which had made him fall and lose consciousness. He looked at the Commander. The dark glasses were gone and he was gazing straight into the eyes of Bairam Khan.

SIXTEEN

When Jalal Baba reached the terrace, he found the seminary workers at the top of the slope. The guards stood in another group. The family had gone indoors. Akbar was on the bench having his leg bandaged by one of the guards. The Commander and he were in discussion. After checking Akbar's condition, Jalal Baba went into the cottage.

'I have known about your movements since you joined the seminary,' the Commander said. 'I received reports about your teaching at the village madrasa, the honey bottling, Dar-ul-Aman management, the football and cricket matches.'

'Why didn't you get in touch?' Akbar asked.

'Your growing influence has become a problem. Your activities smack of secularism. Associating with you would have been improper, possibly heretical. Anyway, renewing ties with persons not of the Taliban order is discouraged. It is against the interest of our cause.'

'You could have sent word,' Akbar remarked.

'Why? There could be no further friendship.'

'Tell me about the reports of executions you were said to have been responsible for.'

'Mostly true...some exaggerated...all justified,' the Commander said.

'So you have changed.'

'Yes, I have seen the truth just as you claim to have, through your so-called transcendence. Oh yes, I've heard about that too. Nothing you have done has escaped me, not even your involvement with the girl.'

'How did you get to know of all this?' Akbar asked.

'It's our business to find out what people do. Stories carry easily in this area. I would not have come here if the question of your marrying the girl had not arisen.'

'But Bairam...sorry...Commander, how does that concern you?'

'After all that has happened today, it should be clear to you why I came. Observing *Pakhtunwali* is of great importance for us.'

'More so than following the faith?' Akbar asked.

'No more of that, Akbar. Let us draw a line. The girl obviously cares for you. She has made a public declaration of her commitment. Besides, you have helped save the life of a Talib by risking your own. I can't overlook these facts. So I'm going now. And I advise you to marry the girl and leave the area. I'm not sure that my decision is right...but I owe it to you, Akbar Ali Samandar. That counts as a matter of honour. One more thing. I hope I don't see you again. If we do meet, you'll find me like the Tarrar Khan you saw earlier.'

He turned to go, then stopped and said, 'Don't mention our past association to anyone. Our leave-taking must be formal, not as old friends.'

The Commander shook hands with Akbar stiffly and walked away. He stopped and knocked at the front door of the cottage. Jalal Baba came out. They spoke briefly, shook hands. Then Tarrar Khan and his guards disappeared among the trees.

After the incident with the Taliban, neither Akbar nor Asmina wanted the marriage delayed. Jalal Baba picked a date for the wedding, falling within the week. Akbar wrote to Lilian informing her about the marriage. Two days before the wedding, Ameera organized a sing-song of bridal ditties at the cottage attended by the few women who lived in the area.

The marriage ceremony took place in the mosque before the *Fajar* prayer, attended by men. The rites were performed by Jalal Baba.

The houseboy stood by for Asmina and gave the responses on her behalf. Akbar wore a green turban for the occasion. After the responses, the match was solemnized and a prayer recited jointly by Jalal Baba and the congregation, invoking the blessing of God on the union.

The wedding feast was served at noon. The cooks at Dar-ul-Aman outdid themselves, serving barbecued lamb stuffed with rice and pine nut, tandoori chicken, chapli kebab and seasoned yogurt. A wedding at Dar-ul-Aman was a unique occasion that the villagers and the Dar-ul-Aman staff would remember in times to come.

In the evening, Akbar walked up to the cave. He saw the sun frolicking with a tracery of clouds above Koh-i-Mor. He washed and cleansed himself at the brook and offered the *Asar* prayer. Sitting in the niche in the cave, he thanked God.

He returned to the mosque to recite the azan for the *Maghrib* prayer and joined the congregation.

Afterwards, he went to the cottage. Dinner was first served to the men. When Jalal Baba and Akbar had eaten, they strolled outdoors while the women had their meal. Later, the men sipped qahwa before retiring.

The newly-weds had been given the room in which Akbar had convalesced. He found Asmina dressed in bridal wear, reclining on a divan, face veiled. When he lifted the veil, she gasped and sat up.

'It's alright,' he said gently, 'you and I are far too close to let such things come between us.'

He continued speaking until she began to respond in monosyllables. He lay down, suggesting she do the same. She held back, so he took her hand in his and stroked her fingers, chatting, until he fell asleep.

He woke up before dawn for *Fajar* prayers and saw her praying, clad in simple attire. She brought him tea, fussing around the room for a bit before lying gingerly on her side of the bed.

So the first day of married life began. Akbar was served breakfast by his wife. He went as usual to teach at the village madrasa, returning for the midday meal to Dar-ul-Aman. After lunch, he dealt with Dar-ul-Aman affairs. Studies and meditative prayer took up the latter part of the afternoon. After *Maghrib* prayers, he returned to married life.

When the evening meal was over, Akbar and Asmina wandered through the trees. He reached for her hand and put his arm round her. That night he held her tenderly, then more fiercely. She stiffened, relaxing gradually. At length they fell asleep side by side.

During the day he found himself assailed by a curious sense of guilt. Doubts arose in his mind. Questions needed to be answered.

But it is not profane, he reasoned. *The desire I felt was caused by closeness to Asmina...can what is natural be profane?*

Such concerns vanished at night. Asmina seemed to feel more at ease with Akbar. Clothes came in the way. Akbar helped her gradually remove them. Even so, she concealed herself – breasts down to the navel. She watched his silhouette while he unclothed. She felt his nakedness around her...then he possessed her as a natural consequence of their togetherness...the initial pain giving way to acceptance. Afterwards they lay still. Asmina lay awake for a while.

She was awakened by the chilly morning air. She tucked the coverlet around Akbar's naked body and went to the hammam for ablutions and a bath.

Ameera came upon her drying her hair and guessed that Asmina had lost her virginity.

Akbar spent the following day in a daze. His mind kept returning to the night before...he recalled the sweetness of Asmina's body...the fulfilment of mutual desire. Jalal Baba noticed how distracted he was.

'It's alright Akbar,' he said, reassuringly. 'You are going through a special experience.'

'It gets in the way of work.'

'Let it take its course. You are blessed. Work has an uncanny way of reasserting its claim.'

Akbar took time off that afternoon to visit the cave. He hoped to recover some sense of balance and equanimity. The need for Asmina had to make way for other things.

There were other, no less relevant forms of fulfilment. Akbar thought of his studies in faith, exercises in meditation and community services. He would have to fit Asmina in where he could.

Jalal Baba had suggested that since Asmina would not be able to live in Dar-ul-Aman, Akbar should stay at the cottage until their home was built. A piece of land, higher than the cottage, close to the source of the spring, was earmarked for the new home. Akbar wasted no time in arranging for the trees to be chopped and the ground levelled.

Jalal Baba designed something like a cottage for them – incorporating features chosen by Akbar and Asmina. It contained a living room, a bedroom, a kitchen, storage space and an outdoor veranda. The hammam and toilet facilities were located close to the spring.

Akbar was excited at the prospect of building his own home where he could start life with Asmina. *Like an ant,* he thought, *we'll build a life together*. He was at the site whenever he found time, urging the builders to complete tasks planned for the day by sunset. At times, he would pitch in and do a shift with them. The expenses were borne by Akbar. As a result, the cottage was finished in two and a half months.

Akbar wrote to Lilian frequently after marriage because he wanted to share this stage of his life with her and also because Asmina wanted him to keep in touch. Her tribal instinct alerted her to the significance of maintaining close ties with kin.

After a spell of rainy weather in late summer, Akbar and Asmina moved to their home. Jalal Baba commemorated the event by prayer.

That evening, Akbar and Asmina were joined at their first meal in their new home by Jalal Baba's family. When the guests had gone, they walked for a while under the trees around their small cottage and caught a glimpse of the moon – large and clear in the mountain air – passing through rain clouds.

Asmina found Akbar one day on his haunches, palms resting on thighs, eyes turned upward, facing a window, absorbed in something that kept him from responding to her. She touched him lightly on the shoulder and found it rigid. She retreated to the veranda. Looking in later, she found him on his fours with forehead resting on the floor in the *sajda* position of the namaz. She assumed he was praying.

Minutes passed with his body doubled over in *sajda*. Curiosity turned to concern. After what seemed like an hour, he rose, ashen-faced, and ran his hands along his arms.

She asked if all was well. He smiled and kissed her forehead. She looked at him questioningly. He paced the room, then spoke of the uplifting spells he experienced in meditation.

'I don't know when such a thing will happen...I have no control over it. Consciousness ebbs. I lose contact with the world. I am drawn upwards. There is peace and love... lightness and much that I cannot describe.'

When he fell silent, she kissed his hands. He drew her close and told her not to think of him as anything other than her husband.

'How can I ignore what you have just told me?' she remarked.

'I told you because I want you to understand that part of my life.

I am Akbar, your husband, and that is how you must regard me, no more, no less. I have human needs and wants and you are the centre of my existence. That doesn't change when I pray or meditate...just as that other part of my life remains with me even when I am with you.'

In the days that followed, he got to know many things about Asmina. She was devout. Jalal Baba had seen to that. She had a sensible approach to religion although she treated its tenets as unquestionable. She could read and write Pashto and Urdu and was sufficiently well-versed in Arabic to read the texts with some comprehension. She had also been taught some maths, science, history and geography by Jalal Baba and such tutors as he managed to find.

Akbar decided to teach her English and sent for books on Urdu literature and fiction for her. He also trained her to operate a computer when Net signals were accessible. The websites opened windows to a world of knowledge for her.

She was an efficient housekeeper, and cooked simple but wholesome meals. She laid out a patch of ground next to the little cottage for growing vegetables and planted some fruit trees.

There was a special affinity between them. They communicated at different levels and enjoyed each other's company.

In moments of affection, he called her 'Mina'. She addressed him as 'Janu' when they were by themselves.

One night as they lay together, Asmina asked Akbar whether it was proper for them to make love in the nude. He was taken aback by the directness of the question. After a pause, he said, 'Some people may call it irregular. But Mina, we lie together like this because it comes to us naturally. Natural responses cannot be bad. They may be questionable at times but to my way of thinking, this thing between husband and wife is not wrong.'

'But people say...' she said.

'I know what they say,' he intervened. 'They say lots of things about how conjugal relations should be conducted. Some of it is outlandish, some suitable for robots, not human beings.'

After some moments, he said, 'If you find it more appropriate not to undress, I'll respect your wishes. I want you to feel comfortable.'

SEVENTEEN

The sound of gunfire, alternating between random shots and automated bursts, was not an unusual occurrence in the Bajaur highlands. The inhabitants had learnt to continue with their activities when distant shots rang out. Concern usually arose when the shots seemed closer, round the corner.

In early autumn, the hills around Kitkot reverberated with machine-gun fire, accompanied occasionally by exploding rockets. Army patrols combed the terrain, often passing by Dar-ul-Aman on manoeuvres. F16 aircraft and helicopters also appeared above the peaks, searching for militant hideouts.

Out in the woods one afternoon while collecting wild herbs, Asmina counted three sorties flying westward. She mentioned this to Akbar when he came home that evening.

Next morning, she was awakened before daybreak by the sound of an explosion that seemed to occur near the village. It was followed by two other explosions. To her surprise, the sounds did not affect Akbar's sleep.

During the day, they heard that unmanned American drones had attacked a militant campsite causing several deaths and considerable damage. Akbar wondered how Bairam Khan had fared and was relieved to hear that although he was injured, he had managed to survive the missile strike.

The destruction caused by the drones was the talk of the village for the next few days. Such incidents were known to take place in the neighbouring agencies of North and South Waziristan which teemed with militants but were rare in Bajaur.

The militants were in the process of setting up an assault staging post near Kitkot when the drones struck. The ground attacks by Pakistan forces were pre-emptive.

There was widespread concern about skirmishes and long-drawn exchanges of fire. The road leading to Khyber Pakhtunkhwa on the south-east and the Afghan border on the north-west was closed periodically for transferring troops and weaponry to embattled sites. Jalal Baba had instructed the people at Dar-ul-Aman to avoid remote wooded areas and hill trails.

After the elimination of their stronghold, there were reports of militants having dispersed in the woods pursued by army commandos. Some shepherds had come across them.

Jalal Baba was woken up one night by a knocking on his front door. Pistol in hand, he went to check. A faltering voice claimed to be a wounded mujahid seeking Jalal Baba's help. It turned out to be the Talib whom Akbar had saved from the wild bees. He was dishevelled and despairing.

'What is it?' Jalal Baba asked. 'Why have you come?'

'Sanctuary,' he said, 'In Allah's name, help us...our Commander is lying not far from here, seriously wounded.'

The wounded militants had been instructed by their central command to assemble at a pass some distance from Kitkot from where trucks were to transport them to safer territory. While the group led by the Deputy Commander managed to avoid the commandos and reach the pass, the

Commander had collapsed midway. As his physical state after the drone attack was too precarious to risk the trek to the rendezvous point, the two Talibs accompanying him decided to seek help at Dar-ul-Aman.

Jalal Baba instructed the houseboy to follow with water and blankets, and set out for the woods with the Talib. The Commander lay on the ground a few hundred yards away, feverish and delirious, in shredded clothes, breathing with difficulty. In the fluttering torchlight wounds were visible on his belly, back and upper legs. The second Talib squatted beside him, cushioning his head.

After trying to feed him water without success, Jalal Baba wrapped him in a blanket and carried him to the cottage. He was taken from there in a hastily improvised sling to Akbar's old room at Dar-ul-Aman.

The presence at Dar-ul-Aman of Dr. Murat Efendic, a Bosnian scholar, who was a general surgeon, made the task of tending to the Commander easier. The doctor, assisted by Janbaz Khan and Jalal Baba, cleaned and dressed his wounds. Dr. Efendic felt that the Commander should be taken to a fully equipped hospital without delay. Jalal Baba pointed out the hazards of doing so.

'There are some medical facilities available at the Constabulary bases,' he explained, 'but the kind of hospital you suggest is located in Peshawar...going there by road will endanger his life. Also, there is the risk of exposing him – and all of us here – to the military authorities. If that happened, he would be treated like the high-profile militants in army custody, and we would be penalized for helping an enemy of state. My concern is not for us but for him. I am bound by duty to report his presence to the authorities. At the same time, I must protect a fugitive who has taken sanctuary on my premises.'

'You are faced, my friend,' the doctor said, 'with a classic dilemma.'

'Tell me what I should do,' Jalal Baba said.

'Whatever you think is appropriate,' the doctor said, 'I can't tell you what is right or wrong but I will help you in any way I can, so you have to tell me what to do.' After mulling over the matter, Jalal Baba said, 'I think we must get him back on his feet before reporting his presence to the authorities.'

'How will we do that? His body needs major repair.'

'If I arrange to get the medical items and assistance you consider essential for him, will you be able to take care of him?'

The doctor sat back, contemplating. His eyes moved over the comatose figure and the objects in the room and ended at the window where darkness was visible through openings in the blinds.

'I believe I can help,' he said finally. Without waiting for a response, he sounded off at great speed, 'To succeed, I will need many things: a portable battery-powered x-ray machine, a portable ultrasound scanner, a ventilator and vital signs monitors, spare batteries or generators for power supply, surgical equipment for abdominal, back and leg surgery, suturing and blood testing paraphernalia, swabs, bandages, adhesives, anaesthetic and muscular injectables, drips, post-operative applications, several medications including blood from a universal donor...also gloves, surgical outfit and two operating theatre assistants...' He stopped only when he ran out of breath.

After the *Fajar* prayer Jalal Baba, assisted by Dr. Efendic, wrote a letter to a leading benefactor of Dar-ul-Aman in Peshawar.

The letter described the Commander's condition and made a request for the items listed by Dr. Efendic to be supplied in secrecy at the earliest. Janbaz Khan was despatched that morning by bus to Peshawar.

Akbar stopped at Dar-ul-Aman on his way to the village madrasa. It was abuzz with news of the Commander. One of the ulema took him aside and narrated the events of the preceding night. Another stopped him in the veranda and recounted a slightly different version. A third alim reported yet another version.

Akbar was puzzled. It took him a while to realize that Bairam Khan was in Dar-ul-Aman. He went to his room and looked in. An attendant watching over the Commander placed a finger on his lips. Akbar nodded, shut the door and left for the village madrasa.

Three days after the letter, Dr. Efendic's listed items reached Kitkot by a special delivery van, accompanied by two medical assistants and two operators for the scanning equipment.

A letter to Jalal Baba from the benefactor from Peshawar, authenticated by his seal of office, explained that the supplies to Dar-ul-Aman were being consigned for 'the treatment of Kitkot residents and other civilians injured in the hostilities between the armed forces and militants'. This ensured safe passage of the medical goods through army pickets.

The Commander's physical state stabilized somewhat due to Dr. Efendic's early ministrations with medical supplies obtained from village sources. Force-feeding with a teaspoon had been a problem. The arrival of the Peshawar consignment made intravenous feeding possible.

During the three-day wait for the goods, Dar-ul-Aman bustled with preparations for the surgery. A room was set aside and equipped as an operating theatre. Hosepipes leading to a sink in the room were installed for the supply of running water. A temporary laboratory for testing and analysing medical specimens too was set up.

Accommodation close to the medical facilities was readied for the assistants. The absence of constant electrical supply was offset to some extent by electricity generators, battery-powered lamps, fans, mixers, shredders and distillers.

The two Talibs were quite overwhelmed by all the activity. Their reaction was uncharacteristic. They wept and kissed Jalal Baba's hands.

When the consignment arrived, Dr. Efendic launched into pre-surgery investigations. Digitalized radioactive imaging of the Commander revealed that the vital organs although battered, were not damaged.

He had however, sustained massive bruising, bleeding and broken bones. There were also multiple muscle and flesh lacerations. Some of the wounds were infected and blood reports revealed infections, but vital functions, although tenuous, were unimpaired.

Dr. Efendic prepared a surgery schedule and discussed it with Jalal Baba and the assistants.

Akbar looked in next morning and said a prayer over the prone figure. When it was light enough, the Commander was moved to the makeshift theatre, and prepared for the operation.

Five hours later, Dr. Efendic came out of the theatre to inform Jalal Baba that he had attended to all the abdominal injuries, including broken ribs, and would resume after a brief rest to operate on the injured back, leaving the legs for later.

Surgery on the back took an additional four hours, largely because of unexpected complications affecting the spinal cord. Despite the onset of darkness, Dr. Efendic intended to return for the third stage of the surgery after another rest. Jalal Baba suggested delaying the procedure till the next morning, but the doctor insisted on completing the task.

'It's better to finish it now while he is still anaesthetized. Returning to the operating table after surgical intervention the day before is risky. Sometimes it's too great a trauma to the system. So far, he has borne the handling of his body well. We should go with that.'

Surgery on the legs was conducted under lamplight. It included addressing compound fractures, setting bones and suturing muscles and tendons. While attending to the legs, Dr. Efendic was faced with excessive bleeding from the Commander's abdomen on account of the earlier surgery.

He dealt with that by redressing the abdominal wounds and transfusing blood. At that point, the vital signs began to falter. To restore the balance, Dr. Efendic installed the ventilator, removing it only when the signs neared normal levels.

When it was over, he thanked Allah and prayed for the patient's welfare. He instructed the assistants before leaving the scene. Jalal Baba, Akbar and some of the ulema waited for him outside.

'It's finished,' he said. 'I thank Allah that all went well... now he needs post-surgical care, rest and recuperation. As for me, this is the highest point in my medical career...

performing such complicated surgery in three prolonged shifts, in such extraordinary circumstances, on such a controversial patient. I shall – with your permission, Jalal Baba – publish an account of it in medical journals on my return to Bosnia.'

Two days later the Commander opened his eyes to a strange room. He noticed the intravenous attachments to his arms and saw Akbar at his bedside. He tried to move but stopped when he felt pain. He tried to talk but only managed to mumble.

Noticing the look of confusion on his face, Akbar steadied him with his hands saying, 'You are in Dar-ul-Aman. You were wounded by a drone missile. Two of your guards brought you here. You have been operated upon, and all your injuries have been attended to. You are quite safe. Now you need to rest and avoid exertion. Stop worrying...everything will become clear in time.'

The Commander's confusion lessened, giving way to concern. Akbar fed him water through a straw followed by a few spoonfuls of broth. A while later he was asleep.

After a week of bed rest and post-surgical ministrations, he was able to sit up and consume solid food. His upper body was bandaged and his thighs were in plaster casts. He was agreeable to being cleansed, sponged and fed by the medical assistants and Akbar, but resisted others, including the two Talibs.

The Commander made speedy progress on account of his innate strength and Dr. Efendic's treatment. Secrecy about his presence at Dar-ul-Aman was maintained by a tacit pact of silence. Some afternoons, Akbar took him around the grounds in a wheelchair. The old camaraderie revived somewhat but an awkwardness remained.

The last encounter had been a vivid reminder of where they stood. The Commander was also uneasy about what had been done for him at Dar-ul-Aman. It bound him to Jalal Baba in a manner he was not ready to face. 'The doctor says I'll be on my feet soon...therapy and removal of the casts should enable me to walk,' he remarked.

'What will you do then?' Akbar asked.

'Get on with life...before I get too used to your ways here,' he said with a laugh, before turning serious, 'I will consult Jalal Baba...but... you must remember that I'm committed to my cause...jihad is my way.'

As his health improved, he became aware of the danger his presence represented for Jalal Baba. Late one frosty night, without anyone knowing, he slipped out of the seminary, accompanied by the two Talibs.

He left a note for Jalal Baba: *For what you have done, only Allah can reward you. Since I do not have the words to write more on the subject, I will say no more. Since I cannot thank you enough for what you did, I will avoid doing so. I owe this life to you and should the need arise, I will give it up for you.*

The mopping-up of the militants continued through the autumn. Their bases around Kitkot and in areas adjacent to the Afghan border had been destroyed, leaving the region relatively free of their presence.

After an evening meal at Jalal Baba's cottage, Asmina asked Jalal Baba how long he thought the hostilities would continue.

'I believe,' Jalal Baba said, 'the army has taken out the militant outpost. The drones broke up the command nucleus.

The F16s and ground fire have also done much damage. The militants have retreated. But there's no certainty that they won't be back...not immediately...next year perhaps. They have to keep on pushing for bridgeheads in order to survive.'

'It has been going on for almost two decades,' Akbar said sipping qahwa, 'and there is no end in sight.'

'You're being naive,' Jalal Baba said. 'How can you put a time frame on guerrilla warfare?'

'Surely it can't go on like this indefinitely,' Akbar remarked.

'It can go on for a long time. A time will come when it will abate but not yet. Too much remains unresolved. The ideal would be a Muslim order...a classical Muslim order of the golden period adapted to the modern civilization.'

'Do you see this as a sort of cleansing?'

'No...let's put it this way...I see a realignment of interests as an inevitable follow-up to this phase...'

'The prescribed clash of civilizations?' Akbar asked.

'Not quite so dramatic but leading perhaps to an acceptance of political Islam.'

'Do you see political Islam as an Al-Qaeda or ISIS offshoot?'

'No, I don't. Such orders will not endure. You cannot impose faith on people by force.'

'So it's not a battle that can be won by idealists?' Akbar asked.

'I didn't say that. I simply doubt whether the single worldwide culture envisaged by these movements can come about.'

'Sounds highly improbable,' Akbar said.

'So we will carry on – as we have always done – and we will chop and change, compromise and strive for an ideal which probably cannot be reached....'

'Are you saying that the differences Allah has made in us will continue to endure?'

'If that is how you understand it.'

Life in the village resumed its normal tempo despite the snow, sleet and rain of winter. On sunny days, Asmina spent time in the snow playing with Ameera's children.

Her marriage was unlike what she had assumed married life to be. As far as she knew, husbands usually dominated wives and wives were deferential. It was different with Akbar and her. He tried to make her feel as an equal partner. They were happiest when together, chatting, laughing, sharing news, thoughts. She missed him when he left their home and was glad when he got back.

While Akbar was away, Asmina happily cooked for him and kept house. She also spent time studying and solving homework problems Akbar had set for her. She was an apt pupil. Her written work never failed to surprise Akbar.

'You must focus on speaking, Mina,' Akbar said in English.

'I...try Janu. I try,' she replied.

'Try harder,' he insisted.

'Trying...trying...hard, harder, hardest,' she muttered.

'No,' he laughed, 'not hard or hardest...simply harder. Okay?'

'Okay,' she replied. 'Now you tell of Karachi house, family,'

'What, again?' Akbar asked.

'Yes...again.'

So Akbar put aside the books and spoke to her in English about Aliya and Kamran, Lilian and his father, and Uncle Ahmed Ali. She looked at some digital photographs Lilian had sent while he spoke.

Far away in Karachi, Lilian looked at pictures of Akbar, Asmina and the cottage while writing a letter to them.

EIGHTEEN

Asmina left the bed, drew a shawl round herself and went out into the early spring night. She paced the veranda for a while and then sat on the doorstep. There was a hint of narcissus in the air.

Sunken eyes and a drooping figure confronted Akbar on the veranda next morning. She excused herself from preparing the morning meal on account of an uneasy stomach. Akbar offered to stay back but she sent him off to work.

He returned in the evening to be told that all traces of her ailment had disappeared. It struck again next morning at the time of *Fajar* prayers and subsided after a bout of retching. When it recurred on the third morning, at Akbar's insistence, Asmina told Ameera about her problem. Ameera laughed, pointing out that that was the price a woman paid for having a husband. 'You're pregnant,' she explained.

She hugged her, advising her not to worry. She told her how to deal with the queasiness and asked to be informed of any unusual developments.

'Wait a few days before mentioning it to anyone,' Ameera cautioned. 'If your symptoms continue, we'll get the village midwife in for confirmation before informing Akbar and Baba. Meanwhile, remember what I've said about taking care...the first child is usually the difficult one. It's like having to carry a bundle of eggs over a bumpy trail without breaking them, so no climbing and no lifting of heavy objects until the fourth month.'

Asmina went home filled with fear. She felt something had now come between Akbar and her. Their life together would be affected by this strange occurrence.

Akbar found Asmina withdrawn. He assumed it was because of her condition but she assured him that Ameera had found nothing wrong with her.

The next three days were very trying. Asmina's nausea returned. She concealed her discomfort from Akbar. Her anxiety was exacerbated by the thought that she would have to cope with the situation for several months.

After a nod from the midwife on the fourth day, Ameera informed Jalal Baba about Asmina's pregnancy. His delight was apparent. He kissed Asmina on the forehead and held her close. It was more than she could bear. She burst into tears. The excessive crying caused Jalal Baba to suspect that something was wrong.

His questioning was initially met with silence. Then there were hesitant explanations punctuated by sobs and finally a touching revelation.

'What Akbar and you have is a special relationship... and the child is a fulfilment of that. You're worried about the child coming between you and Akbar but your worry is baseless. Now go, wash your face. Thank Allah for having blessed your union...and wait here to share the news with your husband.'

The evening sky was dotted with migratory birds flying north for the summer. Asmina watched them while Akbar was praying. He came in behind her and placed his hands on her shoulders.

'Jalal Baba has told me everything. Of course, we will care for our child. What made you think that it could come between us, Mina? It's God's gift to us...belonging to both of us...if anything, it will bring us closer,' he reassured her. 'Whatever happens, you and I will remain together so stop worrying.'

Jalal Baba was critical of the midwife. 'She's slipshod and clumsy,' he said.

'She's been sent by the village dispenser,' Ameera said, 'I'll find out if there's another.'

'Not necessary at the moment...we'll decide that when the time comes.'

Jalal Baba mentioned his concern to Dr. Efendic, who suggested that Asmina should undergo an ultrasound test.

'Can you operate it?' Jalal Baba asked.

'What a question to ask...I can even install the spare batteries.'

'Good,' Jalal Baba said. 'I'll bring the girl down when you are ready.'

'Tomorrow morning will be fine.'

The following morning, Asmina came to Dar-ul-Aman, escorted by Jalal Baba and Akbar. It was the first time a woman had entered the premises. To maintain the Pakhtun tradition of purdah, the visiting scholars stayed away.

Dr. Efendic had set up the equipment in Akbar's old room. Asmina lay very still in the darkened room as Dr. Efendic ran the monitor over her abdomen.

The doctor told Jalal Baba and Akbar to watch the screen. What they saw was an image of Asmina's womb. Jalal Baba was uneasy about viewing something he felt was reserved for the husband's eyes.

He tried to leave, but Akbar, excited by what he saw, would not let him go. As the images changed, Dr. Efendic explained the functions of the viscera on view.

'Everything seems to be in order,' he said.

'Now let's focus on the foetus...my goodness, what's this?' he remarked as an oddly rounded blob floated on the screen followed by another blob, similarly suspended.

'What is it?' Jalal Baba asked,' Is something wrong?'

'No, no, quite the contrary. I'm just surprised by what I see. You, dear Jalal Baba, are going be grandfather to not one but two babies. The mother is carrying twins.'

What followed was stunned silence broken by Dr. Efendic's laugh.

The doctor suggested medical supplements for the early stages of pregnancy. He also said that periodic examination by a gynaecologist would help. That meant her visiting Peshawar. At Jalal Baba's insistence, Asmina and Akbar moved back to his cottage.

'Let her stay with us until she feels better. She'll be spared housework and we can look after her,' he said. 'Besides, on such occasions, a family should be together.'

Their homecoming was something of a celebration. The children could not contain themselves. Ameera and the servants bustled and fussed. Even the old lady beamed and planted a kiss on Akbar's forehead. Jalal Baba was the most excited of all, although he gave little away. Asmina's pregnancy and Akbar's impending fatherhood was all he thought of.

The Samandar family was no less enthusiastic though Lilian's regret at missing out on such an important event in her son's life was apparent. She urged them to come to Karachi for the birth of the twins.

Dr. Efendic's departure for Bosnia coincided with an improvement in Asmina's condition. She felt and looked better, slept longer and ate fuller meals. Her body adjusted gradually to the prospect of motherhood.

Akbar observed the changes, from the glowing face to the small bump. Altered circumstances – underscored by separate beds in place of the divan – required him to adopt a different approach. Intimacy gave way to tender care.

At first, Asmina missed the special closeness but that changed when she felt the foetuses move. She felt deep affection for the unborn children and the stirrings of a strong protective instinct.

That summer, a new group of ulema were expected at Dar-ul-Aman. One of them had donated a collection of antique books, treatises and maps in Chinese to the Dar-ul-Aman library. The works, mostly handwritten, documented the spread of Islam in China.

Three rare Qurans, each from a different dynastic era, with translations in Mandarin alongside the Arabic text, signified the importance of the collection. The books had aroused much interest at Dar-ul-Aman.

There was further cause for excitement. Reports came in about Akbar's success in the Mufti qualification exam. He had topped the list of candidates and was included in the roll of honour maintained by the examining board.

Anticipating Akbar's success, Jalal Baba moved swiftly to the next step – a dissertation at a leading university. *To achieve great objectives* he wrote to Ahmed Ali, *excellence must be enhanced.*

At Jalal Baba's prompting, Akbar applied to the Graduate Studies Board of the Faculty of Asian and Middle Eastern Studies, Cambridge, for research studies on a doctorial thesis titled, 'Exegesis of the Ibn Taymiyyah texts from a mystical perspective'.

The application was forwarded with a mandatory statement on the proposed research and a sample of Akbar's written work of 3,000 words, graded by Jalal Baba. He also nominated Ahmed Ali's old college, Trinity, as one of two colleges for admission for the study period.

Despite the stir caused by these developments, it was business as usual for Akbar. He was busy with the import of the antiquarian Chinese books and the issue of visas for the incoming ulema.

His workload increased unexpectedly when he was appointed Supervisor by the Wafaq-al-Madaris examination board for the Dars-e-Nizami exams, which were to be held at the village madrasa.

He was also engaged in negotiations with the provincial electric power company at Peshawar for installing permanent power transmission lines from the village substation to the honey bottling plant and the entire Dar-ul-Aman complex.

Sizeable orders for honey meant more work for him, as did the appointment of an in-house medical team at Dar-ul-Aman to deal with the common ailments of local people.

The gloom that had pervaded the village during the militant presence started to disappear. More women were seen in the bazaar. Little children played tag in the streets instead of hiding from militants. Strains of music were heard with greater frequency from shops and homes.

It seemed that most of the militants who had survived the attacks managed to get through to the new base, although the Commander – after his departure from Dar-ul-Aman – had left no trail. He had not followed the others in the general retreat. Rumours abounded about him hiding in the woods or being seen in an Afghan marketplace but nobody knew of his whereabouts with any certainty.

Village boys recalled the earlier period by strutting about like the Talibs, with the oldest among them acting as the Commander and making as if to strike terror in his subordinates. References to the Commander made Akbar wonder about Bairam Khan's whereabouts.

The health of the 'twins' – as she called them – enabled Asmina to move about almost normally. She and Ameera kept busy planning and collecting accessories for them. But they could manage only two trips to Peshawar to visit the gynaecologist and to shop for baby items.

Further trips were disallowed by Jalal Baba on account of the bumpy condition of the roads. Instead, transport was arranged for the gynaecologist to make any future visits to the cottage, though Jalal Baba realized that eventually Asmina would have to travel to Peshawar for the delivery.

Asmina took short walks in the woods, usually accompanied by the maid, or the children. Sometimes Ameera went with her or the houseboy followed. Akbar escorted her in the evenings.

Occasionally, she urged him to take her to their meeting place by the cave. 'Later,' he would say, 'after the babies are born. It's not safe at present.'

By midsummer Asmina's physical appearance had altered. She had an unusually distended stomach and the graceful carriage had given way to a waddle. Her breathing was more laboured and she sweated profusely.

The gynaecologist came from Peshawar on a house call, accompanied by technicians who operated the scanning equipment to check developments.

All seemed to be in order except that the foetuses had grown considerably in size and the limited range of Asmina's pelvis could make for a difficult delivery. Her medication was changed and she was advised to rest and reduce her walks.

'Inshallah,' the gynaecologist said, 'you'll be coming to us soon for the birth. You should reach full term shortly.'

Jalal Baba thought it best that Asmina should go to Peshawar the following week and await the delivery, instead of travelling when the birth was imminent.

On the day before her departure, Asmina's afternoon walk with the two children was interrupted by a stabbing pain. She sat on the ground, holding her sides as the children looked on, bewildered.

Within moments, the intensity of the pain made her cry out. She instructed the girl to run to the cottage and fetch her mother and the maid.

The girl dashed off, the boy knelt against a tree trunk watching her. He was fascinated by the reddish trickle oozing from her like a punctured egg yolk.

Ameera and the maid found her lying in a pool of blood. The maid went back to fetch a blanket and whatever help she could find. When Asmina revived, she was being carried to the cottage in a sling by Ameera, the maid, the houseboy and a passing peasant. Her clothes were wet and sticky.

By the time they got her to the cottage, Jalal Baba and Akbar were on their way up. When they heard the news, Jalal Baba froze for a moment. Events seemed to have overtaken them. He realized that he would have to deal with the situation. He sensed that the gynaecologist may not get there in time. Nevertheless he dispatched Janbaz Khan to the nearest picket to request the station commander by radio telephone to have the gynaecologist airlifted to the seminary. There was no Dr. Efendic to turn to, so he sent for the midwife.

Akbar did not believe that anything could be wrong. God was on his side after all, so everything would be well. He raced up to Jalal Baba's cottage, passing the old lady who was sitting outside on the bench praying on rosary beads. All three children were there, tended by the houseboy. The evening sky was rose red.

The inside of the cottage echoed with sounds of pain alternating between screams, moans and racking coughs. Sometimes Asmina's voice rang out, calling on Allah.

Inside Ameera and the maid kept mopping Asmina with swabs. The white sheet was streaked red. Akbar watched in disbelief. There was nothing he could do. Asmina lay, eyes clenched, struggling for breath. Her head moved from side to side, hands clutching and releasing the bed sheet as the pain intensified or ebbed.

When Jalal Baba got to the cottage, Akbar was standing by the bedroom door. Jalal Baba stumbled past, colliding with Ameera.

'What has happened?' he asked.

'There is intense bleeding...it started while she was out for a walk,' Ameera said.

'The babies...the pregnancy...what of that?'

'I think labour has started...there is much movement in the womb.'

'But it's early.'

'Sometimes it happens early.'

'I have sent for the midwife...'

'Thank God.'

'Can you handle things until she gets here?'

'I'm doing what I can...I wish this bleeding would stop.'

'What's the cause of it?'

'Baba, I can't say...but I'm worried about her...she's weakening.'

'Do what you can, my child...everything is in the hands of Allah... I'm going to my room to pray...call, if you need me.'

'Akbar,' Jalal Baba said gently, holding him by the arm, 'come and pray...there is not much we can do here...but we can seek His help.'

Akbar was not to be moved. He was speechless, rooted by the doorway. Jalal Baba's prayers were interrupted by the arrival of Janbaz Khan with the midwife. Her assistant followed with a bag full of instruments required for difficult deliveries.

The midwife demanded hot water, then slipped on a large apron, disinfected her hands and got to Asmina's bedside swiftly.

She observed Asmina's condition, sought answers to questions, examined her with astonishing rapidity and worked out the prematurity of the birth by a quick calculation on her fingers while the assistant laid implements from the bag on a table.

'The babies are in distress...' the midwife announced. 'They have outgrown the womb. They are trying to find a way out but can't do so because the one in front is in a transverse position.'

'Ya Allah,' said Ameera, 'what is to be done?'

'I will have to massage the womb and manipulate the little ones until the one blocking the path is properly positioned.'

No one dared question her plan of action.

'Yes...yes,' Jalal Baba said, 'do what has to be done.'

He stood behind Akbar. Both men felt it necessary to keep at a bit of a distance.

The midwife commenced applying her hands to knead the abdomen like potter's clay. Asmina's body jerked violently and agonized screams filled the room.

'Mina,' Akbar cried out, 'what are they doing to you?' He tried to move forward but was held back by Jalal Baba's powerful grip.

The massage continued interminably, or so it seemed to Jalal Baba and Akbar. Asmina's protests lessened from wild cries to whimpers.

Finally, the midwife stepped back.

'The head of the first one,' she said, 'is now in place... but I don't know whether she has the strength to push. It's going to be difficult anyway. Her hips will be a problem. They are too narrow even for a normal birth. And these babies are large...'

'Please help us,' Ameera sobbed.

'My Lord,' Jalal Baba said, 'this is the hour of our need. We ask for help.'

Ameera knelt beside Asmina's bed and whispered, 'Your babies want to enter the world. You must help them.'

Asmina seemed to stir. Then there was a cry from the midwife.

'I see it. I see the head moving. It's on the way. Allah be praised. It's coming.'

It was a sizeable boy. Within minutes, the midwife had intoned a prayer, cut the umbilical cord, bound the navel, suspended the baby by its feet – head pointed downward – and patted its bottom until it coughed and cried.

Asmina lay still, eyes closed. The blood flow had lessened. Just when the wait began to pall, there was a violent upheaval in the womb accompanied by a drawn-out moan from Asmina. Blood gushed out, spilling over the head of a second infant that was pushing its way out, accompanied by a piercing cry from Asmina which jolted everyone. The midwife uttered a prayer and got busy with the second delivery, hands tugging to free the infant from the tight hold. This time she placed a healthy girl beside the boy.

The midwife looked up from the blood flow muttering hesitantly, 'I'm no doctor, but I think her uterus has ruptured. You should get a doctor at once to examine her. He'll be able to tell you better.'

She straightened up, adding 'She needs blood transfusion and surgery. Make whatever arrangements you can to get help for her.'

Almost twenty minutes later Asmina opened her eyes and looked around the room. The bleeding had eased, the pain had receded. Her body was numb, devoid of feeling. The midwife had finished sponging her. She had on a fresh gown. The bedclothes had been changed, traces of blood removed.

The women pottered about tidying up. Akbar and Jalal Baba stood a step back from the bedroom door. Tense, stone-faced, they waited for the gynaecologist who, according to Janbaz Khan, was on the way.

Asmina became aware of little sounds, like tinkling glass...
and there they were, tiny swaddled kittens, lying by her side.

She tried reaching out to them but was hampered by
weakness. Seeing her look of despair, Ameera brought the
babies to her. She kissed them tenderly and asked Ameera
to place them in the crook of her arm. Her lips formed the
word 'Janu'. Ameera understood and gestured to Akbar to
come over.

In the rosy red light flooding the room, Akbar looked
down at his wife, pale, almost transparent, the lustrous
hair matted. His eyes were fixed on her. He did not see the
babies. He reached for her hand. It felt cold. She drew his
hand towards the infants. He recoiled on touching them.

'Don't do that...you are denying what Allah has given us,'
she whispered.

'You, my Mina are what Allah has given me.'

'Take them from me. If you turn away, you will be turning
away from me. Pick them up and hold them...*now*.'

There was a feverish urgency in the word 'now'. He did
as she asked, cradling an infant in one arm and lifting its
twin with the other.

'Now, recite the azan in their ears,' she said. 'The first
sound they hear should be Allah's name.'

'*Allah hu Akbar, Allah hu Akbar,*' he uttered in their tiny,
shell-like ears. When he had finished, she murmured, 'Now
you have my life in your arms. Hold on to it...hold...on...'

She was silent after that. There was no more to be said.

NINETEEN

With Asmina's death the nucleus of lives drawn together under the influence of Jalal Baba, was on the verge of disintegrating.

Disturbed by the events, the old lady had collapsed on the day of the funeral, lingering between life and death. A red-eyed Ameera devoted herself entirely to the care of the twins, supervising even the feeding by wet nurses. Her own children were left to the care of the maid.

Jalal Baba seemed to have aged overnight, the upright posture giving way to a stoop, the alert dark eyes now sad and cloudy. Akbar had receded into a world of shadows.

Asmina was buried near the spring, at the edge of the terrace overlooking Koh-i-Mor. After the funeral, Akbar spent three days and three nights there, grieving all day long and lying beside the grave at night.

He would have stayed on if Jalal Baba had not dragged him away on the fourth evening. Even so, he returned next dawn for the daily vigil.

For the people closely associated with Asmina, mourning became an individual affair rather than a shared experience. Jalal Baba struggled to pick himself up despite an overwhelming feeling of despair. Ameera held on to Asmina by taking over her children. Akbar was rooted to the grave.

Ulema at the Dar-ul-Aman, concerned about the state of Jalal Baba's family, managed to convince him that Akbar needed to get away.

On the fifth day, a helicopter flight, arranged by Jalal Baba's army contacts, brought Lilian and Ahmed Ali to Dar-ul-Aman. They had flown from Karachi to Peshawar the day before. When Ahmed Ali stepped into Jalal Baba's encompassing arms, a surfeit of feelings welled up.

Lilian, attired in salwar kameez and chador for the occasion, was a step behind Ahmed Ali. When the men had had their moment, she removed her dark glasses and shook hands with the handsome white-haired man held by her brother-in-law. Jalal Baba took her hand and for a moment felt that he was looking into Akbar's eyes.

'You are welcome, Mrs. Javed Ali,' he said, 'I wish our first meeting had been happier.'

'So do I,' she murmured, 'but sometimes events dictate what must be done. I fear we are in such a situation today.'

She looks tired, he thought, noticing the fine lines radiating outward from the bridge of her nose, *and those eyes tell their own tale.*

'I trust Justice Sahib is well, as also the rest of your family,' Jalal Baba said leading them towards the seminary.

'All well thank you, but very distressed by what has happened.'

'Come, I'll take you to Akbar,' he said. 'Can you manage the climb to our homes?' he asked Ahmed Ali, mindful of his heart condition.

'If it's not too steep,' Ahmed Ali said, 'and if I walk slowly, stopping to rest in between.'

When they reached Jalal Baba's cottage, Lilian, remarked, 'It's breathtaking...that distant mountain, the woods and the purity...such a pity, so much beauty overcast by sadness.'

Her attention was diverted momentarily by Ameera's children playing in the foreground of the cottage. They ran towards Jalal Baba calling, 'Baba...Baba.'

Jalal Baba gathered them up, kissed them and introduced them to Lilian. He noticed her looking around expectantly, hoping to see Akbar. He explained that Akbar was at the grave, where they would go after a break.

'It's a steep climb,' he explained, 'for which we'll be better prepared after freshening up and some tea.'

Lilian met Ameera in the cottage, each conscious of the other's stricken state. On seeing the twins lying side by side – one, with arms and legs in the air and the other, sucking its fist – Lilian burst into tears, subsiding momentarily when Ameera led her towards them. Lilian knelt beside the bed, touching, kissing and marvelling at them, smiling and sobbing in turn. Ahmed Ali was also moved to tears at the sight of Akbar's children.

Ameera left them on their own for a bit, returning to ask them to tea. It gave Lilian an opportunity to put her arms around Ameera in quiet thanks for taking care of the twins.

On the way to the cave, Lilian surprised Jalal Baba by her agility in climbing. Her early mountaineering experience in the Cotswolds came in handy. Ahmed Ali decided to wait at the cottage.

Lilian spotted Akbar at once, silhouetted against Koh-i-Mor, gazing at the distant hills. He did not hear them come. He felt a breeze from the valley. The hunting cry of a peregrine chasing a goshawk was offset by lark song closer by.

Lilian approached Akbar and placed a hand on his shoulder. He looked up. Both of them were taken aback. He had not expected to see his mother at the gravesite.

Lilian could not have imagined Akbar looking any older, sadder or more lost. There was no trace of the young man she remembered, bright and full of hope. She was about to speak but instead burst into tears. It helped wash away the pent-up grief.

Jalal Baba retreated to the cave to pray. When he returned, he found mother and son slumped by the grave.

He roused them gently and pointed to the lengthening shadows. Lilian rose, dusted herself and rinsed her face and Akbar's with spring water. Akbar looked at the grave, reluctant to leave. Lilian drew him towards the downhill trail where Jalal Baba was waiting.

Next morning the Samandar family left for Peshawar on their way to Karachi. The leave-taking was a sorry business. A pall of gloom descended on Dar-ul-Aman. Akbar – heavily sedated, still traumatized by Asmina's death – sleepwalked his way through the ordeal.

For the Dar-ul-Aman residents his departure was unreal. It was as if a light had gone out – a blessing withdrawn. The family link with Jalal Baba was severed when the twins were taken away.

Jalal Baba knew only too well that a corner had been turned. Dar-ul-Aman had nothing more to hold Akbar back. His salvation lay elsewhere.

When they were airborne, flight stewardesses hovered around the carrycots, eager to assist. Akbar kept his distance from the infants as he had since their birth. For him, they were linked inextricably with Asmina's death.

Back in Karachi, Kamran's plain speaking eventually struck home.

'Come to grips with reality, Bhaijan,' he said. 'That's where answers lie. Existing in a vacuum is no good. Surely, your faith enjoins living while you have the life to do so.'

Kamran's words came back to Akbar as he paced the garden at night. For the first few days he had lain in bed, dozing, waking and staring at the ceiling – mind in abeyance, movements dictated by instinct.

After Lilian's solicitude had elicited some – albeit fitful – response, Kamran stepped in with his homespun therapy. His gentle hectoring did rouse Akbar sufficiently to take to the garden, at least at night.

Kamran took on Akbar, forcing him to step out of the shadows and face the truth.

Akbar was struck at first by the extent to which he had lapsed in communing with God. It was a turning away occasioned not just by having lost Asmina or the world of Dar-ul-Aman but also by a sense of betrayal – divine compassion withheld – compassion that might have prevented her death.

Gradually signs remembered from childhood surfaced once again – whispers under the trees, a presence hidden by plants, almost within reach.

'You cannot escape Him, as long as He is within you,' Jalal Baba had said.

So the aggrieved lover had to confront the other beloved at last. He railed at Him all night pacing under the trees, wandering through the garden.

It was the cry of a soul that had lost its way – a pilgrim's doubt about the purpose of his quest. Beset by anguish, he felt abandoned, deserted. 'Why', he demanded, 'have You forsaken me? Where were You when I needed You?' The questions remained suspended – until the first light was ushered in by the early birds.

In the dwindling darkness, a remark resurfaced, *You are denying what Allah has given us.*

Puzzling over the source of the statement, he was struck by another reminder, *They are His ultimate gift to us.*

What was that ultimate gift?

More followed: *Our love has brought them into this world. If you turn away, you will be turning away from me...and from our love.*

Then a demand: *Recite the azan in their ears...the first sound they hear should be Allah's name.*

The darkness dispersed. Were these the answers he sought? Time would tell.

When Akbar walked into the nursery, the infants were being bottle-fed. Lilian was surprised to see him. The early hour and his unkempt appearance aroused concern. It was not clear what he had in mind. She drew the baby in her arms a little closer protectively and glanced at the ayah feeding the other. Akbar stood by a window waiting for the meal to finish.

'What is it, Akbar?' Lilian asked casually.

'Just came by to see them,' Akbar said.

'That's nice,' she said lightly, 'you've taken an age finding your way here...and then you've chosen such an unusual hour.'

'I've been praying and felt this was the best time to see them.'

Lilian was intrigued to learn that he had prayed, especially as he had not done so after Asmina's death.

'Is it...is it the first time since...since...?' she asked, hesitantly.

'Yes.'

With the feeding done, the babies were back-patted on their changing table. Akbar looked at them intently.

'This has been a long time coming,' Lilian remarked.

He reached out, stroked the arm of one child and offered his index finger to the other who clutched it. He smiled and bent down to kiss them.

'I'm so pleased this is happening,' Lilian sighed.

'I've made some kind of peace with circumstances...I don't want to hold back from my children.'

'For a start, you should name them,' Lilian said.

'Their names should echo their mother's name,' Akbar said, 'as in...Usman and Asma.'

The atmosphere in the house lightened the following week with the arrival of Aliya from Canada, accompanied by a son of three and a year-old daughter. They were on a holiday visit. Teymour was expected to join them later.

Aliya was delighted to find Akbar at home. She had missed him on her last three visits. For the next few days the upper floor of the house echoed with the patter of little feet, babies' cries and the piano played by Lilian.

When friends and relatives were not visiting, Aliya tried to make up for lost time while Akbar struggled with himself to keep up with her.

She was fascinated by Akbar's account of life at Dar-ul-Aman. He answered her questions, but hesitated when it came to Asmina. Aliya had to coax it out of him in fragments.

'I wish I could have been there,' she said, '...and seen the cave and the spring...your cottage...Dar-ul-Aman and of course, Asmina.'

'It's over,' he said, 'that part of my life is over...'

Associations that had mattered to Akbar were also affected by the change: his parents – and Ahmed Ali – who always had a place in his life; his deep-rooted ties with Aliya and Kamran; the teachers of his youth – the imam and Abdulla Saleh; Jalal Baba – spiritual father and a revered comrade; some of the students he was close to; and associates and teammates with whom he had shared work objectives.

Such associations were now perceived as part of the life that had ended with Asmina. Some were likely to endure, some would be altered, the rest were relegated to the past.

A courteous distance marked his kinship with his father and uncle. While the former took it in his stride, Ahmed Ali took it as a rebuff. Only Lilian got to see the old Akbar from time to time. There was a new edge to the relationship with Aliya and Kamran. The imam and Abdulla Saleh were part of the Beyt-as-Salah reality. Jalal Baba was a reminder of his marriage to Asmina and the lost connection with spirituality and transcendence.

It was difficult for those around him to assess whether he had recovered from her death even though his manner indicated a readiness to take on the world again.

By a quirk of fate, his future course of action was ordained by admission to Trinity College, Cambridge, for a PhD in Asian and Middle Eastern Studies, based on a research paper on the Ibn Taymiyyah texts.

The acceptance of his application was received at Dar-ul-Aman and relayed by an exultant Jalal Baba to the Samandars. Akbar took the information as a matter of course. Javed Ali and Ahmed Ali believed it was a godsend and set about organizing his departure for Cambridge.

Akbar was adamant about bearing the expenses of the Cambridge study course. He had placed most of the salary earned at Dar-ul-Aman in an Islamic investment account which had grown over time.

The Dar-ul-Aman governing board had also paid him a substantial gratuity from the profits of honey production. Occasional royalties from publications and recordings of the azan and *qirat* renderings added to his savings.

'It seems you came home yesterday after years and now you're getting ready to go away again,' Lilian remarked.

'Mother,' Akbar said after a pause, 'I'm looking for a way through this wilderness...it's not here...I know that now after the break with meditation...a part of me having yearned for the peace of that realm ...has missed out...on three separate occasions.'

'I remember Jalal Baba telling me that there is no timetable for transcendence. It comes of its own when one is in a special state of mind. That state of mind eludes me...I seem to be shut out of that plane...wooden feet rooted to the ground...I have been cast out of the order,' he said.

'My darling,' Lilian remarked, drawing him close. 'How sad...to have lost the magic touch...but you will soar again, I am sure you will.'

Shortly before Akbar's departure, Aliya invited her friends for dinner. Most of them were known to Akbar. Old timers like Simeen, Mansoor, Rajab and Nasir attended, along with their spouses. Akbar did not have much interest in them. It was Tooba he was waiting for.

Aliya had almost given up on her when she walked in. Akbar reacted as if touched by a charge. He noticed that she was without an escort. A deep purple sheath encased her slimness. Upswept hair and emerald ear drops emphasized elegant cheek bones and a slender neck.

To avoid the others, Tooba and Akbar slipped into the garden after the initial pleasantries.

'Much nicer here,' she said, 'all you hear are loud voices there...everyone talks at the same time...nobody wants to listen.'

'Is it as bad as all that?' Akbar remarked.

'It's worse...you've been away too long.'

After a while they were chatting like old friends. He found it easier to converse with Tooba than with Aliya. He reminisced about his days at Dar-ul-Aman and of his life with Asmina. She noticed the tears.

'There is little joy in life now...I do things because I have to...can't shake off the burden of living,' he said.

'My poor friend,' Tooba said reaching out to him. 'You have been hit hard...I wish I could help.'

'What about you?' he asked after a while, 'I know about your NGO and of the recognition your services have received far and beyond from international agencies...but what of your personal life...who waits for you?'

'No one,' she said, with a level look.

'Hasn't there ever been anyone?'

'Once...a long time ago...I thought there was someone, but he went away before anything could come of it.'

'So what happens now?' Akbar asked.

'I don't have to be waited for, you know,' she said shrugging, 'at least not unless someone like him comes along.'

PART III
THE FAR COUNTRY

PART III
THE FAR COUNTRY

TWENTY

During the flight to London, Akbar dozed in snatches. Parting with the twins a month before their first birthday had been a wrenching experience – they looked so much like Asmina – he was apprehensive of how much he might miss them.

As for family members, the distancing imposed since his return to Karachi – even for Uncle Ahmed Ali – would lessen the impact of separation.

He lapsed into an extended reverie in the dimmed lighting of the cabin as the plane went forth. A blackened figure was discernible, groping on hands and knees through encircling darkness towards a ring of light. Others of similar hue, further back within the darkened halo, illumined now and again by flickering sparks, crawled forth through slush and sticky sediment in like manner. Some fell shrieking by the wayside and were consumed in a burst of flames. The survivors wailed and stumbled, slipping and scrambling to reach the light. The darkened face of the figure closing in on the light was that of Akbar.

He was roused from the vision by a flight attendant's attempts to fasten his seat belt as rain and high winds buffeted the aircraft. He sat upright as the plane lurched, shuddered and dropped into air pockets. He tried focusing on flashes of lightening visible through a nearby window.

What if the plane went down now, taking us with it? he thought. *That would be a real quandary. Where would I land? Interesting thought...it would of course be one solution to the dilemma.*

He shut his eyes and gripped the armrests. The plane skittered across the darkness, lashed sideways by surges of rain and bounced off course by strong winds. Akbar felt a strange calm. It helped him drift off.

A swarm of bees attacked him. Screaming was of no avail.

Just as he was about to give up, the flight attendant tapped his elbow to enquire about his welfare. The disturbance seemed to have passed, the seat belt sign had been switched off.

So it's not over then, and I am left where I was before these visions came to me...suspended between what has passed and what is to come ...with Asmina's death, everything seemed over...all links severed...the light that shone for a while went out...the end, I felt, was near...but life goes on...and here I am on the threshold of the unknown.

Avebury, the Wiltshire village attached to a Neolithic stone circle, or rather, three stone circles, was a different world from humid, troubled Karachi. But the old rectory, where Akbar's grandparents lived, smelled like another home when roast lamb, roast potatoes and cauliflower baked with cheddar cheese were being served.

He had visited Avebury earlier but this was different. He was there to stay for a while before setting off for Cambridge.

Some years before, his grandfather, the Reverend Dr. Armstrong, had opted for retirement from the rectorship of Avebury and declined proposals for office in the Anglican Church hierarchy. Instead, he and Mrs. Armstrong chose to continue living at the rectory in Avebury, which he had purchased when it was put up for sale.

Dr. Armstrong held a doctorate in theology and had authored two well-regarded books on related subjects. On retirement, he resumed writing a column for one of the national newspapers.

The Armstrongs were pleased to have Akbar visit. They hoped his time with them would be restorative. Lilian had kept them informed about Akbar's affairs. A picture of the twins she had sent earlier was prominently displayed in the living room.

Dr. Armstrong was another one who was drawn to Akbar. He knew of Lilian's unusual experiences with Akbar as a young child and had always been intrigued by the special spiritual quality he sensed in his grandson.

Akbar had always felt at home at the old rectory. Much of his childhood had been spent with his English cousins, romping in the grounds and exploring hidden areas in the rectory buildings.

The house was a late Tudor structure with crossed beams, mullioned windows and a pebble-dashed roof. Parts of the interior had been altered in the late nineteenth- and again, in the mid-twentieth century to keep up with the rector's functions in changing times, but much of the quaintness had survived in the form of creepy asymmetrical passages, darkened oakwood fittings, and creaking floorboards, oddly juxtaposed little rooms serving no evident purpose, a servant's hall, scullery and cellar.

The stables, carriage house and servant's wing had been sold to a developer who converted them into flats. But there was enough land left over for one to imagine what the rectory must have looked like in its prime.

'You are being tested, my boy,' Dr. Armstrong said, as he strolled with Akbar in the shrubbery that early autumn evening. Ash and beech leaves floated to the ground. There was a chill in the air. Smoke from the neighbourhood drifted in, reminding Akbar of the woods around the cottage where he and Asmina had lived.

'I seem to have lost the blessedness,' Akbar confided. 'I feel adrift, deserted now.'

'That's what it means to be human,' Dr. Armstrong said.

'The yearning returns even now to plague me...it hasn't left me... that's when everything looks bleak,' Akbar said.

Dr. Armstrong looked closely at him, 'Perhaps you have been denied access to the special world while being tested ...'

Akbar felt his grandfather might be right. It was reassuring. The anguish dogging him since Dar-ul-Aman seemed to be ebbing at Avebury. If he had to go on without Asmina, he would have to strive for renewed equilibrium. He would have to let go of her. For a moment, he wondered whether her death was designed to draw him to other affiliations, then recoiled from the thought.

'Don't ascribe human values to what is unfathomable,' Dr. Armstrong said, as if reading his thoughts. They were now walking towards the vegetable garden.

Akbar was grateful for his grandfather's company. It was not just the kinship, or the finely etched handsomeness –

so reminiscent of Lilian – that appealed to him but also his gentle way of setting things right.

'Go to Cambridge,' Dr. Armstrong advised, 'when you are in an appropriate state of mind.'

It was with a sense of equanimity that Akbar reported weeks later at the Porter's Lodge at Trinity Great Gate for the Michaelmas term. He was well-rested after his stay at Wiltshire.

The rooms assigned to him were among those kept aside for research scholars in Nevile's Court, an elegant quadrangle set off by the seventeenth-century classicism of the Wren Library.

His unit comprised two furnished rooms – bedroom and sitting room-cum-study – on the first floor, in the south wing. A note left in the room asked him to call at the College Bursary after he had settled in.

The Bursar advised Akbar about the rules for College residents and gave him a booklet containing the layout of premises, features and facilities.

Later, he called on the Master along with four other research graduates who had taken residence that day. Lord Aldenbury was a renowned historian. He received them in a handsome oaken room with gleaming silver cups, shields and photo frames.

A portrait of Lord Byron and a spectacular sunset by Turner were on the walls. Caucasian rugs lay on the floor and the windows opened on Great Court. The Master was in his mid-sixties, distinguished-looking and elegant in a deep blue cardigan. Glasses of sherry were served. Akbar took grape juice instead.

The Master addressed his callers by name and seemed to know enough about them to engage each one in brief conversation. His interest in Akbar was apparent.

'Your academic record is remarkable, Mr. Samandar... and your dissertation subject quite fascinating. When complete, we hope it will rank as a referential authority on Ibn Taymiyyah,' the Master said.

'Thank you Master...one can but try.'

'I would have taken you in anyway Mr. Samandar...even if you had proposed a different thesis topic. I was keen to have a research scholar from Pakistan.'

'Why is that, Master?' Akbar asked.

'Your papers indicate that you are some kind of Renaissance man... that was intriguing...apart from that I also know your country. I have travelled the length and breadth of it...even visited what was East Pakistan.'

'When was that?'

'My first trip took place in 1942 before the partition of India. The Indian government had commissioned a survey of archaeological sites in the northern areas. I had been appointed a member of the commission by Whitehall...or rather, the Home Office.'

'And the second time?' Akbar asked.

'In 1951, the government of Pakistan called me back for a similar exercise in both wings of Pakistan, led by your renowned archaeologist, Dr. Dani.'

When he was leaving, the Master advised Akbar to get in touch with Dr. Carla Berkoff, Fellow of Trinity and specialist in Islamic studies.

Akbar settled into the lifestyle of a research scholar with natural ease. The academic environment suited him. He found this experience different from the cloistered religiosity of Beyt-as-Salah or the rugged monasticism of Dar-ul-Aman.

At Trinity, there was a medieval grandness about the dinners at Great Hall and the architecture of Great Court, New Court and Nevile's Court and a brooding romanticism about the Backs on the River Cam.

For the rest of the year, Akbar moved purposefully between Trinity College and the academe of the Faculty of Asian and Middle Eastern Studies. The Faculty was located in an art deco building on Sedgwick Avenue which was within walking distance of Trinity College.

It came as a pleasant surprise to Akbar that Cambridge was one of the rare cities where walking was the most common mode of travel, rivalled by the omnipresent bicycle.

Akbar's introduction to the Faculty began with a call on Professor Andrew Crowden, Head of the Department of Middle Eastern Studies to discuss the particulars of his research programme.

During discussions, Professor Crowden introduced Akbar to Giles Butler, who had been appointed as his thesis supervisor. Over coffee, Giles briefed Akbar on the guidelines for researching and conducting studies. Later, they visited the Faculty library for viewing available texts followed by a briefing from a specialist on research technology for locating and retrieving documentary material.

At Giles' prompting, Akbar also looked in on the University Library. The fact that he was visiting one of the premier book repositories in the world was not lost on him. It was the largest he had ever seen.

The following day was spent in the shops of Petty Curie, Sidney Street and Market Place, buying things from crockery to stationery. He also acquired a black three-quarter-length gown from a haberdashery specializing in scholars' accoutrements. The gown was essential wear for research students on certain occasions.

Food provisions included biscuits, apples and bananas. A carrier bag crammed with too many apples gave way, scattering the contents. Akbar's attempts to salvage the fruit while hanging on to other purchases, met with little success. He was about to give up when a passing cyclist dumped his bicycle and scrambled all over the pavement to retrieve the runaway fruit. Akbar laughed at the comical sight of the rescuer chasing the fruit between legs of startled pedestrians.

'I'm glad you're amused,' the rescuer said good-naturedly, straightening up to his full height of six feet and pushing back a lock of blonde hair. 'I don't exactly do this for a living.'

'I admire your skill,' Akbar remarked, 'you're so good at it!'

'That,' he said, grinning, 'is because I am really a retriever masquerading as a man for the last thirty-two years.'

They laughed at the remark.

'Thank you Mr...er...Retriever...for rescuing my larder supplies...I am Akbar Ali Samandar, dissertation scholar at Trinity.'

'You could have fooled me. You seem more like Changez Khan of the Golden Horde than Akbar the Great...as for me...I'm just David Kelso-Tanner...a boring old Trinity Don,' he said, waving and pedalling at the same time.

Akbar's pigeonhole at the Porter's Lodge contained two letters – from Lilian and Jalal Baba.

Lilian provided news of the family: his father sponsoring four scholarships in law; Kamran finding a new lady love; Aliya's husband being elevated to company directorship, which necessitated a family move to Montreal; the twins, Usman and Asma, blossoming into little people in the pictures sent by Lilian.

Jalal Baba's letter both soothed and disturbed at the same time. He wrote of matters recalling the life Akbar had left behind. It was comforting to know that despite vicissitudes, Dar-ul-Aman endured...a constant feature on the mountainside.

I was hasty in questioning my ties. They endure...vital as before.

The Master and Fellows of Trinity dined at High Table which ran breadthwise along the north end of Great Hall. Akbar sat at the research students' table which lay adjacent to High Table. For the undergraduates there were three tables running lengthwise down the Hall, one along the east wall, the other along the west wall and the third in the middle.

Food at High Table was served to the dons. The several hundred undergraduates collected their meal from a service counter. Research scholars were also provided table service.

Akbar's gaze wandered from the long rows of begowned undergraduates lining both sides of the dining tables to the arched beams of the early seventeenth-century ceiling and came to rest on an imposing Henry VIII, in a full-length portrait above High Table. He also caught David Kelso-Tanner's gaze on him.

It did not take Akbar long to set up his work schedule. Academic research fell into a familiar pattern, whether conducted at Beyt-as-Salah, Dar-ul-Aman or the Department of Middle Eastern Studies.

His working day started with prayers and a reading of the Quran. The remainder of the morning was spent in rooms at the Department, researching online, scanning, poring over texts, making notes in consultation with Giles.

In the afternoon, Akbar alternated between the Faculty Library and the University Library, taking time out for *Zohar, Asar* and *Maghrib* prayers. Owing to the frequency of his visits, the library staff had become familiar with his requirements.

Work at night in his rooms, with a break for meditative exercises, often kept him up late. He also attended talks and programmes conducted by scholars at Cambridge or other academic centres.

Despite the enduring sense of loss, it felt good to be working again. Since Asmina's death, his life had lacked the earlier elevation to transcendence. He was sustained by old habits – praying and simply following the faith. In such matters, there seemed little difference between the old Akbar and the revitalized one – except for those who knew him closely.

TWENTY-ONE

Dr. Carla Berkoff was in her study when Akbar called. Her flat on Portugal Street was one of those provided by Trinity to teaching Fellows. When Akbar first contacted her on the phone, she was brusque.

'Your name and student ID are all that's needed. I'll leave word at the Porter's lodge when and where you're to call,' she said before hanging up. Following her directions, Akbar turned up at her flat on the scheduled date a few minutes before four in the evening.

'You're early,' she said at the door, 'I like that.'

Carla, barely five feet tall, was small without being diminutive. Her piercing black eyes behind rimmed spectacles were set in a tightly moulded face like that of a Bolshoi ballerina, an illusion heightened by hair drawn severely back.

She shook Akbar's hand firmly. Noting his chestnut hair and grey-blue eyes, she asked, 'Are you really from Pakistan? You look more European than I do.'

Akbar blushed and mumbled an explanation about his mixed parentage.

Taking a chair at a round table and indicating that Akbar should do likewise, she said, 'I see you have chosen to cut the

Gordian knot by getting to Ibn Taymiyyah via the Sufis...a bit like putting a square peg in a round hole, isn't it?'

'I don't see it that way,' Akbar said, 'It's more a question of reviewing the Taymiyyah expositions from a metaphysical perspective...after all, Islamic doctrines are not compartmentalized. Scholarly exercises allow for an overlap and even review by novel approaches.'

'Innovation is regarded as *bidah,*' Carla said, her lip curling.

'Really, Dr. Berkoff,' Akbar remarked, 'that is an unusual observation from an academic of your status...there is no bar on bona fide intellectual enquiry.'

Carla responded instantly.

'You're right, of course, Akbar...it is Akbar isn't it?'

He nodded.

'I was curious about what led to this...was it adherence to Al-Ghazali perhaps?'

'Please Dr. Berkoff,' he protested, 'next you'll cite Hallaj's *An-al-Haq* as the inspiration for my research.'

'No, not that obvious,' she said with a short laugh.

'I suppose I was motivated by the Mutazali belief about the perfect unity and eternal nature of Allah and of the Quran being a successive reality, not co-eternal with Allah, and consequently fair ground for analysis and enquiry.'

'Coffee?'

Carla called out from her kitchen, 'I see from your CV that you researched at Dar-ul-Aman in Pakistan's tribal area.'

'That's right,' Akbar said.

'Any hobnobbing with extremists?' she asked.

It was Akbar's turn to laugh, 'Yes, plenty. We were in and out of each other's pockets and often had tea together just like the coffee we're going to have now.'

'Are you taking the mickey out of me?' she asked, returning with two mugs.

'Of course not,' he said.

'You seem different...not like the usual run of Pakistanis.'

'What makes you say that?' he asked, nonplussed.

After a pause she said, 'Shouldn't I have? But it's true... the ones I've come across haven't impressed me...and the tabloids are full of their unsavoury escapades!'

There was a momentary silence. When they resumed discussion, it was to talk about work. Carla told Akbar that she would be available on appointment for discussions and guidance on his thesis, in the capacity of college supervisor, but the Department of Middle Eastern Studies would continue to remain in charge of his dissertation programme.

He saw her that evening at dinner at the High Table. She was wearing the tweed jacket and skirt he had seen her in earlier, with the addition of a red silk scarf. She did not look at him. He noticed David Kelso-Tanner too further down.

After dinner, he went on a whim to the Porter's Lodge to check Carla Berkoff's profile. She was Russian, thirty-five years of age, a divorcee and the recipient of several scholarships. Her doctoral thesis was on the collegiate institutions of the Omayyads. It had earned her a citation and had been published in prestigious historico-sociological journals.

As the term progressed, Akbar was drawn – quite unexpectedly – into camaraderie with a small group of research scholars, which included Arjun Kumar, an Indian biochemist, Giti Karimov, a Tajik anthropologist and Etienne Pascal, a French classicist. They had come upon each other during dinners at the Hall and gradually elected to sit together at mealtimes.

This was unusual for Akbar. Before this he had never really felt the urge to be close to people on the basis of camaraderie. Former linkages had been occasioned by family ties, demands of duty and love and somewhat differently, the call of other-worldly influences.

His need for the present company was now centred on friendship. He felt the urge for another 'coming together', not as it had been with the family; another 'being with', not as it had been with Asmina, but as with birds of a feather, swooping through the sky together, perched in a row on electric lines, pecking at seed on a shared bird table.

The coming together of the group had been initiated by Arjun Kumar. At dinners in the Great Hall, graduates usually sat singly or in twos. Arjun's eyes swept over the scene one evening, settling on Akbar who was sitting on his own. Arjun headed straight for him.

'I hope you don't mind,' he said, taking the seat next to Akbar, 'I find myself drawn to you.'

'Such a novel approach,' Akbar said, observing his swarthiness, humorous eyes and wide smile, 'will get you anywhere!'

They chatted easily, exchanged personal information and acknowledged a proximity because, or perhaps in spite of, the Indo-Pakistan relationship.

It did not take Arjun long to spot the shy presence of Giti Karimov. There was a strange exoticism about her almond eyes, straight black hair and hesitant manner. She was resigned to being a loner. Arjun's suggestion to join them at dinner came as a pleasant surprise. She was pleased to be asked but was awed by the academic status of her new companions. She found Akbar's credentials especially intimidating.

'I daresay, you could teach me much about Islam,' she said, 'I am an occasional Muslim, despite my traditional upbringing.'

'I can't teach you anything Giti, but I can discuss matters of interest,' Akbar said.

'That sounds priggish,' Arjun remarked.

'Just clarifying the situation,' Akbar said.

Etienne was enticed away from a group of French-speaking graduates. 'Come and chat with us,' Arjun told the plump, puzzled classics scholar busy with his second helping of Trinity's fabled crème brûlée. Etienne took time over joining what he saw as a slightly bizarre cabal. They had almost given up on him when he turned up one evening and placed himself firmly between Akbar and Arjun.

The part of the table they occupied became a sort of nucleus often joined by others, drawn there by the chatter and laughter. Carla, David Kelso-Tanner and some others at the High Table could not help but notice the animation.

Laughter was rare for Akbar. It was not that he did not feel like laughing. He just did not give in to it often enough. Now with his new-found friends it came more readily.

The conviviality carried through from dinner in the Great Hall to sports, art and entertainment – events picked out for them by Arjun. Trips to theatres, galleries and soccer matches were fitted in with their work sessions. Having fun was no longer a rarity for Akbar.

'What does it take,' Arjun remarked, 'to appreciate that God too has a sense of humour...not to mention awareness of the absurdities of life!'

Occasionally Akbar visited key Islamic centres and mosques, accompanied by one or more of his mates.

Sometimes they indulged in what Giti called 'halcyoning' – taking part in outdoor events in keeping with the weather. Hiking was one such popular pastime. At times they lit wood fires for barbecues.

For the Christmas holidays, Akbar went to his grandparents in Avebury, taking Giti and Arjun along. Etienne went home to France. The vibrant log fires in the rectory were a cheering change from the blandness of college heaters.

Mrs. Sommers, a retired cook, had been reinducted into the household for the season. Her presence ensured a well-laden table and a regular supply of Christmas specialties. The rectory hummed with the comings and goings of Avebury parishioners friendly with the Armstrongs.

The festivity was heightened by the arrival of further offspring of the Armstrongs – Akbar's uncle and aunt – with their families. Akbar was very fond of them.

Christmas Eve at the rectory was a traditional event. It started with mulled wine and singing songs with Mrs. Armstrong on the piano, followed by a dinner of turkey, trimmings, mince pies and Christmas pudding, rounded off by exchanging gifts around the Christmas tree. The service next morning at St. James' Church was conducted by the incumbent rector. Akbar thought it was beautiful.

'You look happy,' Dr. Armstrong said after Christmas lunch, kissing the top of Akbar's head.

'I'm more at ease now, Grandpa.'

'Have you found a solution?'

Akbar paused before replying.

'I sense an accommodation of sorts...between the reflective self and ...the controlling force.'

'Really? When did this come about?'

'I felt the first stirrings when I was staying at the rectory before going to Cambridge...I feel it more positively now...It's this place Grandpa...the rectory...the trees...your presence... you and Grandma.'

He walked to a window that looked out on to the garden.

'Let us thank the Lord.' Dr. Armstrong said, 'you in your way, I in mine.'

Before returning to Cambridge for the Lent term, Akbar and his friends spent a day at Bath, taking in the Georgian elegance of the resort town. Another day brought them face-to-face with the Neolithic starkness of Stonehenge. On the way back Akbar remarked, 'So many ways to worship God...four thousand years ago the Druids had their own way of doing so...All faiths aspire towards a single source of inspiration...'

Cambridge was colder when they returned, January and February being the coldest months. To keep warm, Akbar walked briskly – often breaking into a run – from Trinity to Sedgwick Avenue, and back.

He was anxious to get to work, scanning a treasure trove of Sufic commentaries on literalist traditions that Giles had located. The excitement of discovery kept him darting between faculty and university libraries and the writing table in his study.

His thesis had reached an interesting phase. Giles kept track of authorities which he regarded as appropriate for Akbar's bibliography. They were largely opinions of post-thirteenth century Sufi scholars on the works of Ibn Taymiyyah and his disciples, Ibn Qayyim Al Jawziyya and Al-Dahabi.

Carla was of the view that Akbar should broaden the scope of his enquiry to include commentaries on literalism by scholars predating Ibn Taymiyyah.

'Referencing such information makes research meaningful,' she remarked. To make her point, she gave him a list of authorities going back to the ninth century which were not accessible online, though hard copies of some were available in private collections in England.

Returning one evening in gathering twilight over snow-covered fields on the far side of the River Cam, his mind on documents scanned earlier, Akbar stopped near Trinity College Bridge, held back suddenly by an invisible force.

A tingling sensation starting from his toes travelled to his brain, setting his body aglow. In a dark landscape devoid of people, trees and shrubs loomed large like shadowy watchers. Around him, the snow glistened. Sounds gradually magnified of water flowing, foliage rustling and night creatures calling. His senses were flooded, as if charged by lightening with a divine ecstasy that radiated from the core to the extremities of his being in a surge of unparalleled sublimity. It passed in moments...and the hand that held him back, suddenly let go.

He lurched and tottered across the bridge dazedly, as if suddenly aroused from deep slumber, and entered the gateway to the cloisters under the Wren Library. On the way to his rooms, he recalled the date. It was the twenty-seventh of Ramadan – *Lailatul-Qadr* – commemorating the end of the revelation of the Quran.

During the remaining weeks of winter, the 'halcyoning' continued. Ice-skating on the Emmanuel College pond or on the frozen parts of the Cam was especially popular. There were also snowball skirmishes in Great Court, choral singing at bonfires in some colleges and the glory of the madrigals at King's College Chapel.

Winter's end brought on the Oxford/Cambridge Boat Race on the Thames on the first Saturday of April. It was watched by the four from Hammersmith Bridge.

Almost imperceptibly, the snowdrops gave way to crocuses, drawing tourists, who made their way through King's College, St. Johns and Trinity to the River Cam to gaze on clusters of white, purple and yellow flowers dotting the Backs.

Spring at Cambridge has a special flavour which affects old and young and those in between. It was the season for the four to go punting on the Cam, leaving behind memories of mists and rain, murky twilights and overheated rooms.

Their favourite punting course lay under the Bridge of Sighs at St. Johns, along the Trinity Backs, beneath Clare Bridge, past the perpendicular Gothicism of King's College Chapel, under the Mathematical Bridge (attributed to Isaac Newton), on towards Mill pool, bypassing swans, river fowl and other punters.

'You seem miles away,' Etienne remarked one afternoon, looking up at Akbar who stood poised in the stern of the punt, pole in hand, gazing over meadows bordering the Cam. They were heading for Grantchester, a rural retreat a few miles from Cambridge. Akbar was very far away just then.

Where is the ecstasy? he wondered. *What more can I do? I observe rida...complete resignation to Allah's will...why then am I denied? A brief vision...a glimpse on Lailatul-Qadr... is all I got.*

The episode had thrown him off course. He had taken it to be a sign of progression to a higher stage. He waited for a further sign, which failed to come...*Fana-fi-Allah*...negation of the human self and affirmation of the divine self. Whatever it was, it would not let him go, nor, it seemed, would it let him *in*. It was there. It was real. Perhaps, it was playing with him.

His friends sensed Akbar's anxiety. They assumed it was related to his work. He stayed away from dinners at the Hall.

Etienne decided to do his own checking. On the landing by Akbar's room, he noticed that the outer oak door was half open. So he knocked on the inner door. Getting no response, he turned the handle and slipped in.

At first, he could see no one but heard a voice chanting, '*Allah hu, Allah hu, Allah hu.*' He then saw a figure in a salwar kameez, lying face down on a prayer mat, arms and legs outspread. The voice seemed to emerge from deep within the figure.

Realizing it was Akbar, Etienne knelt and turned him over. Akbar's eyes were open, staring into space, his lips repeating the phrase, '*Allah hu*'...his body was rigid.

Bewildered, Etienne considered getting help from the Porter's Lodge. As he got up to go, Akbar fell silent, his eyelids clamping down like those of a doll and his body became limp. Etienne placed a cushion under his head. Akbar opened his eyes after a while, just as the afternoon sun pushed its way through the scattered clouds.

'Etienne,' he said seeing the concern in Etienne's eyes, 'I'm all right...don't worry.'

Later, they sat by a window overlooking Nevile's Court in awkward silence, embarrassed by their involvement in the strange encounter.

'What you saw was not a sign of illness or a mental aberration...it's...a state of being,' Akbar finally said, 'but...I want to explain what this is, when we are all together.'

After dinner they settled in a corner of the graduates' common room. Akbar opened up about himself from childhood to Asmina's death.

There was silence when he finished. They were awed by the account.

'You're like a Jedi knight,' Arjun exclaimed, breathlessly.

Akbar laughed. 'Not quite...I doubt whether I would find my way in a Star Wars situation.'

'But, you are...an...elevated person...like the Sufi masters we have in Tajikistan,' Giti said in an undertone.

'Listen,' he said, 'there are two sides to life...the temporal and the spiritual...yes, I've had more exposure to the spiritual than most people...but it runs parallel to my everyday life... which I share with you...and in which I am as special or ordinary as any of you.'

'Phew,' Arjun exclaimed, 'I also know of the Sufi or Yogi thing back in India. Imagine my coming all the way to Cambridge to be stuck with a closet Sufi...but since we are stuck with you,' Arjun said, after their second round of coffee, 'I suppose we'll have to live with your weirdness.'

'No other option,' Akbar said with a shrug.

'I would imagine,' Arjun said, 'Saints and holy men need time off too for coming down to earth, that is...that's where you'll find us.'

'Shut up Arjun!' Giti said, 'don't mock him.'

'Doesn't bother me, Giti,' Akbar said, smiling, 'let him have his fun. I'll have my moment.'

'What's it like...this transcendence, my friend?' Etienne asked in French, with great interest. 'Do you know when the moment is upon you?'

'It cannot be planned,' Akbar said, 'It occurs during meditation...it takes one over.'

'And...what happens then?' Etienne persisted.

'How can I describe something that is not of this world?'

'What can you recall?'

Akbar thought hard before speaking,

'It's like...there's no time, gravity, temperature, air, water...one is there...not there...one is everywhere...there is no self...self is all there is...'

'How wonderful!' Giti exclaimed.

'But you should know that the experience has eluded me since...since Asmina's death.'

'Why...why so?' Giti asked, reaching out for Akbar's hands.

'Her death threw me off course...I seemed to have lost my way...it has been difficult to revert to that special plane.'

'*Comme c'est tragique*,' Etienne remarked.

'Yes...it's been devastating...I pray...I meditate...that's what I was doing when Etienne came upon me...but I get no further.'

'Paradise lost,' Giti murmured.

'Perhaps,' Arjun said, trying to lighten the mood, 'but look what your temporal life has got you...three down-to-earth mates...who have at least made you laugh.'

'I suppose I should count you lot among my blessings,' Akbar said.

'How will we know,' Arjun asked at the door, 'when next we meet, whether it's Jekyll or Hyde?'

'Well, you'll just have to keep guessing,' Akbar said.

TWENTY-TWO

King's Parade was awash with afternoon sunshine. May had been like that. Exams were in progress. Undergraduates were everywhere. Akbar was heading for Sedgwick Avenue. Two figures at some distance were walking in his direction. They came closer and he was brought up short. Aliya, in a checked trouser suit and Tooba, in a printed silk tunic, stood before him.

'Couldn't have been better had we planned it...' Aliya said, laughing as they hugged.

'We've taken you by surprise,' Tooba said.

'Completely.'

Recovering himself, he suggested that they go to the Copper Kettle for coffee.

'We're staying overnight at the Double Tree Hotel,' Aliya said, 'we came by coach...it's back to Avebury for me tomorrow and Tooba returns to London.'

'We hadn't planned this,' Tooba said. 'It was a spur of the moment thing...finding ourselves in England at the same time – Aliya to introduce her children to your grandparents and I to attend a conference dealing with NGO affairs – so we decided to take time off and pounce upon you...which I think we have done effectively.'

She was pleased to see Akbar. She noticed the healthy glow, the trimmed beard, jeans, T-shirt and the wrap-around knotted scarf.

'Just as becoming as your madrasa look,' she said.

'You look quite marvellous yourself,' he said, glancing at her dimples.

'When you're done with the mutual admiration,' Aliya said, 'perhaps we could talk about things of common interest.'

The conversation ranged from Karachi matters, the Samandar family, the twins, Tooba's NGOs to Aliya's life in Canada and Akbar's year at Cambridge.

Akbar decided to skip work, and took them for a tour of Cambridge. That evening, he excitedly introduced his visitors to his friends during dinner at the Garden House Hotel.

Next morning, all of them gathered in his rooms for coffee before going punting, which turned into a riotous event leading onto lunch at the pub on the Mill. They all trooped off to the railway station in the afternoon to see the girls leave – Tooba took a train to London and Aliya to Avebury.

'I think I know about friendship now,' Akbar confided to Tooba as she boarded the train. 'It's what I feel for these three persons you have met briefly...I imagine that's the kind of thing that exists between us.'

'It's what has existed between us since that day at the beach many years ago,' she replied, waving goodbye.

Later Akbar pored over a collection of folios containing ornately decorated pages of eighteenth-century Qurans at the Wren Library. He smiled as he remembered how his sister and Tooba's punting attempts had almost landed them in the Cam.

'Private joke?' David Kelso-Tanner asked stopping by Akbar.

'Oh, hello,' Akbar looked up. 'You could say that.'

'Haven't seen you here before,' David said.

'Haven't been here much...it's quite beautiful...I had to find an excuse to work here...it's not enough to come just as a visitor.'

'You found some work then?'

'Yes, my tutor Carla told me about these documents.'

'Carla Berkoff?' David asked.

'Yes...she suggested I check them out.'

'You're dealing with someone formidable'

Akbar asked with a grin, 'Do you know her?'

'Not personally, but she makes her presence felt at Fellows' meetings.'

'I daresay...she also makes her presence felt at tutorials.'

'Your field of study...and hers...is fascinating,' David said, taking a chair.

'You think so?' Akbar asked, observing the wide-set cheekbones amidst the planes and dips of a fine face, highlighted by a pair of soulful eyes.

'Islamic studies have a distinct appeal,' David remarked.

'They are...absorbing.'

'Listen,' David said, as a thought struck him, 'when you're done...if it isn't too late, shall we go off and have a chat at a pub or over coffee?'

Akbar agreed.

They occupied a corner table in the Copper Kettle. University folk and visitors could be seen through the glass front, strolling on King's Parade in the long summer evening.

David's interest in Islam dated back to field trips made in his undergraduate years to archaeological sites at the outer reaches of the Roman Empire, located on the boundaries of northern Iraq, north-eastern Turkey and north-western Iran. He had been a volunteer at the digs at a base camp in Talafer, a border town in Iraq.

'Despite differences between natives of the three countries,' David related, 'their allegiance to Islam was inspiring...I found the ways of the Bedouins of the Shammar tribe that straddle Iraq, Turkey and Iran, most impressive...I was befriended by a young sheikh who headed the branch based near Talafer. His kinsman headed the branch in Iran; the head of the Turkish branch was another cousin... tribesmen crossed borders freely with herds of sheep, goat and camel...all that area comprised one territory in their eyes. It was an existence not of this world...stark white deserts... blazing sun...starry nights...where else would God have sent a special message?'

'Mystical backdrop for the romance between Arab nomadism and English iconoclasm given full rein by T.E. Lawrence, Thesiger and Lady Esther Stanhope,' Akbar remarked.

'Now you're making fun of me,' David said.

'Wouldn't do that, David...it's grudging admiration, more likely.'

'If you had seen and absorbed the desert as I have, you too may have wanted to give up the world for that.'

'Why didn't you pursue your dream?' Akbar asked.

'It's a boring story,' David remarked, looking away, 'my father – distinguished civil servant and acclaimed sociologist – felt I had fallen under the spell of Professor Alex Atherton, Director of the excavation. I learnt later that there was bad blood between them. Father insisted I give up plans to study archaeology and take up history instead. In short, I was made to quit the Middle East.'

'Big step,' Akbar remarked.

'Dreadful. He threatened to leave me without the means to continue at Trinity if I persisted with my obsession...to break his hold I tried for a scholarship but lost out to someone better. I was left with no option at the time but to follow orders. So here I am,' David said with bitterness.

'Do you dislike history that much?' Akbar asked.

'No, no, quite the contrary. It's the next best thing. I shudder to think what I would have done had it been sociology.'

Akbar laughed, 'At any rate, history is close enough to archaeology...you're fortunate in that.'

'I suppose so, but it's the linkage between Middle Eastern archaeology of the pre-Judaic and post-monotheistic cultures that interests me...and of all the different strains, I find Islam the most interesting.'

'Why Islam?' Akbar asked.

David paused, watching three old ladies make for the door.

'Because it is not archaic...or elitist...or racist...the only nationalistic aspect is the use of Arabic language...which was unavoidable because the message had to be conveyed in a tongue that could be understood by the people for whom it was meant...and what a tongue...none other like it...a perfect formulation of divine configurations.'

'That's an amazing observation,' Akbar remarked.

David continued, 'Islam is modern...timeless...prescribing a way of life and professing to be part of life...enjoining communion with God at specific times of the day and calling for a fresh commitment on each occasion – with congregations of labourers shoulder to shoulder with executives, sinners next to saints...equally balanced.'

There was a long pause. Akbar asked, 'Why have you not converted?' 'I have thought of doing so – often,' David said, 'but hold back in case it becomes no more than a badge of faith...I will adopt Islam when I am prepared to make that commitment...I need to close in on it. Perhaps I'm waiting to...to...fall in love...so to speak.'

'And how is that supposed to happen?' Akbar asked

After a pause, David said, 'By the influence of persons like you.'

'Like me?' Akbar asked with astonishment.

'Yes, why not you?' David replied, 'I know of the transcendental episodes...I sensed it at our first meeting. Since then, reports have made the rounds.'

'I don't know what to say,' Akbar said.

'I have a confession, Akbar. It may make you cross. It may even put you off, but I admit to having researched you online.'

'Why did you do that?' Akbar enquired, puzzled. 'Surely we know each other enough for you simply to have asked.'

The chat lasted for three hours, ending only after the sun had set. It was nine by the time they got back to Nevile's Court.

There was buoyancy in the air during the last weeks of the Easter term. Exams were over. Results were displayed on notice boards outside the Senate House. Colleges celebrated the end of the academic year by holding May balls on their premises at which professional bands from London performed. The merrymaking lasted till dawn, followed usually by punting.

Akbar attended the Trinity May ball which was held under a marquee in Nevile's Court. Arjun had booked a table for twelve. Giti, wearing a dress flown in from Tajikistan, was paired off with Akbar for the evening. Arjun and Etienne escorted their girlfriends. All the men, including Akbar, were formally attired in black ties. The women wore ballgowns.

The ball opened with the Master leading his wife to the floor for the first dance. They were soon joined by others. In the marquee, boisterous undergraduates held sway. Sounds of laughter mingling with music and popping champagne corks drifted from the cloisters to the Backs and across the Cam.

Akbar was persuaded to take the floor with Giti. He was reluctant to do so largely because he did not know how to dance. At length he agreed. His awkwardness gradually abated with guidance from Giti. He soon mastered the basic steps and managed, with his athleticism and grace, to give an appearance of ease.

He caught sight of the pale arms and shoulders of Carla Berkoff in a severe black sheath with jagged coal black feathers arching back from her temples. David Kelso-Tanner, looking tall and elegant, swept by with Lady Aldenbury on his arm.

During one of their turns around the floor, Akbar and Giti passed the Master's table to which David had returned after the dance. He smiled at Akbar, raising his glass. Following his glance, the Master called out, 'Akbar Ali Samandar, I am sorry for interrupting but do see me before you leave for the summer break.'

On the Monday following the May ball weekend, Akbar was reminded by a note from the Master to call before 1 pm.

He did not have to wait long.

'I have here a letter for you from the Trinity governing council,' said the Master, 'which I would advise you to read.'

The letter informed Akbar of the grant of a scholarship for the entire duration of his thesis.

'Congratulations, Akbar Ali Samandar,' the Master said, shaking his hand, 'The council has received a very positive report on the work you have done this term. It's a rare grant for a researchist but Trinity is well served by your effort. I'm personally very pleased.'

By mid-June, Akbar wound up work at Cambridge and went to Avebury for a few days before travelling to Karachi for the summer vacation. Finding his grandparents looking somewhat frail, he suggested that they should consider moving to one of the empty flats built where the stables used to be, to forgo having to maintain the somewhat larger expanse of the rectory.

'Over our dead bodies,' Dr. Armstrong said. 'We have no plans to move until it is time to go, besides, there's nothing wrong with me. It's your grandmother who has been running a slight temperature.'

'Do you want me to stay for a bit?'

'No, no. You go home. Lilian must be longing to see you... not to forget the delectable twins.'

'I'm staying Grandpa, until the doctor gives you both a clean bill of health...despite the twins.'

TWENTY-THREE

It was a hot sultry day in July that greeted Akbar when he finally flew to Karachi for his vacation.

The oppression was offset to some extent by sea breezes blowing monsoon clouds across the sky – fluffy white or sun-tinged – that would turn a glowering grey by August. Karachites cherish the breeze. The mood of the city lightens when the first raindrops fall, but turns to despair when the storm-drains fail and the streets are flooded.

Ahmed Ali and Kamran met Akbar at the airport. They recalled the time when he had departed for Cambridge with an unkempt beard, a caseful of books on Islam and a depressed state of mind. The Akbar who emerged from the terminal had a short, trimmed beard, the hint of a smile playing on his lips, dapper in drainpipe jeans and a loosely knotted scarf.

His uncle and brother greeted him hesitantly but were soon reassured when he enfolded them in tight hugs. The warmth with which Akbar met them was unexpected. The brooding brusqueness had been magically replaced by an open friendly demeanour and an endearing smile.

They left the terminal building with Akbar walking in the middle, one arm around Kamran, the other encircling Ahmed Ali.

As the car eased into the highway, Akbar found the familiar mix of dilapidated chawls, overloaded buses and haphazard traffic quite off-putting.

How old will they be now? he wondered, cheering up at the thought of the twins, *two months short of two years, I think.*

He looked forward to seeing them but not without some trepidation. They would have grown into persons by now, albeit little ones. How would they react to a father who had been absent?

He saw Lilian first at the front door, then the youngsters, one on either side. His father stood a step behind.

Akbar greeted his parents with mixed emotions. The twins watched, bewildered, as the stranger, whom their Dadi referred to as their Papa, hugged and kissed Dadi and Dada repeatedly.

Then he bent down and scooped them up, one in either arm. He kissed them and nuzzled them and called them by their names. They looked at him shyly, giggling when his beard tickled them.

He did not leave them for the remainder of the day. He stepped with awe into the nursery that Lilian had set up with their playthings and learning toys. He played with them when they dashed about indoors or in the garden. He helped Lilian bathe them and get them ready for bed. He sat with them through their evening meal. He read them their favourite story and prayed with them. He watched over them long after they had fallen asleep. He felt engulfed by a deep love that seemed to be drawn from his lost love Asmina.

Despite the outpouring of love, he was the stranger waiting to be let in. The family had grown into a tightly knit unit during his absence. The twins looked upon Lilian and Javed Ali as their parents and Kamran as a sort of sub-parent. Dada and Dadi were like Papa and Mama to them, and Chacha a step away from Papa.

Akbar's presence was viewed as an intrusion, as he discovered the next morning when the novelty of the 'stranger bearing gifts' had worn off. His appearance at the nursery was met with resentful glances, followed by cries of protest when he approached them.

'You'll need more time to win them over,' Kamran said. 'At the moment, they're more ours than yours, bro.'

'Don't worry,' Lilian said, 'it'll change...they may not be quite eating out of your hand now, but they'll start to soon enough...you'll see.'

There was a revival of bonding however, with his parents. At the time he left for Cambridge, Akbar's relations with them had been marked by misgivings brought on by his personal anguish, isolating him from his family.

It was different now. The spell in Cambridge had changed that. Barriers had fallen; he had reconciled himself to his circumstances; and there was a renewed sense of purposefulness in his research and meditation, despite limitations. Within these parameters, he found life liveable, people approachable and relationships possible.

To ascertain if his brother had truly come home, Kamran suggested an afternoon of cricket in the backyard. After a preliminary protest, Akbar fell in with the plan. It turned into a boisterous game with staff and family members. There were run outs and boundaries – and much laughter. Time stood still for a while – only Aliya was missing from the window upstairs.

Instead of her, were two little spectators, excitedly clapping, bobbing up and down and clamouring to join the game. Lilian had little choice except to send them forth with an ayah.

When the game was over, they sat with their father and uncle for tea like little grown-ups. Lilian had baked scones. Akbar reached for honey. The bottle he held was labelled *Dar-ul-Aman Honey*, and in finer print, *Ain-al-Akbari Brand*.

Watching him, Kamran remarked, 'We get regular supplies from Jalal Baba...I thought you knew.'

When Akbar put down the bottle, Kamran held up another bottle saying, 'If that surprised you bro, take a look at this.'

The bottle Kamran that held contained a transparent golden variety of honey, labelled likewise as *Dar-ul-Aman Honey* with the finer print reading *Asmina-pari Brand*.

'They're both delicious...the first one is rich and fruity, the second light and floral.'

Another surprise followed a few days later. A letter from Jalal Baba advised that the Dar-ul-Aman Trust had decided on acquiring Akbar's cottage at a price that had been assessed by accredited evaluators and were awaiting Akbar's instructions for forwarding the proceeds.

The summer sky was heavy with thick clouds. One afternoon when the heat was especially stifling, Lilian tried to make it easier for the children by setting up a kiddie pool in the garden filled with cold water.

Akbar observed them through the trellis, cavorting and splashing in the pool. As he watched, a sudden strong gust of grit-laden wind from the west blew through the trees, the leaves flapping violently, covering surfaces with a dusty coat. Lilian hurriedly called the children in and hastened to close the windows before the dust storm developed.

The intensity of the wind increased – bending boughs, snapping branches and blowing away objects in its path. It raged for a while, knocking down hoardings, banging doors shut, crashing window panes, snapping power lines and disrupting traffic. At length, a wind-driven drizzle followed. Gradually, the wind weakened and dropped.

The drizzle became a downpour. The rain, a blinding sheet of water, soon grew into a deluge. The garden was flooded within minutes with rainwater gushing down from higher ground. The roads resembled canals with water coursing down their surfaces and the house looked like an island in choppy waters.

Through the crashing rain, the children, who had been confined to the upper floor looking out the window, caught sight of a mini-van at the gate. Cries of 'Tooba Khala...Tooba Khala,' rang through the house. The van sputtered into the drive. Tooba, in a drenched safari jacket and trousers, jumped out and rushed in.

Her presence was the magnet that brought the twins bounding downstairs with two ayahs in tow. They jumped on Tooba, knocking her down. All three rolled over one another on the carpeted floor while Akbar looked on amazed. Lilian smiled and remarked,

'See, how she brings rowdyism into the house, whenever she comes...and how those rascals respond to her!'

'She has an uncanny ability to draw people to her,' Akbar remarked. 'She did it to my friends in Cambridge after one meeting and now she has bewitched my babies.'

'Although, the twins are irresistible...as you can see,' Tooba said over coffee in the veranda, 'I didn't have to court them.'

They were relishing the cool air brought in by the rain through openings in the trellis.

'They sidled up to me when I happened to call on your mother one afternoon with an abandoned baby in my arms. They stayed with me through the visit, poking and prodding the infant. The next time I called, they clambered all over me looking for the baby, even wanting to check in the car... that's all it took for us to become friends.'

'Wish I had that kind of equation with them...I envy you,' Akbar said.

'It'll come...don't push it,' Tooba replied, getting up to dry her clothes. Akbar noticed the absence of make-up and the short boyish haircut.

'Why?' he asked, 'the hair, I mean...not that this doesn't suit you, but still – why?'

'More suitable for the work I do,' she said.

Distracted momentarily by her dimples, Akbar said, 'Tell me, about it...your humanitarian work, I mean.'

'Grandiose words,' she shot back, 'the task is quite dehumanizing...the scope is as vast as...the world itself... there's no end in sight.'

'What is it you do that is so unsettling?' Akbar asked.

'In a word...we deal with human misery.'

Akbar got an idea of what Tooba meant when he accompanied her on field trips to Kasba Colony, Machchar Colony and some Lyari River settlements. On one such trip, the accompanying team included a guide, a doctor, a disinfectant sprayer, a film cameraman and six persons carrying food, water, clothes and other articles.

'The malaise is not confined to these areas...a stroll in any of the two thousand odd slum settlements around our city will bring you face-to-face with it,' Tooba, explained. She was clad in a safari outfit, knee-high boots, surgical gloves and a veiled hat resembling a beekeeper's headgear.

The alleys they entered were narrow, blotting out the daylight. The homes lining either side, when not crumbling, were black with filth and marked with stains that included fingerprints of excrement and rotting food.

Open drainage channels with foul-smelling sludge ran along the middle of the alley streets. Remnants of excreta lay on either side of the drains. Fly-ridden garbage heaped everywhere, constricted whatever open spaces there were in the settlement. Rats, cats and the occasional dog scampered through the alleys, unheedful of humans.

'It's more or less like this in urban slum settlements all over the country,' the doctor observed. 'Citywide slums and displaced persons' camps are the fastest growing habitations these days.'

'Its no better in the rural areas,' Tooba added. 'Agricultural tracts of land between most cities have now been taken up by large industrial plants that spew toxic waste and... spread disease...'

Her voice trailed off.

The guide led the team to what appeared to be a junkyard. Broken, rusty machine parts littered the ground, partly submerged in festering remnants of rainwater.

Everything seemed black – the water, the ground, pieces of wreckage, more garbage. In the blackness, objects began to stir amongst the debris. It took Akbar a while to realize that they were human beings – skeletal, half-naked men, women and children.

'That,' said Tooba slowly, 'is human misery.'

'This,' said the guide, clamping a clothes peg on his nostrils, 'is hell.'

Akbar watched as the team ministered to the residents of the black yard. Tooba was occupied with making notes in a register containing the particulars and case histories of the wretched beings.

She seemed to know most of them. When attending to them, she would place a hand on their shoulders or arms or pat them on the head.

In a lean-to, on one side of the yard, the doctor examined patients and handed out medicines. Disinfectant was sprayed. Food, water and clothing were distributed amongst scrawny arms and blackened hands lined up beside the lean-to. When the book work was complete, Tooba sat on a folding stool, head in her hands.

'Don't you feel well?' Akbar asked approaching her.

'I'm fine, just waiting for women with female complaints, to discuss their problems.'

After a while, she said, 'Akbar, you have greater experience of...God than I do, so tell me...isn't attention to the wants of "the needy, and the wayfarer and those who ask"...a form of righteousness?'

'It is so,' Akbar said, 'yes, I'm sure it is. It is what the *Sura e Baqara* says.'

'These people,' Tooba said, 'have as much a right to life as you and I...yet their circumstances make for death rather than life.'

'But do you see an end to this?' Akbar asked.

'No,' she said, 'at least not until we have a long-term policy directed specifically to resolving this.'

'And...meanwhile...?'

'We deal with the fragments of humanity we come across...and try to instil in them a sense of purpose, a reason to live...It's the best we can do,' Tooba said.

'How do you do that?'

'That's a long story. I will tell you some other time.'

'Come,' she said after a bit, 'let me introduce you to my family.'

She led the way to a burnt-out chassis of a bus inside which the movements of some more black figures were discernible. The cameraman followed.

At the front end, a woman lay upon a tattered mattress feeding a baby from flat, sagging breasts. Tooba bent towards her. The woman murmured in rasping tones that the eldest son was away at work with a municipal sewage-cleaning team.

Her husband, a full-blown AIDS patient, lay in a shrunken heap in a corner. Two naked children crawled awkwardly on the rusty metal floor. Two teenagers sat, sightless by a window, covered in flies. A young girl distributed food and water to them.

'This is Dina's family – or really my family,' Tooba said. 'Dina, the mother, is suffering from several ailments, which are not life-threatening, but they are so enervating that she has to rest every few minutes. The two boys, Bugoo and

Tamba, were born blind. In fact their eyes were missing... and that's how they've been. The two little ones suffer from rickets. The three who are whole, include the eldest son for whom we found work, Nari, the girl you see serving the family, and the little baby. I wanted to take Nari with me, hoping to send her to school and provide her a wholesome life, but you will be surprised to learn that she turned me down – despite her mother's insistence.'

'Why?' Akbar asked

The cameraman focused his lens on Tooba to catch her response.

'She felt it was her duty to stay and look after her folks. With her gone and her brother at work, there would have been no able-bodied person to tend to the family.'

'That is remarkable,' Akbar said

'Amazing where one comes across nobility of spirit,' Tooba said. 'What's more, she's quite stoical about her situation. It may surprise you to know, they are not without hope because they have comfort in having recourse to at least one breadwinner...the boy for whom we found work...that is what we do...we harangue public and private agencies to employ at least one able-bodied person from our families in despair...who then become the fulcrum for the survival of their less fortunate kin.'

'Do you know what the faith of this family is?' Akbar asked.

'Sumar, the husband is a Muslim, as far as I know...Dina is probably a Hindu...or may be a Christian...but, given the kind of life they have, does it matter what they believe in? The very poor can't really afford a religion.'

TWENTY-FOUR

At the time of his departure the twins were with him at Karachi airport. He recalled how Asma, yanking her hand from Kamran's grip, had rushed across to him crying, 'Papa,' just as he was about to enter the terminal. Usman followed a moment later, breaking loose from Tooba's hold. Then they were upon him, clinging arms wrapped around his neck before being drawn away

Blinking back the wetness in his eyes, Akbar approached a food counter for sandwiches and coffee. At the bar, he was reminded of the dinner with Tooba on his last night at a seafront restaurant overlooking the Indian Ocean.

'Are you waiting for me to marry you?' he had asked. Turning her gaze from the flapping wings of gulls skimming over waves illuminated by restaurant lights she said, 'Not really...I'm not exactly waiting to marry anyone...it could have been you...but you went elsewhere...soon after, the idea of marriage got sublimated into the things I do now...and that's the way it's been.'

'Don't tell me, there weren't others...proposals, I mean.'

'There were...some...keen enough suitors...but they didn't move me...anyway, this kind of talk will be of academic interest soon...'

'Rubbish, how old are you?'

'Same as you...twenty-eight.'

'That's not old.'

'Who said I was old?'

'That's what I thought you meant.'

'I was merely pointing to statistics...honestly Akbar, I'm not focused on marriage...there's much more going on...it's what we make of ourselves that matters...how we live our life.'

'What if I get married?' Akbar asked suddenly.

Pat came the response, 'What if you do? I don't know about you, but I'll still regard you as a friend...an especially close one...can't expect more.'

Akbar's flight reached London four hours later than scheduled. He was met at the airport by Arjun and Giti in Arjun's newly acquired sports car. Their presence helped banish the loneliness that had dogged him all the way from Karachi.

His rooms in Nevile's Court felt like home away from home. He had brought back photographs of the family on this trip. He set about displaying them in his rooms – the parents, siblings, Asmina, Jalal Baba, Ahmed Ali and the twins playing with Tooba.

Anxious to disperse the ghosts of Karachi, Akbar plunged into research and data accumulation for the dissertation. He decided to start working on the layout of the written submission. Autumn was back and the academic year was underway. Scarves, sweaters, top coats, boots, gloves and umbrellas were being readied for winter.

Carla Berkoff had left a message at the Trinity Porter's Lodge for Akbar to get in touch for the first tutorial of the course scheduled for this stage of his dissertation. He called by phone and was given an appointment to discuss some notes he had made during the summer break.

On the day fixed, he was delayed at the University Library duplicating documents Carla had asked for. He tried calling to inform her about the cause for delay but got no response.

A speedy taxi got him to Portugal Street eventually. He rang the doorbell and waited. He rang twice after that, and was about to use the knocker when the door opened on a barefoot Carla in a black silk kimono, hair piled up. Her kohl-rimmed eyes gave her a mysterious look. The red gash of a mouth looked lethal. The smell of brandy and aromatic cigarettes hung in the air. Langourous notes from *Norma* floated from somewhere within. Never having seen this side of Carla, Akbar was at a loss for words.

'Akbar Ali Samandar,' Carla said in deep tones, 'you are intruding on my private time.'

'I'm sorry Dr. Berkoff,' Akbar said, 'I got delayed getting these duplicated,' he said, holding up the documents from the University Library.

'You should have called,' she said.

'I did...but there was no response.'

'I switch off if a call is more than five minutes late.'

'I'm truly sorry Dr. Berkoff.'

'You've already said that,' she said with a slight sneer.

'What else can I say?' he remarked, staring at her bright red toenails.

'This is the first time since the start of the tutorials that you have been late, so listen carefully. I allow scholars in tutelage three lapses. This is your strike one. If you slip up two more times, I will suspend your tutorials. Now go away, I'm busy. Leave your vacation work with me. You can come tomorrow at five.'

Akbar hesitated a while, then said, 'Five tomorrow evening will be problematic...Dr. Frankenheimer is conducting a seminar at the Department at which I am the first responder. May I come earlier?'

'I'm not concerned about your other commitments. If you can't make it at five, I have no time to spare this week,' she said, waving her hands. 'Next week I'm off to the Norfolk Broads. So it'll have to be the week after. Call me when I get back and I'll give you time then.'

'Dr. Berkoff...I'll come tomorrow at five.'

'Okay,' she said, shutting the door in his face.

An angry Akbar strode back to Trinity in biting rain. He had put up with Carla's overbearing attitude for over a year, but her manner that evening was hard to take.

'She's a damn good tutor,' he complained to David, 'but she also gives the impression of being a man-hater, or a Paki-hater or an Akbar-hater...I can't tell which.'

'She's just a bitch,' David said. 'She flies off the handle at the drop of a hat...a touch off-balance, I hear. Everyone gives her a wide berth. Drop her. Take another tutor.'

'Can't,' Akbar said, 'she's better tuned to my work than the others.'

'She's got you by the short and curlies, my boy...I tremble for your privies.' Akbar reddened slightly at the remark.

The next day, a black turtleneck sweater skirt outfit and pulled-back bun hinted at a business-as-usual approach. She dealt deftly with his vacation work.

'Your work is commendable...these papers,' she said, referring to the sheets before her. 'They contain passages of ingenuity...there is uncanny understanding of Ibn Taymiyyah's thought processes and mystical parallels. A few pieces could do with some rewriting...and one or two dropped altogether to avoid getting mired in dead ends. All said, it's interesting material, though. If you get it together – as seems likely from the structured samples I've seen – it should be an original study of some merit.'

'Amazing, Dr. Berkoff,' Akbar remarked, grinning, 'that's the best thing I've heard in ages...and I thought you had something against me.'

'Akbar,' Carla said, straightening, 'I recognize good work and give credit where it's due...it's all to do with work and study...my reactions do not have a personal angle. I don't have time to like or dislike scholars in my tutorials. You're simply a student like any other.'

'I understand, Dr. Berkoff,' Akbar said. 'Please overlook what I just said. Perhaps, now we can focus on the variations you have in mind for the written approach.'

Taken aback, she paused before speaking of a set of seventeenth-century commentaries on Ibn Al Arabi penned by a Moroccan monk.

'I came to know of their existence recently,' she explained. 'I'd like you to examine them for data that may be relevant to your thesis. The text is mainly in North African Arabic and Latin, but parts of it, I'm told, include commentary in French... with your language skills, you shouldn't have a problem.'

'I'd be very interested,' Akbar said.

'Well, you'll have to go to Bisley,' Carla said, 'a village near Stroud in Gloucestershire. The manuscript was acquired earlier this year by Professor Arfan Gibrilliac. He is an archivist who maintains an impressive collection of historical documents at home. Let me know,' she added, 'when you can go and I'll call to tell him you're coming. He is well known in academic circles but keeps a low profile, preferring privacy... It may interest you to know that after spending a year in a seminary in the Atlas Mountains, he returned as a Muslim.'

'That is interesting,' Akbar said, 'and possession of those manuscripts makes him more so.'

When Akbar told David of the proposed trip, he offered to drive him to Gloucestershire.

'How did she react when you told her about me?' David asked, as they set off.

'She made a face and questioned why it was necessary to take you along. I told her you would drive me there and help me find Professor Gibrilliac's home. She finally got the general idea...and called the Professor to tell him that there would be *two* visitors.'

'Bitch,' David said.

'I don't think she likes you much either...asked me how well I knew you in her condescending tone. I said you were a friend,' Akbar remarked, rolling his eyes.

David chuckled. He was excited, as Akbar was, at the prospect of viewing the seventeenth-century handwritten tract.

'I never imagined that the Cotswolds were so breathtaking... my mother claims that they are unbeatable,' Akbar said as the car drove up hills and down vales, passing market towns that had flourished during the Industrial Revolution and picturesque villages dotted with homes and cottages built of Cotswold stone.

'We're passing through some of the best countryside in Europe,' David said. The car sped past snatches of red, gold and brown foliage dotting the Gloucestershire landscape.

Professor Gibrilliac's home turned out to be a renovated seventeenth-century manor with outhouses, distinctive because of the proverbial Cotswold stone.

A man who looked like a gypsy sauntered up to open the gate. David drove down a gravel path to the front of the house. A gardener moved about the grounds, spiking dead leaves. A heavy oak door swung open on a sturdy woman of East European origin.

'Please come,' she said in accented tones, 'I tell Professor you here.'

Professor Gibrilliac, at seventy-two, had an ascetic appearance and a ragged beard.

'I have agreed to show you the manuscript, Mr. Samandar,' he said, staring at Akbar pointedly, 'because Dr. Berkoff has spoken highly of your project. She seems to have great regard for your capability.' Akbar smiled.

'She regards you as an exceptional scholar...I have heard her use that description only once before.'

'Dr. Berkoff is too kind,' Akbar said.

'We'll have tea first,' the Professor said, waving off Akbar's embarrassment, 'then you can take a look at the manuscript.'

After a meagre fare of tea and biscuits, the Professor – not a man of many words – led them to a dark oaken library with book-lined walls and a polished table surrounded by chairs in the centre. He proceeded to a spiral staircase in one corner which led to a loft overlooking the library where he kept archival material. The manuscript was placed within a four-legged glass-topped case. Akbar was made to wear gloves before he was permitted to handle the faded parchment containing bold Kufic writing. A latter-day handwritten copy of the text lay beside the manuscript.

Akbar's request for a duplicate version of the copy was turned down by the Professor. He told Akbar to peruse the copied version in the loft for as long as he required and make his own transcript from it, which called for a handwritten exercise since there was no duplicator in the library.

'The manuscript will remain locked but the copy will be on this table and remain accessible to you,' said the Professor. 'I'm going to my study now...it's the first door on the right on leaving the library.'

After two hours of work – Akbar poring over the copy, David scanning other documents on display and looking through books on the shelves – Akbar fell in with David's suggestion of an overnight stay in Bisley as more time was needed.

When told of the plan, the Professor hummed and hawed but eventually agreed to let him in the following day. He gave Akbar a key to a little-used side door to the house which opened into a corridor leading to the library with instructions to use it the next day.

In the latter part of the evening, Akbar and David walked from the lodging house, where they were staying, to the manor. Akbar intended to use the remainder of the evening for copying the lengthy text without disturbing the Professor's household. They brought sandwiches and coffee with them. No one was about when they got to the manor or when they went in by the side door.

Akbar positioned himself by a window in the loft to catch the evening light. When it became dark he turned on a small table lamp while David dozed in an armchair.

After a while, footsteps followed by shuffling and scraping below alerted him to the presence of people in the library. He continued with his work ignoring the sounds. There were muted murmurs below.

A door opened as someone – seemingly significant – arrived. Chairs moved. Without any warning, the murmuring below was interrupted by a greeting uttered in a loud voice followed by a response, in Pashto.

Akbar leapt up. He crept to the railing of the loft and peered down. His eyes fell on the unmistakeable figure of Tarrar Khan embracing and kissing a burly Central Asian man with a handlebar moustache and a bushy beard. Akbar saw the Professor bolt the door.

Among the twelve persons seated around the table, Akbar noticed the Professor, the housekeeper, the gatekeeper and the gardener. A meeting, chaired by the Professor, seemed to be underway. David, aroused by Akbar's sudden reaction, came up from behind, giving him a start.

'What's going on?' David asked.

Akbar clapped a hand on David's mouth. 'Don't make a noise,' he whispered, 'I'll explain later.' For an instant, Akbar felt a sense of déjà vu. He recalled the darkened upper floor of Beyt-as-Salah, the parapet, and the scene that had played out in the imam's chambers.

'You are welcome to my home, General Tamar Gugushvili,' Professor Gibrilliac said, beaming at the Central Asian person.

'Happiness mine,' the General replied in guttural tones with a grin that raised the tips of his moustache upward to the corners of his eyes.

A knock on the library door led to the unbolting of the door and the entry of two gypsy-like women carrying trays of baklava, kous-kous, kebbeh and other delicacies. Two men followed with a samovar and a trayful of small cups.

'The miserable codger!' David remarked, 'all we got were crummy biscuits.'

'Shut up,' Akbar whispered, 'otherwise they'll know of our presence.'

'Why the cloak and dagger?' David asked, frowning.

Akbar paused before replying, 'If my guess is right, a terrorist plot is being discussed.'

'What!' David remarked, paling, 'are you serious?'

'Wait and see.'

'But...but...shouldn't we do something...inform someone...' David spluttered in rising alarm.

'Not yet,' Akbar said, 'we know nothing...stop fidgeting David and keep quiet please...we can't move until they clear out...so let's stay put and gather what information we can, then decide on appropriate steps.'

'If we get out of here in one piece.' David mumbled.

The attendants served tea and savouries to the persons at the table.

'We must disperse soon,' Professor Gibrilliac said at last, calling them to order, 'now let us get on with reviewing the targets proposed by High Command and appoint teams to organize the attacks. Time frames for the attacks will be set by High Command after approval of plans. Tarrar Khan... whom all of you have met...is High Command's emissary. He has brought us instructions from the leaders.'

'We have list here,' Tarrar Khan said in pidgin English, taking out some papers from a briefcase.

They all turned to listen to him.

Akbar nudged David and whispered, 'I know that guy.'

David look appalled, 'How do you know such people? You aren't one of them...are you?'

Akbar smiled, 'You recall my stint in FATA. Who do you think lives there – elves and dwarves?'

David looked sheepish.

'I have known Tarrar Khan since then.'

'High Command wanting major public destruction like 9/11 or the Mumbai attack,' Tarrar said.

All present, including the two in the loft, listened intently.

'Seven targets chosen. Attacks on school, hospital, department store, airport terminal, hotel, cinema and open marketplace,' he stated. David and Akbar were shocked by the information.

'So we must appoint seven committees from among ourselves,' the Professor said. 'Each committee will prepare a comprehensive attack plan for a designated target within a month from today. At the month's end we will send all the plans to High Command for final orders.'

Seven committees, each comprising individuals picked from those at the table, along with the four others who were in attendance, plus some more who were named but were not in attendance, were appointed. Each committee was assigned one target and was tasked with preparing a plan of attack.

The discussion continued for a while, concluding about an hour later. The Professor led the guests to the dining room for supper. This gave Akbar and David the chance to creep down from the loft and escape unnoticed.

TWENTY-FIVE

Akbar and David spent that night and most of the next day at Stroud for registration of a report with the police on the terrorist threat to national security. In view of the seriousness of the event, the Chief Constable of Stroud took over the investigation from the police chief at Bisley. Akbar and David were whisked off to Stroud in police transport for rendering a detailed account of their chance eavesdropping on the conspiracy. A police driver followed with David's car. The manor was raided by a joint team from the Counter-terrorism Command of the London Metropolitan Police and MI5.

Akbar and David were interviewed separately by officials from Counter Terrorism and the MI5 about the events at the manor. They were also questioned exhaustively about their personal histories.

Profiles were made. Akbar's life story raised eyebrows and provoked awkward queries but he remained composed throughout. David, on the other hand, was shaken by the interrogation.

The manor incident was put down as an accidental discovery of a sleeper cell run by Professor Gibrilliac, representing a prominent terrorist organization. The persons who had attended the meeting at Bisley were identified as delegates from smaller cells operating under cover in different parts of the country.

General Gugushvili was a Chechen commander who had been smuggled into the UK, presumably for overseeing operations. Several delegates had left the manor by the time the raid was conducted. The authorities reacted promptly by putting a tail on them. Professor Gibrillac and two of the persons Akbar and David had identified were arrested on being found in the manor during the raid. The housekeeper, General Gugushvili and Tarrar Khan were among those who had got away.

The few reporters who managed to get to Stroud Central Police Station, were kept waiting until an official report, approved by the Home Secretary, was put out.

At the insistence of the legal advisor of Trinity College – whom the Master had contacted, following a call by Akbar from Stroud – the police withheld particulars of the Cambridge men from the press.

Sketches of the conspirators' faces based on descriptions given by Akbar and David were circulated countrywide. Before leaving for Cambridge, Akbar and David agreed to go to Scotland Yard and Thames House at Millbank, when called. They also undertook to make themselves available for questioning at Cambridge, if necessary.

Driving back to Cambridge, Akbar recounted the Beyt-as-Salah and FATA incidents in response to David's queries on his terrorist encounters. By time they got to Cambridge, Akbar could tell that the ordeal had unnerved David. He was jittery and reluctant to let Akbar go. So Akbar stayed with him until he fell asleep.

Akbar was in two minds about disclosing their role in the Bisley escapade to Carla, until events took over. Reports in the media on the unearthing of the terrorist plot, along with a hint about those who discovered it, hit the headlines, leaving him no option.

'Difficult to believe,' she said. 'Professor Gibrilliac an Islamic terrorist...impossible.'

'Why the epithet "Islamic"?' Akbar interjected.

'What do you want me to say...Jewish?' she spat out.

'Why not mention the name of the terrorist organization mentioned in the report...it would be more accurate.'

'Don't tell me what to say, Akbar. I choose my own words.'

'In this case, Dr. Berkoff, I think you are wrong...very wrong.'

'Why are you so defensive about the Islamic aspect... of terrorism?'

'Because it has its origins in the political strategy of a particular sect of Muslims...terrorism per se is not part of Islamic dogma or practice...even the word "jihad", at its core, implies no more than fighting for the faith...without recourse to terror.'

'Do you actually believe, Akbar, that the rest of the world perceives it that way?'

'Perceptions can be wrong,' Akbar said, 'we know how wrong those Jewish tribes were when Moses came down Mount Arafat, tablets in hand.'

'Is world opinion wrong when it sees the threat as a Middle Eastern and South Asian one? Is it mistaken when it identifies the perpetrators as Muslims whose declared purpose is conquering the world? Who else is responsible for this culture of violence and hate?'

'Why are you always so negative about Islam, Dr. Berkoff?' Akbar asked in exasperation. 'Is it simply a mindset or your upbringing?'

'You're being personal, Akbar,' she said.

'I'm sorry, Dr. Berkoff, but you drove me to it.'

There was an extended pause during which they glared at each other.

'I won't hold it against you' she said coming up to him, 'for it seems that when not tutoring, we spar on subjects unrelated to the thesis.'

'It seems that way to me too,' Akbar said.

'Well, I can't change my views and nor, I think, can you. So, if it's all the same to you, we'll carry on with the arrangement but try to focus more on the dissertation.'

'That suits me. Dr. Berkoff.'

'For a start, I think it's about time you called me Carla.'

In the aftermath of the Bisley terrorist conspiracy, Akbar and David faced further interviews in Cambridge and in London at Scotland Yard and the Security Service headquarters. Tracers placed on General Gugushvili, the housekeeper and Tarrar Khan did not yield results, but most of the other delegates were apprehended. They were identified by Akbar and David from a line-up that included decoys. Then they were charged and remanded for trial.

Particulars of Akbar and David were not revealed to the press on account of an understanding reached between the Master and the Home and Education Secretaries.

To save them from being exposed to death threats for testifying at a trial, the Director of Pubic Prosecutions decided to hold in-camera trials of the accused persons.

At the end of the Michaelmas term, Akbar visited his grandparents in Avebury. Both of them had been unwell. Dr. Armstrong had slipped a disc which required bedrest and Mrs. Armstrong was under observation for suspected recurrence of the earlier malignancy. Their second daughter, Emma, who was younger than Lilian, was staying over to help out.

'Aunt Em,' Akbar said, kissing her, 'nice finding you here.'

'Marvellous, darling,' she said 'it's almost a year since last I saw you. You look well. Cambridge seems to suit you.'

Christmas at the rectory on this occasion was somewhat muted on account of the condition of the Armstrongs' ill health and lengthy rainy spells. Emma's family did come for the event but the exuberance of the year before was missing.

Halfway through the Easter term, Professor Crowden reviewed the dissertations in progress at the Department of Middle Eastern Studies. In subsequent discussions, problems inherent in the thesis in review were aired and the standard of the work, based on research notes, written observations and oral expositions, was assessed. Akbar's presentation, mentored by Giles Butler, was eye-opening.

'As a rule,' Professor Crowden said, 'the gestation period for a thesis is three years – it may even go on longer, but in this case, we seem to have a before-term product in the making. There isn't more to be said except carry on, Messrs Butler and Samandar, in the splendid postgraduate work you're doing.'

Akbar celebrated by cooking a Pakistani meal, taught to him by Asmina, for his friends in the makeshift kitchenette on his landing. The lamb biryani, chicken curry and spiced potatoes were polished off by his delighted guests who insisted that the food tasted better than what was served in the Indo-Pakistan eateries. Leftovers were whisked off to David's rooms before Arjun could get at them, giving rise to taunts about Akbar's soft corner for dons over research graduates. It was true – Akbar *had* grown closer to David after the Bisley incident.

The trials of the accused in the terrorist plot took up much of Akbar and David's time. They were summoned to London when court was in session to testify as witnesses for the prosecution. Part of the defence strategy was to cast doubt on the veracity of Akbar's testimony.

A high-profile legal team had been engaged for the defence of the accused and large sums were spent on checking Akbar's background. Investigators had been sent to Pakistan and Pakistani lawyers engaged to assist in the investigation.

Although Akbar had made it a point to keep his family in Karachi informed about the entire episode, these events had the effect of exposing Akbar's identity. As a consequence, it did not take long for death threats to be sent to his family in Pakistan. This caused much consternation at the Samandar home. When Javed Ali and Lilian got to know what had provoked them, they became even more concerned.

Besides adopting precautionary measures, not much could be done. Extra guards were posted and surveillance cameras put up at the Samandar residence. Family members now travelled in four-wheelers with tinted glass and armed security guards riding fore and aft.

Drivers were instructed to avoid crowded sites, manholes, strange objects lying on the road, vehicles parked on roadsides and to check undercarriages for explosives before each journey.

Despite these measures, Javed Ali's vehicle was blown up one morning by a remote-controlled bomb placed in a dustbin when it slowed down to enter the Sind High Court premises. The force of the explosion flung the passengers far enough from the vehicle to be spared serious injury but the shock reverberated through the legal community and made headlines in Pakistan. Death threats were not to be taken lightly.

'You were just lucky,' a shaken Lilian said to Javed Ali. 'All the precautionary steps failed.'

The trials were held in camera at the Central London Criminal Court . The defence attempted to discredit Akbar's evidence by fostering the impression that he was an ex-terrorist who had fallen out with his group on account of rivalry with his cell commander.

Despite adducing evidence relating to Akbar's education at Beyt-as-Salah, his internship at Dar-ul-Aman, his marriage to a tribal girl and his fame as a presenter of Islamic TV programmes, the defence plea for striking his evidence from the record for mala fides on grounds of unreliability, failed. The Bench found substantive proven material on record corroborating the testimonies of Akbar and David.

At the conclusion of the trials, the accused were convicted and sentenced to varying terms of imprisonment. The propriety with which the proceedings were conducted left minimal grounds for appeal.

'Well that's that,' David said.

'Is it?' Akbar remarked.

'What do you mean?'

'Think about it.'

As they stepped out of the Old Bailey, they were accosted by a horde of reporters and cameras. They were pursued relentlessly by the media over the next few weeks and despite desperate attempts to maintain privacy, their life stories soon became public knowledge. It got to the point that the administration at Trinity had to arrange for special measures to protect them from the media and unwanted threats to their security.

TWENTY-SIX

After a tiring session at the Department involving reclassification of research references, followed by a dreary tutorial with Clara, Akbar strolled on the Backs for a while. His meandering eventually led to David's rooms. A note attached to the door mentioned that he had gone to his father's cottage at Grantchester. A hand-drawn map of the location of the cottage was attached, along with a message urging Akbar to get there.

He arrived in Grantchester by bicycle, and found the front door of the cottage ajar. It led to a cheerful living room with comfortable furnishings. There was no one on the ground floor. He did not venture upstairs, assuming that that too was devoid of people.

The search for David led him to the garden which lay at the back of the cottage alongside the river Cam. The voice of Placido Domingo in an aria from 'Cosi Fan Tutte' soared from a maze of paths and hedges situated at the bottom of the garden.

Another voice was audible too, striving to sing along with the tenor. It was David's. Akbar wound his way through the maze to the central part, where on a platform bearing three truncated Corinthian columns, a disc player and a goblet of red wine, David lay on an exercise mat, exposed to the afternoon sun.

Akbar recoiled at the sight of David in the nude. David's reaction was more measured. He did not display surprise at Akbar's sudden appearance. Instead, he got up slowly, reached for a towel draped on a column and wrapped it round his waist. Eyes averted, Akbar attempted to apologize. David smiled, patted him on the shoulder and said, 'What's the matter...never seen a naked man before?'

'It's not that,' Akbar stuttered, 'I...I...did not expect...'

'Hadn't expected me to be in the buff...I often do that when I come here, especially when no one's around. My father, who is the only family I have, rarely visits...so I get the place to myself...that's when I lie all day long and watch the Cambridge sky, as Rupert Brook admitted to doing... Great heavens!' David exclaimed, breaking off. 'You've turned crimson.'

Akbar felt the heat rising to his ears.

'What is it with you, Akbar?' David enquired, 'I'm a man no different from you...so why this reaction? I hadn't planned on surprising you...it just happened.'

After a pause, Akbar mumbled, 'I guess...the unexpectedness...the intimacy.'

'What intimacy, Akbar? We're friends, man...you can see me exposed just as I can see you...it's all the same...this occurs between friends...doesn't mean a thing...'

'Let's...let's drop the subject,' Akbar said, 'perhaps I've overreacted.'

'Of course...you have...and that surprises me because you're so composed in most situations.'

They decided to treat themselves to cream tea, honey and cakes at the Orchard Tea Garden.

'Specialty of Grantchester,' David said, as they took a table under an apple tree. 'It's what everyone does when they come here...tourists, Cambridge folk and even the locals.'

Later, they walked beside the river and through meadows bordering the banks which David described as Rupert Brook country. They passed cottages tucked away in meadow greenery or peeping out of rural cul-de-sacs and country stores straight out of storybooks.

'There are more Nobel laureates settled in Grantchester than anywhere else,' David added. 'They're all imbued with the Rupert Brook sentiment: "But Grantchester! ah Grantchester! there's peace and holy quiet there."'

'Stay for supper,' David said, when Akbar made to leave, 'I have soup – carrot and coriander – and scotch salmon with garden green salad, freshly baked brown bread and dairy butter, followed by Grantchester apple pie. Not as exotic as biryani and chicken curry, but it's the best I can offer.'

'It'll be dark by the time we finish,' Akbar said.

'Stay anyway, you can spend the night here if it gets late... say your prayers in the garden or indoors, just as you like.'

After supper they sat out in the garden watching traces of late evening light surrender to a sky pricked by stars. A hush fell over the garden, interspersed with sounds of night creatures and the gentle lapping of the river.

'The spirit of Rupert Brooke rides high in Grantchester,' David said, sipping his wine. 'The flowing water and our being here remind me of "The Old Vicarage":

"How Cambridge waters hurry by...

and in that garden, black and white,
Creep whispers through the grass all night;"
Or more appropriately:
"and green and deep, the stream mysterious glides beneath,
Green as a dream and deep as death."'
'Is that how you see yourself,' Akbar asked, 'a latter-day
Rupert Brooke?'

David chuckled, 'That would be presumptuous...I don't
have his poetry...remember, I'm just a history don and a
desert buff, not a Bloomsbury luminary...but yes, I am aware
of him when here...I can't help but see Grantchester in the
light of his verse.'

'You're a romantic,' Akbar said, beginning to see
Grantchester through David's eyes.

'We'll go punting tomorrow to Lord Byron's Pool,' David
said after a while. 'It's a secluded spot...very picturesque...
ideal for a swim.'

'What do we do for swimwear?' Akbar asked

'Don't need it. We can skinny dip.'

'What?!' Akbar exclaimed.

'That's what people do at the pool...Lord Byron initiated
the tradition when he was at Cambridge. Other notable
persons have done it too. Rupert Brook for instance, went
skinny-dipping with Virginia Woolf.'

'This...fixation with nudity...is a very English thing,'
Akbar said.

'Why are you such a prude?' David asked, 'we're close
enough to go skinny-dipping if we wish...I'm not ashamed
of my body...are you?'

'It's not a matter of being ashamed, David. It's just not
done where I come from...besides, I see no good reason for it.'

There was a pause.

'As you wish...I shall probably write a book about you one day, bringing in the Bisley episode to highlight your proclivity for misguided terrorists.' Both of them laughed.

They shared a bedroom with beds beside a window open to the sky.

'Tell me about yourself, Akbar...I've waited for the right opportunity to ask you,' David said.

Once more Akbar recounted his story. For some reason, he wanted David to know everything about him, so he repeated events as if reliving them. During a pause, when describing Asmina's death, he became aware of David lying beside him with his head on his shoulder.

'Don't...don't move,' David murmured, placing a hand on his chest, 'I just want to be close while you tell me about yourself...I have been here all along...sharing what you went through...visualizing the people you came across...and even trying to meditate like you...'

'How could you?' Akbar asked, surprised to feel David's tears on his neck. 'Unless you practise meditation?'

'Emotionally, I am a Muslim...it's my mind that must accept that reality.'

'But meditation and transcendence...can't happen by proxy,' Akbar pointed out.

'I meant that I sensed the struggle you described just as if I was undergoing it.'

The sound of a night bird trailed through the stillness of the night. Moonlight streamed in through the windows. Akbar wanted to move away from David but something held him back.

'Don't speak of Asmina's death,' David said, stroking Akbar's chest gently. 'It's far too painful. Tell me about the coming of the twins and what happened after that.'

And Akbar did so. He told him of the aftermath of the death, the retreat to Karachi and the move to Cambridge.

When he became aware of David kissing his neck and whispering words ending with, '...love for you,' Akbar realized that a threshold was being crossed signalled by the stirring in his loins.

He sat up and said, 'I can't do this, David...this is not for me...you must let me go.'

David fell back with something like an entreaty. Moments passed before he spoke again, 'Stay with me...and remain my friend.'

Akbar bent forward touching David's forehead with his lips, and said, 'Your friend always...I can't afford to lose you.'

It was close to morning when they went to sleep. By that time they had come to a better understanding of their relationship.

Akbar pedalled back with a growing sense of bewilderment.

How could I have been so naive, not to see where this was going? Not to gauge David's feelings...or even mine? Not to nip it in the bud?...If only I had Uncle Ahmed Ali's insight, I could have handled this better, but Uncle, dear Uncle I am now so far removed from you as to have lost you somewhere in the misty recesses of my mind...so I must find my own way...

'Ya Allah, forgive me,' he pleaded pedalling furiously, 'for losing my way...for being drawn to forbidden thoughts and deeds...for betraying you.' He recited *ayats* to allay his sense of guilt, but the formulaic invocations failed to still the uneasiness within him.

'Where are you, baby?' Akbar said to Asma on Skype...as a final exercise in exorcism. 'Get Dadi to fix the camera on you...ah, there you are...pretty girl with pretty ribbon.'

'Ribn *thoo, thoo*,' she said, tugging at it with displeasure.

'She's unhappy when her hair is tied up,' Lilian said off-screen,

'They're gorgeous, Mama,' he said, beaming.

Then Lilian came on, 'You should do this more often... you've no idea how excited they are...'

'It's a matter of timing...when I have the time, it's usually quite late in Karachi. And I'm at work when it's okay for you.'

'I know darling, but do try.'

Akbar spoke to his father, Ahmed Ali and even Kamran, despite the clamouring of the twins for exclusive chats with their father. When he finally logged off, his mind was more at peace.

Akbar's resumed sense of equanimity was short-lived. His Aunt Emma informed him that Grandmother Armstrong's recurring fever signalled the appearance of a secondary malignancy. She would require radiotherapy, which could be administered in Avebury initially, but would eventually necessitate her transfer to a special treatment centre.

Akbar felt depressed on the way to Carla's for his tutorial. When he turned up, she was trying to hustle her ex-husband out of the door. She had been squabbling with him about a jointly-owned property. Akbar's presence gave her the excuse she wanted.

'Ah, you're here at last,' she said, 'about time...we have less than an hour to complete the review on Shams Tabrizi and the Qalandars. It must be done now...'

Akbar nodded, trying to look concerned.

'Nicholas,' she said, 'you must go now...call me from London before leaving for Prague and I may have some answers for you.'

'You're a ball-breaking pain in the arse...' Nicholas yelled, ignoring Akbar.

'Shut up,' Carla snapped, 'you don't have to be coarse.'

'I won't be put off by your yelping.'

'Get out, you poof,' she shouted, pushing him out and drawing Akbar in through the front door – which she banged shut on Nicholas.

'I've told him not to come here...to communicate by telephone or email...but he insists on foisting himself on me...'

'Your treatment of him in my presence may have set him off. The abuse may have upset him,' Akbar ventured.

'He deserved it,' she said, shaking with anger, 'he's a crummy bisexual...been cheating on me for years.'

'I'm sorry,' was all Akbar could manage.

'Yes, I'm sorry too,' she said, 'and now he wants to give my half of the flat we shared to someone...who he is coupling with...the flat goes to his pretty boy over my dead body.'

Akbar was at a loss for words.

'I suppose I should apologize for all this...but I'm afraid you walked into it,' she said, placing a hand on his arm.

'I can leave if you like,' Akbar said.

'What good will that do now,' she said smoothing her hair, 'stay...and talk...we can skip work for the time being.'

Akbar was not sure where this was leading. She fetched him coffee, and poured herself a large glass of brandy.

'Let's discuss your work, Akbar,' she said, lighting a cigarette, 'I've talked about it to the gnomes at Trinity...and you'll probably be offered a teaching fellowship.'

'That's a huge step...thank you Carla.'

'Will you accept it?' she asked.

'I don't know...I haven't focused on a future course of action.'

'What's the good of it anyway?' Carla said, switching to her challenging tone after the first few sips of brandy, 'one more Muslim scholar at large.'

'What do you mean?' Akbar asked.

'What use are all the Islamic scholars littering the academic world?'

'Are you on to your Islam bashing again?'

'I'm not an Islam basher...in my opinion it's by far the best religion we have...' she said.

'Then why aren't you one?' Akbar asked.

'Because I lack commitment,' she said.

Odd coincidence, thought Akbar, *David cited the opposite reason for not converting.*

'Then why your grouse against Islamists?' he asked.

'They've done nothing for their cause, nor for the problems they face ...ironically, the best religion in the world... has devolved on the worst people on earth...it's God's joke on the world'.

'That's a nasty thing to say...' Akbar said.

'It should have gone to the best people...the elite,' she said.

'And who are they?' he asked, despite himself.

'The Jews,' she shot back.

'This is insane,' Akbar said, getting up to go.

'No,' Carla said seizing his shoulders, 'you need to hear what I have to say for your own sake...'

'But this is a one-sided argument,' Akbar said helplessly.

'It's the truth,' Carla said, 'If you find the worldly success of Jewish people difficult to swallow, consider their individual achievements...the highest achievers are Jewish...scratch the surface of any significant human endeavour and, more likely than not, a Jew will pop out.'

Akbar listened in silence.

Carla went on undeterred, 'As for the Muslim world... it is justifiably lambasted for a variety of ills ranging from corruption to human rights abuses and poverty.'

'I don't see why I should go along with this,' Akbar said, with rising desperation.

Carla paused, eyes on Akbar.

'Ha,' she yelled, 'you're all the same...you Muslims... can't face the truth about yourselves in your scramble to get to paradise...your stricken face says it all...can't take it from a woman anyway...and I thought you were different... but you're no better than the rest...dishonest and fake...for all your humbleness and piety...you're just a fake, Akbar... fake...fake... fake!'

She was topping up her next glass of brandy when Akbar left the flat.

TWENTY-SEVEN

Akbar was seething with rage on the way back to Nevile's Court. He had stormed out of Carla's flat to avoid a confrontation.

She's exactly what the husband called her...all her anger at him...that frustration...vented on me...

In the normal course he would have talked to David to help restore his objectivity. Yet he shied away this once on account of the sense of guilt he recalled after the Grantchester episode.

Does that continue to haunt me? Come on, David's still a friend...he was so at the time of my visit...I looked upon him as a friend even as he lay beside me...and he continues as a friend... whose advice I can seek.

At the Copper Kettle, David listened to Akbar's words over coffee.

'Before going off at a tangent,' David said, 'tell me how much of what she said...is true...rather how much do you accept as the truth?'

'There is some truth to it,' Akbar admitted at length.

'Be fair, Akbar,' David interrupted, 'quite a lot's true... some statements are conjectural and some are opinion... her's...but there's not much to challenge.'

'Perhaps so, but the way she lashed out...with a face twisted with bitterness and hate...there's...nothing redeeming about her.'

'Well, I told you about her volatility...Seems the husband agrees with me...but seriously, Akbar, it's not what she said, it's how she said it that's got to you...'

David's comments did not help. Carla's barbs had struck home, stoking a host of concerns: the wretchedness of the umma, the absence of excellence in Muslim leadership, the lapsing of his transcendental powers. He was angry with Carla for the insults and wounds she had inflicted, for the blood she had drawn. She had even had the last word, striking at all he stood for. He could not leave it at that. He had to voice his objection. She owed him an apology. He would confront her.

The doorbell rang a few times. There was no response. It reminded him of that earlier occasion. Rapping the door with the knocker did no good either. He turned to go. Then, as before, the front door swung open and Carla stood there in a purple kimono, barefoot, swaying slightly.

'My Muslim nemesis,' she said, 'come to wield the scimitar.'

Akbar was at a loss. He felt he ought to say something reflecting his state of mind, but all he could manage was, 'I'm sorry Carla,' feeling that he had lost this round too. 'I see you're not prepared for visitors...I'll come later,' he finished lamely.

'You're not going anywhere, my friend,' she drawled. 'You've come on a visit...haven't you?' And again, as earlier that day, she pulled him into the flat and slammed the door.

'Carla,' Akbar protested, 'this is not a good idea...I came to talk. But you're not up to it...so let it go...there'll be another time.'

'I'm up to anything you throw at me. This is as good a time as any,' she said defiantly.

'You're out of order now, Carla as you were then,' Akbar muttered. 'My word...out of order,' she mocked, '*so propah*... say what's on your mind...tell me my remarks were vile...I was obnoxious...for telling you like it is...'

She lit a cigarette that exuded a strange herbal odour.

'I'll tell you why you won't speak,' she continued, 'because it's all true...and because you don't have the balls to say otherwise.'

Akbar got up to go. Though she was a small woman, she pushed him back with force. He fell into a chair, jumping up instantly. She came at him, arms raised as if to strike him. They grappled with each other. There was a glint in her eyes. Her mouth was set.

Suddenly, they were on the floor, struggling furiously. It appeared like a fight to the death...each one out to destroy the other. Then all at once – inexplicably – his mouth was on hers.

It happened in a flash. A violent madness fired their beings. They tussled like bloodthirsty savages, forcing their bodies together...her taut frame like an arched bow against his sinewy hardness...each taking possession of the other with a rage that seemed to make the room shake. The rage that welled up in Akbar wanted to destroy her...to still the vicious tongue that taunted him and all he stood for...to subjugate the superiority with which she reduced him to nothingness, by asserting his manhood over her. They were out to devour one another. Time stood still as they vented their anger...slaking a limitless thirst.

When it was over, Carla, kimono all but in tatters, disengaged herself, disappearing for a while, as the morning light broke through. She came back, with a mug of tea and buttered scones. Akbar sat up in a stupor, consumed the scones hungrily, took the hand she offered and kissed it. She looked at him intently, saluting with her free hand.

He returned to Trinity stunned by what had happened, and found his way to the Backs. He spied Giti on the opposite side on her way to the Department of Anthropology. She waved at him. He looked away.

His thoughts were focused on the night, struggling to grapple with the questions.

How did the copulation come about? He thought he knew himself. So where did the animalistic rage come from? Had he moved so far from the ideal...being condemned now to scrambling with the blackened crawlers who were burnt alive in that fateful dream? Was there a way back for him?

Or was it a need...to be with a woman...after being with David...falling prey to a frenzy as overwhelming as the exhilaration of ascendance!

Then came the big question.

What of the quest...is it lost?

Followed by a curious response.

Carla's words have stripped bare the debacle – the failure of the umma to keep faith with Allah...is it also bedevilling my search, confined as it is to self-attainment of union with the Ultimate... is that a failure of the same order?

To regain some semblance of equilibrium, he buried himself in work. It helped. He realized that at a practical level some adjustment had to be made in the working arrangement with Carla. They agreed to carry on with the tutorials on Trinity premises. The reason for the changed venue was not discussed. Both acknowledged that the thesis was the best part of their association...perhaps the best work either of them had done.

All thoughts addressing his concerns were driven from Akbar's mind when he received news of his grandmother's admission to a hospital in Long Melford in Suffolk. It was a special endowment institution subdivided into two units, one for the treatment of children, and the other for the treatment of patients over sixty years of age. The children's unit was called the Alistair Waterton Centre after the endower's eleven-year-old son who had died of bone cancer. The unit for the older folk was known as the Lady Hester Waterton Centre. The hospital, built on farmland owned by the Waterton family, now formed part of the endowment.

Mrs. Armstrong's condition was precarious. The initial breast cancer had been excised by surgery, leaving her relatively healthy for many years. Secondary malignancy had developed in time, affecting a lung. Mrs. Armstrong required specialized treatment which was more readily available in the private sector than under National Health.

The objects of the Hospital trust included subsidized treatment for Church officials and their families. Mrs. Armstrong was admitted to the hospital under this proviso. Charges exceeding the subsidy were to be met by her health insurance cover.

She was allowed a personal attendant. Dr. Armstrong stayed with her for the first two days, followed by Emma, who was succeeded by Dr. Armstrong's daughter-in-law. Akbar also offered his services. His turn came soon enough.

Mrs. Armstrong's room on the second floor was cheerful. The windows looked down on landscaped grounds with rambling paths, herbaceous patches and watercourses flowing into a garden pool, beyond which was a gazebo, a maze and the front gate. Fields of ripening corn and wheat, dotted with clumps of trees, spread out on either side of the hospital grounds.

Mrs. Armstrong lay against pillows piled up on her bed, book in hand. She was pale and drawn, but managed a wan smile when Akbar walked in after taking over from his aunt. She was happy to see him.

He quickly got accustomed to wheeling her to the radiation unit for therapy and back, limp as a rag doll. He watched her hair fall. He held her free hand during the intravenous chemotherapy injections. He fed her, ran a bath for her and watched her as she dozed.

A sense of peace pervaded the room. On the second day of his watch, Akbar observed the sun setting over the fields from his prayer mat. Without warning, the sky turned rose red...like the evening when Asmina left him. He watched transfixed. Against the backdrop of the darkening sky, he saw a person rise from tending a prostrate figure...it was the girl Nari tending to Dina. The vision was seared into his mind, dissolving into a burst of light that engulfed him and extended to the horizon. He felt weightlessness, as if drifting upwards, borne on the wings of *Al Buraq*.

When he came to later, a full moon lit the sky. Mrs. Armstrong was looking at him with a smile, 'I have been watching a luminosity radiate from you, now reflected by the moonlight,' she remarked. Then as an afterthought, 'Is it your faith...Islam, that brings this out in you?'

Akbar paused caught unawares by her question.

'Grandma, Islam is the faith into which I was born, also the one in which I am schooled...so, yes in that sense it is by reference to Islam that I access these phenomena, and I am also conscious of...having been designed to operate within... within the parameters of my time and place in the history of creation. At the same time, I am aware that there is so much more out there and beyond that is unfathomable by human reckoning that we are fortunate to have been given certain rules and wherewithal as a birthright...to turn to for learning those rules...rules that can help us find a way to the source.'

'That good fortune you refer to my dear Akbar', said Mrs. Armstrong, 'is called the benevolence of God...however miniscule our reality may be in the scheme of the universe, He has not overlooked providing us with the means for ultimate salvation.'

After a spell of rain the next day, Akbar wheeled Mrs. Armstrong to the hospital grounds in the late afternoon. He pushed the wheelchair along garden paths while they chatted. She asked him to stop at certain spots to take a better look at flowers and shrubs.

'Just like a natural setting,' she remarked, 'that group over there,' she said pointing to a clutch of long-stemmed flowers resembling narcissi, 'I wonder what they're called.'

Akbar asked a gardener with a swarthy complexion if he knew the name.

The man replied in a familiar accent, 'Not knowing, sir.'

On a whim, Akbar questioned him in Urdu about which part of Pakistan he came from. Startled, the man began to reply in Urdu, then clammed up and moved away. Akbar suspected he was an illegal immigrant, anxious to conceal his identity.

Further on they came across two of his mates who also seemed to be Pakistani. It struck Akbar that the hospital may not be averse to hiring cheap labour. The nursing staff included Filipinas, Africans and Central Asians.

Back in Mrs. Armstrong's room, Akbar called his grandfather and later his aunt Emma to report on her. They were also able to chat with her. Talking to them cheered her.

As dusk approached, Akbar prepared for the *Maghrib* prayer. He turned on the TV for Mrs. Armstrong and began to lower the window blinds. His eye caught some movement in the corn stalks growing alongside the hospital boundary fencing. When he looked again, the crops appeared unruffled in the fading light.

After his prayers, the nursing aide brought Mrs. Armstrong's evening meal. All of a sudden, the lights went out, leaving the room in relative darkness. The blackout lasted for several minutes. The lights came on and went off again, blinking at intervals. Even when they had steadied, there were moments of fluctuation and darkness.

'Some problem with the supply,' the nursing aide said. 'The engineers are dealing with it.'

Awakening early the next morning for the dawn prayer, Akbar heard the sound of footsteps running past. Opening the door slightly, he caught a glimpse of two staff members disappearing down the corridor.

Later, he sat by the window reading the Quran and reciting special prayers for his grandmother. His attention was drawn to voices in the hospital grounds. It was drizzling. In the pre-dawn darkness, he saw a row of workers receiving instructions from a person who was evidently in charge.

After serving his grandmother breakfast, Akbar went to a cafeteria on the ground floor. On returning, he readied his grandmother for consultation with a specialist. While they waited to be called, the lights went out again. Daylight offset the interior darkness to some extent.

Then an accented voice came over the public address system: 'This is Commander Tarrar Khan. Jihadi fighters taking over hospital in the name of New World Islamic Order. People on all floors now hostage. They be ordered to stay in their place. My guards come to you soon with instructions. Do as told or you be shot.'

Akbar froze. The voice was one he had heard before. He knew the name only too well. The threat was real. The plan that was first discussed at Professor Gibrilliac's was now being implemented.

'What is it Akbar, dear? What's this all about?' Mrs. Armstrong asked, visibly alarmed.

'Don't worry Grandma,' he said, holding her hand, 'we'll have to wait and see...I'm sure it'll get sorted out.'

While he was speaking, the door opened and a heavily built hospital matron came in, followed by a girl in jeans and polo neck top, carrying an M16 assault rifle.

'You to stay here,' the woman said in accented tones.

'What if we need medication or food?' Akbar asked, 'Can we get through to the nursing staff?'

'Nurses, doctors and medical workers all hostage in staff rooms at duty stations. Patients in rooms. No movement allowed this floor, ground floor, upper floor...if you leave room, you...shot by guards watching corridor...'

Her words were interrupted by a signal on an advanced communication receiver carried by the girl. She snatched it from the girl's hand, switched it on, responded to the caller and left.

Akbar recognized her as Professor Gibrilliac's housekeeper. He wondered whether she remembered him, but there had been no sign of recognition.

From the windows he could see militants unrolling wire along the base of the hospital building. Another team was busy attaching charges to the wire at twenty-yard intervals. The telephone was dead. Even their cell phones were inoperative.

He opened the door and tried peering down the corridor, only to have the attempt cut short by warning shots. He was at a loss – they were trapped in the room. Mrs. Armstrong, watching him pacing the room, motioned to him to sit beside her.

'Akbar, dearest, calm down and don't put yourself in harm's way... we'll just have to get through this.'

There was not much that could be done and there was no diversion to offset the mounting anxiety. The TV too was dead. Mrs. Armstrong suggested that Akbar should read the Quran aloud and translate the passages he read in English.

The recitation got underway but was interrupted by the sounds of a scuffle and an altercation behind the door. Akbar jumped up to check. Mrs. Armstrong tried to stop him, but he opened the door a chink and peered out. A medical worker, most likely a doctor, was struggling with two militants who were trying to drag him along the corridor.

'Stop it,' he yelled, 'I wasn't running out...I was going to see a patient on life support...'

'You quiet,' one of his captors yelled, 'you come with us...'

They half dragged, half carried him down the corridor. After a while there was the sound of a shot. Akbar and his grandmother looked at one another in silence.

There was another sound, of a door opening and closing, followed by warning shots and a woman's voice calling out,

'Don't shoot...I need a nurse...I must see a nurse...'

More scuffling followed...and again...a shot. Akbar got up troubled. He went to the window to check on movement outdoors. His eyes fell on five bodies laid out on the grass below. Three were nurses in uniform and two men in surgical gowns.

By noon there was no sign of Mrs. Armstrong's lunch. Akbar brought out packets of biscuits, potato crisps and chocolate from his overnight bag along with a container of coffee.

Mrs. Armstrong drifted off to sleep in the afternoon. Akbar wondered how much longer they would remain in suspense. Two more bodies had been added below. The silence grew ominous.

Then without warning, there was the sound of police sirens closing in on the hospital. Craning his neck out of the window, Akbar could see them lining up outside the front gate. Ambulances too could be seen. He assumed that someone from the village had stumbled on the situation at the hospital and alerted the authorities.

The sirens continued even after reaching the hospital. After what seemed like a long-drawn wait, an exchange of gunfire rent the air. It was sporadic, moving between the hospital and the front gate.

An explosive outburst resounded through the air followed by shouts and cries. One of the police vans had been blown up by a grenade launched from the second floor. *This is serious business,* Akbar thought, *grenade launchers...what on earth will they do next?*

As if in response to his query, Tarrar's voice came on the public address system: 'See what we do...if you attack us, we destroy you.' There was a pause. Sounds of an altercation in lowered tones drifted over the public address system.

Then, the voice again, addressing the government forces: 'Put guns away...or we shoot children first, then old persons.'

The police response came via a loudspeaker: 'What is it you want?'

Tarrar replied, 'Nothing from you. We will destroy hospital... this is war...war of New World Islamic Order on Kaffir people.'

The police response to that was interrupted by repeater shots from the ground and second floor. A warning came through eventually, 'Put down your weapons and come out with your hands raised...if you don't do so within fifteen minutes, you will be attacked by our forces.'

Sounds of continuous exchange of fire had awakened Mrs. Armstrong, who watched Akbar pacing the floor. The anxiety was overwhelming. They had no access to their neighbours or the hospital staff or any sense of what was going on outside.

Almost fifteen minutes later, the sound of Chinook helicopters indicated that the Army's 22nd Special Air Service had joined the action. Akbar watched the helicopters draw closer. The police announced their arrival, adding that helicopter gunships were also on the way to support the ground attack.

The presence of the Chinooks had different effects. For the police it meant the availability of special forces for attacking the terrorists. Police officers moved about, clearing landing space for the helicopters. A barrier had been set up to keep reporters – who had not been long in turning up – along with relatives of patients and inhabitants of Long Melford, away from the line of fire.

For Commander Tarrar and his strategists, the arrival of the reinforcements was a matter of concern. The wiring of the hospital premises had not been completed.

Evening shadows lengthened, adding to the darkness in the rooms. The shooting continued, accompanied by cries and sounds of masonry crumbling after being hit.

On the prayer mat, Akbar begged for sense to prevail. As he placed his forehead on the prayer mat in *sajda*, three massive explosions shook the room, knocking down objects, shattering the glass windows and deafening the occupants.

Mrs. Armstrong slipped out of bed and sat beside Akbar on the prayer mat, laying her face on his chest. He put his arm around her and drew her close.

Footsteps at the door caused them to look up. The door opened and two nurses and a young doctor stood there, dishevelled, shoeless.

'We've managed to get away,' the doctor said, breathlessly.

'We're trying to get to the police lines. Do you want to come with us?'

Akbar demurred. He knew his grandmother would not be up to it.

'You have no idea what they'll do,' the doctor said. 'Those explosions blew up the children's hospital.'

'Oh no,' Mrs. Armstrong said.

'I think, they've botched it up though...only half of it has been destroyed. We must go now...the corridor is empty while they are running around trying to find out what went wrong with the explosions.'

'Good luck,' Akbar said, watching them race down the corridor. He left the door slightly ajar.

In the aftermath of the explosions, children's voices could be heard screaming. Akbar spotted some of them running towards the gate, half-clothed and barefoot, through the exchange of gunfire.

The Special Forces Support Group had launched an assault on the terrorists. A full-scale battle was underway. Helicopter gunships hovered in the air while the terrorists targeted them with rocket-propelled grenades.

A series of footsteps overran the corridor. There were hostile footsteps. Remarks, some in English, punctuated the air: 'Hurry finish wiring'; 'This corridor, this corridor must be wired'; 'English forces attacking'; 'IED now set'; 'Remote ready'.

Akbar panicked, *how many improvised explosive devices have these devils managed to get?*

A volley of shots echoed through the corridor – fired from one end and returned by the other. A gunfight was on in the corridor.

'They break through,' someone yelled. 'English troops in corridor.'

'Stop them,' said another. 'Detonate...detonate in Allah's name,' screamed a female voice.

There was a shot nearby. The door was kicked open and two people fell in. One of them was the woman in matron's uniform. She had been hit, and was being supported by a man. He placed his M4 assault rifle on the floor and laid the woman beside it. Akbar drew Mrs. Armstrong into a corner. The man struggled with the woman's bullet-proof vest and tried to resuscitate her but got no response. After repeated attempts, he drew her eyelids down over her lifeless eyes and uttered a prayer, then remarked in Pashto, 'You were a great fighter, a great companion, a great mujahida...find your way to heaven.'

When he looked up, Akbar was staring once again into the eyes of Bairam Khan. His face was bearded and drawn, the hair longer. There was a wildness in his gaze.

'You,' Bairam said, straightening up. 'Akbar Ali Samandar... you have dogged my footsteps since that truck ride...'

'I can say the same about you,' Akbar said.

Mrs. Armstrong looked from one to the other, sensing the tension.

'Who is the woman?' Bairam asked.

'My grandmother...she is a patient here.'

'Well, it's right that you are here at the finish: Everything ends now...you and I will face death together

'What are you talking about?' Akbar asked.

'You know what I'm saying...I'm going to blow up this hospital and all of us in it...with what I hold in my hand...' he said, holding a cell phone aloft. He had barely finished speaking when Akbar lunged at him in desperation. The move knocked Bairam off his feet, sending his night-vision goggles and cell phone flying across the floor. Bairam reached for his TT pistol and shot wildly at Akbar, missing him. Mrs. Armstrong screamed. Akbar leapt on Bairam, who was struggling to get up. They grappled on the floor for control of the pistol. Mrs. Armstrong tried to get to the door for help. There was a shot. Then silence. Bairam pushed Akbar off him.

Blood was gushing from Akbar's abdomen. Mrs. Armstrong rushed to where he lay. Bairam looked from side to side, then went down on all fours to retrieve the cell phone from under the bed. Through a haze of pain Akbar saw him pick up the cell phone and check the keypad. As Bairam raised his other hand, forefinger poised to push the buttons, Akbar reached instinctively for the M4 rifle and pulled the trigger.

EPILOGUE

The Waterton Hospital siege at Long Melford was viewed as a major terrorist attack in the Western world. It had taken three months of planning and forty-five militants, seventeen of whom were embedded as hospital employees. The remainder reached Long Melford by various means of transport in the three days preceding the siege.

Explosives, ammunition and other equipment such as night-vision goggles, bulletproof vests, electric wire and advanced communication equipment, had been brought to Long Melford over a four-week period and secreted in the hospital premises by militants posing as storekeepers. Getaway vehicles for militants who managed to escape were parked beyond the fields.

The hospital had been selected on account of its location in a remote, sparsely populated area. The surrounding countryside of crops and open spaces devoid of construction and people was considered ideal for an incursion. The hospital buildings were wired by the militants with a series of electrical circuits. These were set with charges primed to detonate in conjunction with an explosive placed within each circuit.

Three out of six explosives had gone off in the children's centre destroying half the building. Bombs in the elderly patients' centre did not go off because Bairam Khan was prevented from triggering the switch.

The siege lasted for fourteen hours. It ended with a storming of the hospital premises by British forces supported by tanks, armoured personnel carriers and helicopter gunships.

Two hundred and three persons, including thirty-eight militants and twenty-two special forces men were killed. Five militants were arrested. Two escaped but were being pursued. The hideouts and areas of operation of their cells were being traced.

Mrs. Armstrong was transferred to another hospital. Akbar too, was taken by ambulance to a hospital where a bullet lodged in the right side of his abdomen – missing vital organs – was removed.

Upon recovery, he headed for Cambridge after the official debriefing on his interaction with the militants during the siege. He received a letter of thanks from the British government for having prevented the bombing of the hospital and saving lives. There was also an official undertaking not to reveal his role in the incident, to prevent reprisals.

'We have a celebrity sitting with us this evening,' Etienne said at dinner in the Great Hall.

'Celebrity,' Arjun remarked, 'that's small beer...we have a national hero with us...single-handed destroyer of the militant horde.'

'And don't you ever forget it,' Akbar said playfully.

'But honestly, Akbar,' Etienne said, 'what was it like...the suspense in the hospital?'

'Suspense, you say,' Akbar replied, 'more like hours of boredom, waiting in the hospital room, then a few...fireworks.'

'The hero's way...sublime nonchalance...' Arjun sniggered.

'I'll tell you about it over coffee,' Akbar said, serious now, 'it was fearful, not knowing what would happen.'

'It must have been,' Giti said. 'Finish eating...we'll talk about it later.'

For a moment, Akbar glanced at the High Table and caught David raising his glass to him. He reciprocated the gesture. Carla was not at the High Table that evening, but the Master was present and acknowledged Akbar's presence with a discreet wave.

After dinner, Giti remarked, 'I sense a restlessness...in you. You keep looking over my shoulder when we talk.'

After a pause, Akbar said, 'That's astute of you, Giti...I am distracted. I'm not quite sure why...but it's there...the feeling that I'm not doing enough. It's a search for something...'

Towards the end of the academic year, Professor Andrew Crowden called a meeting of the team working on the Ibn Taymiyyah thesis at the Department of Middle East Studies. Giles Butler, Carla Berkoff and Akbar attended.

They discussed the programme status. They felt that the dissertation was almost complete. There were a few areas which needed revision and some more research, but most of the work had been done.

Professor Crowden told Akbar that he could, if he wished, apply for time off, returning for limited periods during the third year to add the finishing touches.

The news came as a great relief and Akbar finally realized the reason behind his restlessness. He had feeling for some time that he had completed his work on the thesis for the present and it was time to move on.

'So, you want to get away from the University for a bit?' the Master asked Akbar at their final meeting.

Akbar paused before replying, 'That's how I feel.'

'Have you any future plans?'

'Nothing specific at the moment...perhaps, after I've given the matter some thought, I'll have a better idea. Have you any suggestions, Master?'

'You should bear in mind,' the Master said 'that we have plans for you here at Cambridge, in Trinity. So I trust you will not walk away from us.'

'Of course not,' Akbar said.

'How do you see yourself, Mr. Samandar?' the Master asked, 'as a scholar engaged in academic work or a religious visionary or an activist?'

'Meditation alone doesn't work. That has to be combined with activism. I fear I'm not doing enough...more likely just addressing current issues and reacting to situations I come across.'

A call from Tooba on Skype took Akbar by surprise. She had just collected the twins from their nursery school, so it did not take long for the piping voices and smiling faces to get on the screen.

Though Tooba and the twins were separate entities, in his mind they were linked.

It is time, Akbar reflected, *to focus on that situation.*

He was beginning to realize that Tooba's presence in his life would provide continuous rapport with the twins...a family...a home. It was just what the twins needed, what he needed too. There were other reasons for wanting Tooba by his side...his desire for a soulmate...a female counterpoint to the maleness he had been endowed with...a partner in the field of human redemption to which he intended to devote his life...an anchor for the restive corporality that dogged his earthly existence. He needed her, in short, to make him whole.

She said that she did not want to marry him. She only wanted his friendship, 'a voluntary association' which she felt would be jeopardized by marriage.

When he pointed to the social problems they would face with an arrangement outside marriage, she countered with the suggestion that they did not have to live – only *be* – together.

It was not enough for Akbar. He sought a union, a bonding, a belonging.

'How long does this search for the self go on?' Tooba asked. 'There are two children...waiting for you all the time.'

'Odd, you should mention that...'

'Why is it odd? They have a right to your time.'

'Draw your prickles in, Tooba...I was about to tell you that I'm coming back...I've decided to pack it all in and return to base.'

'For how long?' Tooba asked.

'For as long as it takes to become a parent...'

'And how much longer besides?' she questioned.

He paused before replying.

'That depends on you.'

'How come?' Tooba remarked.

'I want you in my life,' he said looking at her on the laptop screen.

'Is it not enough that I feel closer to you than to anyone else?'

'No...we must belong to one another.'

'I used to feel like that once...'

'You are the twins for me,' he said with a suddenness, 'you are the world for me.'

'But when you ascend, you leave the world behind...you leave us behind.'

'When I am called to communion, I surrender myself to it and a light shines on my soul.

'In time you will ascend higher...until you are lost to us...I'm told it is the way.'

'It is one way,' he said.

'Is there any other?'

'The way that goes beyond the self...you have shown that to me.'

'I...I don't understand?'

'You showed it to me that fateful day when you took me to your family...'

In response to her uncomprehending look, he said, 'To Dina's family.'

'Is it an involvement you seek?' she asked.

'An involvement with the world into which I was born...a world much greater than the self... where standing up for those doomed to a life of wretchedness is the best one can do. It is a world to which I can draw the attention of those like Shaista Sabzwari who made an unwitting icon of me...'

'I wonder at that,' she remarked.

'My yearning for the light *and* my need for you, have brought me to this pass,' Akbar said.

'How do you know that it will work?' she asked.

'I will guide you towards what I know...and you will lead me to your world.'

'Is it as easy as that?' she wondered.

There was a moment's silence.

'When two persons wish to come together, there is always a way.'

ACKNOWLEDGEMENTS

The writing of *Prodigal* involved some knowledge of the world of Islamic academia and mysticism. I was guided in this task by the invaluable scholarship of Shaykh Muhammad Harun Riedinger, a Sufi Master of Austrian descent, whose knowledge of historical references, authorities, developments and texts provided me with the insight required for the narrative.

Entry to the mysterious realm of FATA was facilitated by Jamal Shah and Omar Khan, without which the tale would have been incomplete.